DO YOU THINK THIS IS STRANGE?

Do you think

2016

this is strange ?

AARON CULLY DRAKE

BRINDLE
& GLASS

Brindle & Glass Publishing Ltd.
brindleandglass.com

LIBRARY AND ARCHIVES CANADA CATALOGUING IN PUBLICATION
Drake, Aaron Cully, 1967–, author
Do you think this is strange? / Aaron Cully Drake.

Issued in print and electronic formats.
ISBN 978-1-927366-38-7

I. Title.

PS8607.R26D6 2015   C813'.6   C2014-908202-9

Editor: Colin Thomas
Copy editor: Cailey Cavallin
Proofreader: Grace Yaginuma
Design and cover image: Pete Kohut
Author photo: Cristie Hasselbach

We gratefully acknowledge the financial support for our publishing activities
from the Government of Canada through the Canada Book Fund and the Canada
Council for the Arts, and from the Province of British Columbia through the
British Columbia Arts Council and the Book Publishing Tax Credit.

The interior pages of this book have been printed on 100% post-consumer
recycled paper, processed chlorine free, and printed with vegetable-based inks.

This book is a work of fiction. Names, characters, places, and incidents are either
products of the author's imagination or used fictitiously. Any resemblance to
actual events or locales or persons, living or dead, is entirely coincidental.

1   2   3   4   5   19   18   17   16   15

PRINTED IN CANADA

For Natalie.
How could it be any other way?

MY MORNINGS

Listen: I have troubled dreams. It takes me hours to fall asleep. I wake suddenly, then wait to feel tired again. Sometimes, I sit and stare at the wall until daybreak.

In the morning, I'm more tired than I was the night before. It shouldn't be that way. Other seventeen-year-olds have to be dragged up from a slumber, like fish from the ocean deep, but I'm awake at first light.

During the day, I stare into space. I experience regular microsleeps, short bursts of suspended animation, a symptom of long-term sleep deprivation. My micro-comas can last the blink of an eye or seconds or minutes. My body continues on, but there are blanks left behind in my memory. Sometimes, my day is infested with these lice of the mind.

But the morning is an oasis in the desert of my life. After I wake, I don't get out of bed. Although tired, my mind is quiet, with thoughts slow like molasses, and I like it. I listen to the quiet of the house, where the only sounds are the buzzing of the wires in the walls, the settling of the foundation, and the birds making small talk in the backyard.

Freddy's awake, they say.

In my lap, a thick almanac, my favourite book, *The Twentieth Century in Review*. Its pages are ragged, its cover torn and taped and torn again. I sit and slowly turn the pages. Two pages forward, one page back. Two pages forward, one page back.

Rhythmic. Like a song.

I stare at the drab olive-coloured wall across the room. The last picture came down nine years ago. Now there is just a flat and featureless surface before me. We sit together, my bedroom wall and I, and regard each other, our similarities of character, our shared smoothness, our emptiness from top to bottom. The day will fill me quickly enough. But for now, I am empty.

What is our status? the wall asks.

Green, I reply. Our status is green.

Do you think this is strange? I stare at the wall and see a clock that isn't there. I can picture anything I want. I can see the plains of an ancient African valley, the sun breaking over a distant dormant volcano. But I don't. I can focus my eyes on infinity, picture the night sky and tumble into the void, a passenger on a rock suspended in the middle of the cosmos. But I don't. I can see grand epics. But I don't. Every morning, I picture a digital clock, with red hours and minutes, stretching from floor to ceiling. I watch it pulse, tagging the passage of time. No matter when I open my eyes in the morning, this clock tells me that it's 4:32. It's a nice starting point. I like to watch the minutes tick over. It doesn't bore me. It's one of my Favourite Things.

In the morning, I am silent. I am motionless.

I am a deer.

Three years, one month, and four days ago—I was fourteen years old—an idea burst into my head: what is it like to be a deer in a city? The thought threaded itself into my mind, kicked at the walls, bumped shoulders with the other threads, then fell dormant. It still pops its head up, at odd intervals. I haven't been able to shake it.

This thread began when I was riding a bus to school, my head leaning against the glass, watching the raindrops streaking the window. As the bus pulled up to a stop, I glanced up the road to the intersection and saw a doe standing before a crosswalk, caught on the wrong side, across from the forest. It eyed the other side of the road, while the cars rushed by like spawning salmon.

That deer is going to die, I thought.

I looked away. Then looked back.

So there was the beginning of a realization. A deer at the intersection. Standing, waiting, almost dead, and only alive because it hadn't yet jumped into the street.

I burst from my seat, bounced off people in the aisle, and lunged for the closing door. Throwing a hand out, I caught the door before it closed, then squeezed my way out.

As fast as I could, I ran toward the intersection, bolting ahead of the bus. When I got there, I pressed the crossing button. Immediately the light turned yellow. Behind me, I heard the squealing of the bus's brakes, and then the light turned red. Traffic came to a stop.

The deer stood still for a moment, looking at me, before it stepped into the street.

It looked *both* ways first.

And then there I was, standing alone in the rain, watching the doe, while the traffic knelt before it. Halfway across the road, it broke into a gallop.

The bus honked. I turned, and the doors opened. The driver motioned for me to get back on. As I climbed the steps, the bus burst into applause. The driver nodded and said, "Good job."

Someone gave up their seat for me, and I took it. A man in a black fedora said, "Imagine that. It waited for the light to change. That's one smart Bambi."

"Bambi was a boy," I said and immediately regretted it. Black fedora looked at me, a quizzical expression on his face. I was likely a disturbing picture. I wore a longshoreman's cap to cover bandages on my head. My right eye was so purple it was black. I had four stitches on my lip.

"So what?" he said, and I didn't answer. I stared straight ahead.

You don't have to answer, the threads said. *You don't have to answer. Just be rude and get on with your day.*

I stared at the clock out the window. The sounds of the bus drowned away. I let time skip before me.

———

This is my memory, of the day when I first realized I am a deer. The doe crossed the street, the people cheered, and I had no idea why it merited celebration. But I tumbled and tipped the thought through my mind, and the best theory I could come up with was this: *the deer doesn't belong but still tries to fit in.* People appreciate it when someone tries to fit in.

3

Here was the deer, trying to adapt. Here was the deer, trying to live its life in an implausible world. Here was the deer; it learned how to cross the street. That was good enough for now. The only thing it cared about, at that moment, was crossing the road in one piece. I think people should live their lives guided by this principle: *try to cross the street without getting hit by a truck.*

I realized that my goal for the day wasn't so different from a deer's. If the deer gets through the day without getting hit by a car, its day is green. My day is green when I get through it without being hit by a conversation. I have such a difficult time talking to people that the problem is the conversation itself, not the contents of the conversation.

Avert the collision. Avoid the conversation. Problem solved.

There are times, however, when a conversation cannot be sidestepped. When that happens, the best strategy is *never* go off script. Scrutinize a blank spot on a wall or stare into the distance, and watch the clock tick. When spoken to, answer succinctly. Never volunteer an opinion; opinions never work out. Add only facts. Contribute nothing else.

Be a *deer*.

Seventeen years into being me, it's reasonable to expect that I would never deviate from this strategy. But I can't help breaking away from it every day. It's one of the things I don't understand about me: I can't keep my mouth shut.

And here I was now, even as I knew that I should keep quiet, even as I knew that I must be a deer. Here I was, about to open my mouth.

At *this* moment, I sat before the school principal, and we discussed whether or not I should be expelled.

I opened my eyes. It was midday. My status was red.

I sat before the quote-headmaster-unquote. He was a stern man with thick black glasses over a prominent nose. He dressed regally and walked the halls of Templeton College in long robes. His cap had a tassel.

He was the headmaster but he wasn't. His correspondence, his signature, his business cards called him Headmaster Edward McClintock. But he was a school principal. Headmasters live in England. This wasn't England.

The walls of his office were chocolate brown, decorated with portraits of past quote-headmasters-unquote in robes and caps and tassels. McClintock's picture wasn't on the wall, for he was still here. To be honoured on the walls of the office one had to retire, or be promoted to the board of executives, or be fired for reasons sealed in a binding mediated agreement.

The key thing was that one had to leave.

I sat across from his desk, in a chair designed for discomfort. Beside me sat Bill, silently fuming, shuffling in his own uncomfortable chair. He looked down into his hands. They clenched and unclenched while McClintock spoke in a slow, methodical voice. It was deeper than his regular voice, affected to communicate the gravity of the situation. Bill glanced at me occasionally as McClintock spoke and no one in the room was smiling.

McClintock read, aloud, a six-page document that explained why I was being expelled. The words washed over me: the disruptions, the disrespect, the starting quarterback, the concussion, the last straw.

Chad Kennedy acquired a concussion because he fell. He fell because he lost his balance. He lost his balance because I pushed him, and, according to McClintock, it was only relevant that I pushed him. It wasn't relevant that he pushed me first.

It certainly wasn't relevant that Chad Kennedy was the school's starting quarterback. It was so insignificant that McClintock noted its irrelevance four times in his six-page document.

Everything was irrelevant except that I didn't fit in, had never fit in, and it would be best if I didn't fit in somewhere else. That wasn't in his document, but I inferred it.

As he read the pages of his decision aloud, I stared out the window behind him and pictured a large clock behind the trees, burned into the front lawn of the school. The minutes fell as always: 4:32. 4:33. 4:34. When the clock ticked over to 4:35, I noticed McClintock was looking at me, expecting me to answer him, but I hadn't heard what he'd said.

Now would be a good time to say something conciliatory, I knew. *Stick to the script*, the threads advised.

"Could you please repeat yourself?" I asked.

He cleared his throat. "I said—"

"Just the last sentence."

He glowered at me. Bill sighed with exasperation.

"I said"—he spoke slowly—"what is so interesting outside my window, Mr. Wyland?"

I didn't answer. Instead, I stared at the top of his desk.

"Although I appreciate the circumstances of . . ." He paused and drummed his fingers in thought. "The circumstances of your, let's call it your unique condition—"

"Why should we call it my unique condition?"

"Mr. Wyland, it's neither relevant nor appropriate to discuss—"

"It's autism," I interrupted. "It's not Voldemort."

McClintock stared at me, his fingers gripping his report so tightly the tips were paste white. He said nothing about Voldemort. Instead, he cleared his throat.

I don't think he liked Harry Potter movies.

Later, as we drove home, Bill told me I was a Real Case.

"Voldemort," he said. "Jesus, Freddy, where do you come up with that stuff?"

"I didn't," I said. "J.K. Rowling did."

He shook his head. "You're a case, you know that? A real case."

"A case of what?" I asked.

"Exactly."

"Don't drive over manhole covers, Bill," I reminded him.

"You could call me Dad once in a while, you know."

"I know," I said.

———

Here is what McClintock did instead of explaining why my autism and Voldemort were similar. He laid his report on the table and aligned the pages against the palm of his hand.

"Be all that as it may," McClintock began, then said nothing, and I think he wanted me to agree that it may, in fact, be all that.

"The point is, Mr. Wyland, you were daydreaming instead of taking this seriously. Autism or no autism, it doesn't excuse you from the responsibility of polite society. At a time as serious as this, I expect you to be less interested in what's going on outside the window and more interested in what's going on inside my office."

He picked up his judgment papers and tapped them on the desk. "Having read the reasons for my decision, do you have anything to say?"

Stick to the script, the threads urged.

"It's impossible for me to say no."

That's not part of the script.

He adjusted his glasses, waiting.

I continued, "In order for me to tell you I have nothing to say, I have to say it, which means I have something to say."

"Jesus, Freddy," Bill—I mean *Dad*—said and massaged his temples.

"All right," said the quote-headmaster-unquote. "Do you have nothing to say?"

"In order to tell you I have nothing to say, I have to say it. Therefore—"

Bill put his hand on my arm. "Okay," he said. "You made your point." He turned to the quote-headmaster-unquote. "He has nothing to say."

Quote-Headmaster-unquote McClintock took a solemn breath.

"Frederick," he said, "do you have anything you wish to say, regarding your expulsion from Templeton College?"

"I have nothing I wish to say," I replied.

He tapped his papers one more time. "If that's all, then—"

"Not to you," I said.

He gaped at me.

My father snorted. Later, he would incorrectly diagnose McClintock with a strange medical condition.

"That guy had a serious stick up his ass," he told me.

"Sticks aren't serious," I replied.

———

The rain stopped just before we left the *principal's* office. I walked with my father across the school parking lot. As we approached the car, I slowed my pace, my frown deepening. The left rear tire was on the white line of the parking space. The paint was recent, and the line almost glowed. It was unmistakably there. My father looked at me, at the car, at the tire, at the white line. He sighed.

"Not now, Freddy," he said. "Not now."

"You probably could have backed up and drove in straighter," I told him.

"And you could have not been expelled," he answered. "I guess that makes us even, doesn't it?"

"There's no correlation between the two."

He took his keys from his pocket. "Right again, kid."

I skirted around to the passenger door, careful not to step on the line.

"Can we stop for ice cream?"

"The car, Freddy," he said through gritted teeth. "Get in the car."

———

Listen: The rain began again and the wiper motor went *whirrrr, thump*.

"Why did you hit him?" my father asked.

"Because he tried to hit me," I replied.

"Why did he try to hit you?"

"Because he tried to hit me." Out of the corner of my eye, I saw

8

my father slump with frustration. I added, "Before that, I pushed him. Before that, he pushed me. Before that, I told him that he was standing in front of my locker."

Whirrrr. Thump. Whirrrr. Thump. Whirrrr. Thump.

"That's it?" he said at last. "That's what caused you to hit him?"

"Yes," I said.

Whirrrr. Thump. Whirrrr. Thump. Whirrrr. Thump.

I didn't tell my father the reason we had a confrontation: Chad Kennedy was blocking my access to the locker, by holding Oscar Tolstoy against it.

It was evident that Chad was comfortable in this position, but that Oscar wasn't. It was further evident that there was a disagreement under discussion. Oscar was against my locker, his feet a couple of inches off the ground, Chad's right forearm across his chest, and he was trying to explain early marketing of baseball cards.

"Oh my God!" shouted Chad. "Can't you just shut up about the baseball cards!"

I didn't mention this to my father because it wasn't relevant. I was not trying to influence the conversation Chad Kennedy was having with Oscar Tolstoy.

This is what I told my father: "He was blocking my locker, and I told him to move away from my locker."

"By *hitting* him."

"No," I said. "By telling him to move. I hit him because he tried to hit me and I wanted to warn him not to hit me anymore."

"Why didn't you just *tell* him that?"

"He wouldn't have listened."

"Christ, Freddy," my father said. "He didn't listen to you even when you hit him!"

That night, I sat in bed, legs crossed, *The Twentieth Century in Review* pressing comfortably on my lap. I turned the pages slowly and stared at the wall.

Two forward. One back. Two forward. One back.

A new school was not a light matter. It wasn't going to be a private school, either. Public schools have public parking lots with faded lines and manhole covers. I don't like public parking lots. I don't like faded lines.

I don't like manhole covers.

My new homeroom might not have comfortable chairs. My desk might be on the wrong side of the room. I would need a new locker, and it might be on the wrong side of the hallway.

The logistics were *appalling*.

Not surprisingly, I had trouble falling asleep. When the early morning came, it found me in the same place, legs crossed, my book still on my lap. Three of the pages ripped out during the night. My wrists sore.

I was too agitated to listen to the birds gossip. I tried to stare at the wall in front of me, but the clock kept resetting itself. And the olive green wall was disconsolate. *Get up and get on with your life, son*, it told me. *There's no comfort here.*

I took my book from my lap and climbed out of bed. I showered, brushed my teeth, and slouched downstairs. Pouring a bowl of Cap'n Crunch cereal, I sat at the kitchen table, chewing slowly, staring straight ahead.

I heard the stirrings of my father, the flushing of a toilet, his groggy steps down the hall. He shuffled into the kitchen. As he walked past me, he ruffled my hair.

He made coffee and stood at the counter while it brewed.

I poured another bowl of Cap'n Crunch.

"One serving only," he said, not taking his eyes off the coffee pot.

"I'm hungry," I told him.

"No, you're not." He poured his coffee. I dumped the cereal back into the box. As I did, I pilfered a small handful and shovelled the cereal into my mouth. He frowned at me but said nothing.

After he sat down, he said, "You can stay home today. I have to make arrangements to get you into another school."

I looked past him at the scratched kitchen drawer. The handle was loose.

"You know," he added, "I'm losing a full day's wage because I have to find you a new school. Why am I always coming to get you out of situations like this? Why, Freddy?"

He waited, expecting an answer.

"Where's Mom?" I asked.

He slammed the table with his fist so hard that the cereal box fell over and spilled cereal everywhere. A muscle in his jaw clenched and unclenched. He stared at me, breathing heavily through his nose.

I put my spoon down and sat, staring at the wall.

4:32. 4:33.

One week after I was expelled from Templeton College, Bill drove me to my new school, stopping one block away. He swept his arm in a grand gesture.

"There you go," he said. "Hampton Park Senior Secondary."

"It's not a park," I said, clutching my backpack to my chest.

"Nothing escapes you, does it," he said. "Now go."

"Okay." I didn't move.

He knew why I was reluctant to move. "They know you're coming. Go to the office. They'll tell you what to do." He smiled slightly. "I'd come with you, but I thought you might prefer not going into your new high school with your daddy holding your hand."

"I don't want to hold your hand."

"That makes two of us."

I got out of the car.

"Freddy," he called to me. I stopped but didn't turn around. "Try not to get expelled too quickly."

"Okay," I answered and carried on.

My new life awaited.

Hampton Park Senior Secondary was unremarkable. It was a public school, scrupulous like a public school must be, with budgetary trade-offs like floors getting swept at the end of every second day. The neighbourhood was aging, and its children grown into teenagers. It was the closest to my home, and the quickest at which to register.

I held no opinion about the school at which I was now enrolled. There was nothing about it on Wikipedia, and its Facebook page was no more and no less remarkable than any of the thirty representative high school Facebook pages I examined as reference points.

There was no football team of note, so there was no face to the school. There was no central auditorium in which an arts program could flourish. There wasn't any kind of website for the school council, probably because there wasn't anything interesting happening at the school.

I was going to be a new faceless person at a faceless school. Quite likely, everyone here would see me as just another ant in the colony. The school was probably ripe with cliques and friend packs, and I would be marginalized and ignored for the rest of my final school year.

I was excited about the prospect.

All I had to do was find corners in the school where I wouldn't be bothered. All I had to do was find corners where the scent was lost to the rest of the ants.

As it turned out, at least one corner included a comfortable sofa chair. Jim Worley insisted it was magic.

Jim Worley was my assigned counsellor. I was his *counsellee.* He referred to me as his patient.

"I'm kidding, of course," he admitted. School counsellors are not trained doctors; they require nothing more than a bachelor of education. Anything beyond that is duck sauce.

"Sit," he said and motioned to the sofa chair in the corner. "Just sink into that thing." He patted me on the arm before he realized he had just touched me. He drew back his arm quickly. Not knowing what to do with his hands, he shoved them in the pockets of his pressed jeans and stood in the middle of his office, rocking on the balls of his feet.

As instructed, I sunk into that thing. It was not standard school-district issue. It was a chair he personally brought to his office so that students might feel more comfortable. I know this because it was one of the first things he told me. He was proud of his duck sauce sofa chair.

"Comfortable, isn't it?" he asked. After a few moments of silence, I inferred he was expecting a reply.

I ran my hands over the fabric of the chair. "Did you make it yourself?" I asked.

He shook his head. "No, Frederick," he said. "It was made by master craftsmen in *China.*" He raised his eyebrows and nodded, a pleased look on his face. "Do you know where China is?"

"It's across the South China Sea from Taiwan," I said as I looked at the tag on the cushion. "Which is where this chair was made."

He was silent. After a moment, he cleared his throat, then moved behind his desk.

Jim Worley told me he was going to be my scheduled conversation. He had to satisfy his duties as my educational assistant, and a simple check-in each day would suffice. Therefore, after lunch I was to check in.

"Every day," he said, "I want you to report your status."

"Okay," I replied, looking for an open space on the wall to project my clock.

He sat with a sigh as if sitting down was a great physical accomplishment. "How are things today, Frederick?"

"Yellow."

He smiled. "Excuse me?"

"I'm here against my will."

He nodded slowly. "I see. Let's try and fix that."

"Okay."

I stared at his desk. His smile remained. After a moment, it flickered. He tapped his fingers.

"Well," he said. "Good luck with the day."

"Goodbye," I said, standing up. "I'll see you later."

At first, the days at Hampton Park were nondescript, as I predicted. Students were equally as reluctant to engage with me as I was with them. The school was infested with cliques, and the moats between them were wide and deep.

I went through the motions of the day, sitting at the back of my classrooms, speaking only when asked a direct question, refraining from eye contact, an open book near me at all times so that I would appear to be occupied.

Periodically, someone—usually a girl—would try to have a conversation with me, but I was a veteran of such affairs and could handle the occasions deftly.

"Do you want to partner for this lab?" I was asked several times in chemistry.

"No," I replied each time, until my teacher, Mr. Pringle, told me to stop.

My peers crashed on me like waves from the surf, but I kept them from breaking over me. I stayed silent. I answered shortly and sharply. I was left alone.

Lunchtimes were particularly concerning. The school was crowded, and there were few places to be alone, few places where I could sit with my book on my lap and turn pages, staring at the clock.

I was unable to shake the feeling of being watched. In the halls, at lunch, I had this overwhelming sense that someone was watching me. With so many students everywhere, someone probably was. It bothered me, and the threads filled up my mind quickly.

Fortune favours the less discerning, and I quickly discovered that the lunch table beside the janitors' lunchroom was never occupied. It was a place where I could eat my lunch without being bothered.

But places like that were few and far between, and a lunch table was only of use at lunch. I was concerned with how awash the school was with social entropy and the inevitability of being around someone wherever I went. I knew I needed to find a way to get away from my classmates.

That's when I discovered Jim Worley's sofa chair as an area of refuge.

On Tuesday, two weeks after I arrived at Hampton Park, an incident of interest occurred.

When I stopped by to see him each day, I usually told him my status was yellow, and he accepted it and said nothing else on the subject, turning his conversation to a more mundane topic. Before long, however, he could take no more and admitted he didn't understand the colour system.

"Explain it to me," he said. "Take your time."

"I can do it quickly," I told him. He waited. I stared back at him.

"Yessss," he began, "that's not quickly."

"If my status is green," I told him, "then there are no blocking issues. Everything is continuing as expected."

"And if it's not green?" he asked.

"Then it's yellow or red."

He nodded as he spun a pencil between his fingers. "Can you give me an example of something that makes your day red?"

"Conversations with strangers."

"What makes your day yellow?"

"Conversations."

He frowned. "Like this one?"

I didn't answer.

"What else, besides talking to people?"

I looked around his office. Each wall had a bookcase, jammed solid with hard and soft covers. There was no bare wall, nowhere to cast my clock. It bothered me, but I didn't want to mention it, lest we travel down a path of more questions and explanations.

On the back of the door, though, there was a poster, ripped in places, faded, with one corner broken free of its tack. It was a picture of a kitten hanging from a branch, looking directly at the camera, with a terrified expression. The caption underneath said HANG IN THERE, BABY!

I pointed to the poster. "When I first came to your office, I didn't like that poster."

He was surprised. "What's wrong with it?"

"I wondered what became of the kitten."

"Okay, that's good, that's good," he told me. "Wondering is a wonderful thing, Frederick." He leaned toward me and said slowly, enunciating each word, "That's why they call it *wonder*ing."

"I don't wonder about it anymore."

"Why not?" he asked.

"Because I found out."

The pencil he was spinning came loose from his grasp and fell to the floor. He bent down to pick it up. "You found out what happened to the cat in that poster?"

"I did."

He sat up, holding the pencil, and pursed his lips. He looked at the poster. He looked at me. He looked at the poster. "How in the world did you do *that*?"

"Wikipedia," I said.

He stared at me, expectantly. When I didn't continue, he asked, "Well, what did you find out?"

"The 'Hang in there, Baby' picture of the kitten is a cultural icon," I said, "and has been in circulation since 1973 when a group of supporters presented it to Vice President Spiro Agnew."

Don't say anything else, the threads advised.

He stared at me, waiting, and the threads and I counted the seconds. *Five, four, three, two—*

Jim Worley said, "But how does that tell you what happened—"

Answer now.

"The kitten in the picture would be, by now, a forty-year-old cat."

He nodded. "I guess it would."

"There are no documented cases of forty-year-old cats."

"No," he agreed.

Five, four, three, two—

"What became of the kitten?"

"It died."

His stapled smile ripped at the corner.

That was fun, said the threads.

Yes. Yes it was.

Then the phone rang. Jim Worley said, "Excuse me" and answered the phone. As he talked, I sat in the chair and stared at the haphazard red clock my mind painted across his bookcase. Out of the corner of my eye, I saw a book, an oversized book, poking out from the top shelf. I stood up and walked to it.

The Twentieth Century in Review.

I took it down from the shelf. Opening the cover, my fingertips ran over its smooth pages. The book had been rarely opened and the coolness of the pages drifted up like a meadow's scent. I turned a page.

I turned another page. I turned it back.

Things happen for a reason.

No they don't.

Then why not leave?

In a bit.

I fell backward into the sofa chair and turned the pages. Two forward, one back. I did it again. Then again, and the threads in my mind chattered among themselves and resolved themselves, and I began to listen to the humming of the fluorescent tubes in the ceiling.

When I looked up, Jim Worley was sitting in his chair, leaning forward, watching me, a small smile on his face.

"You've been doing that for twelve minutes," he said.

"Yes," I acknowledged.

"How do you feel?"

"My status is green."

He nodded. "Okay," he said. "Because it was yellow when you came in."

"I like this book," I said.

"You can have it if you want."

I shook my head. "I have one at home."

Jim Worley was quiet.

"You know you can come here any time you want to read that book."

"Okay." I stood up. "I'll come back tomorrow."

"But you have to talk to me first. No more of this one-word answer baloney you've been feeding me. After that, you can stay as long as you want, Freddy, except you can't miss a class."

I put the book back, then let my fingers run down its spine.

"And I'll leave you alone when you read it," he added.

"Okay," I said and sat back down. I put my hands flat on the comfy sofa chair and looked it. "This is the most comfortable chair in the world," I said and hoped he would agree with me and that would be the end of it. Perhaps this chair could find a place on my list of Favourite Things.

I have sanctuaries—places in my life where I can feel silence. Where, for a few moments at least, the threads are pacified. Sedated.

My bed in the morning is a safe zone. As long as the quilt covers my feet, everything is paused. As long as I sit still in the morning, and let the birds argue in the backyard, everything is fine.

Jim Worley's office was another one of these places. After sinking into his special chair, he would bid me close the door and our session would began.

Session. His word. Not mine.

But it afforded me a break from the school day, which was good enough for me. He could call it anything he wanted, as long as I could sit and not spend much effort answering difficult questions.

Lately, I had taken to not even knocking. I opened the door and walked in.

"How has your day been?" he asked me as I sat down.

He barely looked up from his work anymore. I called it work simply because it made it easy to describe what he was doing when I walked in. Sometimes he was reading a book. Sometimes he was typing furiously. Sometimes he was leaning over a drawing pad, his arm hiding it from any prying eyes in his empty office, laboriously drawing something out. On those times, when I walked in, he looked up at me with a startled expression on his face. I suppose he looked chagrined. I didn't know why, and wasn't even a little curious. After all, I lived in a glass house. Maybe even a glass mansion. There was no logic in me calling attention to his curious habit of making covert sketches and diagrams, not when I think about going home, sitting in bed, and putting *The Twentieth Century in Review* in my lap.

One man's favourite thing, and all that.

"My day is yellow," I said after finding a comfortable position on his chair, after sinking down into it like a corpse into a bog.

He made some flourishes with his pencil, regarded what he had just completed, folded the paper, and put it in his top desk drawer. Looking up, he pondered me. "Yellow," he said. "It was yellow yesterday, wasn't it?"

"Yes."

"And the day before that."

"Yes."

"And the day—"

"Yes."

We regarded each other.

"How are classes going?"

"Good."

"Yellow?"

"Okay."

He leaned back and put his hands behind his head. Kicking his feet up on the desk, he said, "You want to know what I think about this yellow thing, Frederick?"

"It's Freddy."

"It's Freddy to everyone else," he chided. "But we have a different relationship. You are—"

"—your client."

He frowned at me. "I was going to say friend."

"Oh."

"Do you think of me as a friend?"

"No."

"Why not?"

"You have none of the characteristics."

His eyebrows raised. "What would those characteristics be?"

"We don't laugh together."

He nodded. "When was the last time you laughed?"

"Nine years, eight months, seven days ago."

"That's pretty specific."

"Yes."

"I guess you haven't had any friends since then?"

I didn't answer.

He cocked his head. "Oh?" he mused. "Have you had friends?"

I was silent. My eyes fell on a scattering of muffin crumbs on the side of his desktop, and I wondered, If I were to sweep the crumbs to the floor, how long would they remain there before a janitor swept them up?

"Freddy," he said softly. "Who has been your friend?"

"I've had three friends and one of them wasn't my friend."

"Which one?"

"Oscar Tolstoy was my friend. He wasn't my friend."

"Why not?"

"He annoyed me."

"Friends can do that." He smiled. "Who was your second friend?"

"Jack Sweat."

He shook his head. "Who is Jack Sweat?"

"He's not my friend anymore."

"Why?"

I didn't answer. He nodded, understanding. "So how about the third?"

I opened my mouth to answer, but my voice was lost. Jim Worley frowned and leaned forward.

"Frederick?" he said to me. "Are you—"

A ding. A voice over the PA system. "Jim Worley to the office."

"Ah!" he said, apparently pleased. "Looks like my ship has come in."

"You don't have a ship," I said.

"Turn of phrase," he replied, standing up. "I have to go." He put his pen in his inside coat pocket and picked up a notebook. "Close the door behind you when you leave, okay?"

After he left, I sat in the chair staring at the muffin crumbs.

Do it, the threads urged.

Stop it, I said. You're not supposed to be here. This is my place, not yours.

Just do it, then.

I stood up and walked to Jim Worley's desk. They were the remains of a oatmeal muffin. A red sticky piece of fruit clung to one crumb. It may have been a raspberry oatmeal muffin. I swept the crumbs to the floor and noted their position. Now we wait, I thought to myself.

The class bell rang. It was time for chemistry class.

Just before I left, I lingered over his desk for a moment. Then, without any prompting from the threads, I opened his drawer and looked at what he had been sketching before I came in.

It was Minnie Mouse, but she wasn't wearing her dress. She was lying on a couch, looking directly out of the paper. She was up on one elbow. A necklace hung between her breasts.

Draw me like one of your French mice, was the caption.

Definitely on the spectrum.

CHURCH, BEFOREHAND

My list of Favourite Things has memories pinned to it. They are vignettes, perfectly remembered episodes. It's like opening my eyes, and I am there again.

My first and only time at church is a favourite memory and the oldest thread in my mind. I'm repeatedly opening my eyes as a seven-year-old, in a life and death struggle with my mother to not put on my Sunday-best clothes.

At the time, I had not yet met Jesus. Many people recommended that I get to know Him, but I had yet to be introduced, and my mother decided it was time for me to make His acquaintance. I remember struggling with my mother, who held my mask in the air, as I jumped frantically, trying to snatch it back.

"No, Freddy," she said exasperated, pushing me away. "You are *not* wearing this to church."

I argued. I yelled and demanded. I howled for my mask. They let me wear a mask on weekends and *it was the weekend.*

"You can't go to the church with a mask on," my father told me as he watched from my bedroom door. "Jesus might think you're a mugger."

My father could afford to be unconcerned about church: he didn't have to go; he'd already met Jesus, so there wasn't any need to return.

"The guy doesn't say all that much," Dad had informed me the night before, between forkfuls of spaghetti. "You end up doing all the talking."

"I don't want to do all the talking to Jesus," I said.

My mother glared at my father. "Church isn't really like that, Freddy," she said. "You don't have to say anything. You can just sit and listen."

"I don't want to just sit and listen."

25

She paused and took a breath. "Well, we'll try it and if you don't like—"

"I don't like it."

"If you don't like it when we go to church—"

"I don't like it when we go to church."

"Freddy!" she said sharply. I looked down at my plate.

"He already knows he doesn't want to go to church," my father said, his mouth full of pasta. "The kid's smarter than you think."

In the morning, my mother remained determined in her decision that it was time I made the Lord's acquaintance, so it was time to go to church. I was alarmed at such a serious breach of my Sunday routine. Our battle was epic.

Mom ordered me to the bathroom; I ran away.

She carried me; I pounded at her back.

She struggled to brush my teeth; I resisted.

She tried to comb my hair; I cried in agony.

She tried to fit me into my best clothes; I squirmed.

"I want to wear PYJAMAS!" I shouted at her.

She tried to soothe me. "You can wear pyjamas when we get back, sweetheart."

"I want to watch DORA!" I rebutted as I twisted my arm loose from her grip, desperately trying—and succeeding—to remain shirtless.

She took a deep breath and grasped my wrist firmly. "I know, sweetheart," she said. "I know you want to watch *Dora the Explorer*. And you can. After church."

"But listen: I want to watch it *now*."

"Can't argue with that logic," my father said, sipping his coffee as he leaned against the door jamb.

"Well," my mother said crisply, "maybe if you helped me get him dressed, you could go watch your football game. Or would you rather I gave up, and the two of you can watch cartoons instead?"

In the blink of an eye, he pinned me down and she forced a shirt on me. I screamed mercilessly the entire time. I continued wailing even after I was dressed, even after he picked me up, squeezed me like an anaconda, took me to the car, and strapped me into my booster seat.

"Have a great time," he told me and patted me on the head.

"I don't WANT to have a great time," I shouted back at him.

I don't know why this is a Favourite Thing, but it is, by the very fact that I continue to revisit it. By the very fact that I continue to think about it; by the very fact that it still sits, a thread in the corner of my mind, and that I still wonder why this memory is so important.

Favourite thing number 27.

I was correct. I didn't like church.

I didn't like the pews. I didn't like that they wouldn't recline. I didn't like that they were called *pews*.

I had to sit beside strangers. Everything smelled like turpentine. The organist was loud, and her timing was off.

As the minister spoke, I fidgeted and tapped a rhythm on the pew in front of me. My mother gritted her teeth, then finally gave me a hymn book. After that, I sat quietly, half listening to the choir, half listening to the congregation as it shuffled and muttered in prayer and cleared its collective throat. I was happy with this arrangement. I flipped pages.

The sermon ended and I quickly stood up to leave, but my mother put her hand on my arm. "Not yet, Freddy," she said and bade me wait with her until after the congregation spilled out the doors, into cars, and meandered off to Denny's for brunch.

The minister came and sat with my mother. He smiled at me. "I'm pleased to meet you, Freddy," he said and offered me his hand. I regarded it with suspicion.

"I'm here against my will," I said, then turned and ran away.

As they talked, I raced up and down the rows, my hands sliding across the tops of the pews, making motorboat sounds with my mouth. I had no reason to make the sounds, but I liked the resonance in my head.

"Things happen for a reason," I heard the minister tell my mother.

"No, they don't," she replied. "No one's told me what the reason is, and I don't care about the reason." She lowered her voice to a sharp whisper. "I just want my son back from wherever he goes in his head. I want him present. Not some of the time. *All* of the time."

The minister put his hand over hers. "This is the spot where

God comes in," he said. "In the void between what the world is, and what you want the world to be. You can draw meaning from it, or draw nothing from it." He flickered a kind smile. "I always think it's better to draw meaning."

I ran my hand over the wooden seats, the dips and bumps, moulded from years of butts sitting, butts standing. People standing to say hallelujah because maybe God did something good. People sitting to say amen because maybe God will do something good.

Things happen for a reason, the congregation murmurs. But that's not right. Things just happen. The reason is assigned to the happening, and only after the happening. And like pigeons in an experiment, the congregation flaps its wings and looks for pellets to fall from the sky.

This memory doesn't make me happy. But I haven't filed it away like so many others. I return to it again and again. Despite it not being a happy thing, it remains a Favourite Thing.

Not all Favourite Things have to be good things.

———

It was my last and only time at church, the last time my mother tried to force me into a freshly ironed shirt on a Sunday morning. I think she sat, said amen, and God didn't do something good. I think she resented Him for it. I don't think she bought into any of it. Even if things happen for a reason, who says you have to like it? And you certainly don't have to give thanks.

I don't spend a lot of time trying to find the reason in things. Perhaps my life would be different if I flapped my wings periodically and expected pellets to fall. I'm not a pigeon. I'm a deer.

But if I *were* a pigeon, I might say that there was a reason I was expelled from Templeton College. I *might* say that I left Templeton for a reason.

Saskia.

It was time for us to meet again. My new Favourite Thing. My old Favourite Thing.

There was only one thing that wasn't boring about group therapy: Saskia Stiles. Ten years ago, we were in the same social group. We spent hours playing cards and Taking Turns. Twice daily, we practised entering the room. We greeted each other with a How Do You Do and How Are You?

This is what I learned: when entering a room, you are expected to say something from a list of sentences:

Hello, everyone, my name is Freddy. (If you know the people in the room, you do not have to give your name.)

Isn't it a lovely day? (I don't like this one; often it isn't a definitively lovely or non-lovely day.)

Did you have a good day? (This should never be used in the morning.)

How are you? (How are you *what*? I always wondered.)

Where the hell is my coffee? (This was not on the list of expected sentences at Excalibur House, but when my father discovered the list in my backpack and looked over the speech balloons filled with questions asked by smiling, waving stick figures, he added this question to the end. When I used it at Excalibur House, they called it unexpected behaviour and made me sit for seven minutes in the Room with the Bathtub Full of Plastic Balls.)

I was good at remembering the scripts we repeated each day, better than most of the people in my group. Saskia had no trouble remembering responses but struggled with remembering which one to use appropriately.

Nevertheless, she loved the game. It was exciting. She received immediate feedback for a job well done. She got to repeat the scripts again and again. If she did especially well, she got to read her favourite book. Sometimes she could sit with her interventionist and they would write a poem.

These games didn't interest me. I found no challenge in identifying the characteristics of the moment, in order to decide the appropriate sentence to use. Within a split second, I could compare the criteria with the circumstance and choose the correct response.

They bored me.

Saskia, on the other hand, was always excited to play. Each time I entered the room, she smiled as wide as she could.

"Say, 'Hello, Freddy,'" prompted her interventionist.

"HELLO, Freddy!" she shouted, with joy. "HELLO! How was your DAY?"

The more she said it, the more excited she became, jumping up and down, her wrists flapping up at shoulder level, palms opening and closing. She looked like she was trying to fly.

In a way, she was.

For hours at a time, we greeted each other, and played games, and said polite things. We excused each other a lot.

My favourite game was building a block tower with her before I knocked it down. It was a script, in which I next apologized, and in which Saskia next said it was okay. She loved the game to the point where she trembled with anticipation as I built the tower. Just before I tipped it over, she stepped back, her hands in the air, flapping. Then I knocked it over.

"Sorry," I said to her. "It was an accident."

"Say, 'That's okay,'" prompted her interventionist.

"That's okay," she replied, hopping up and down, "I FORGIVE you, Freddy!"

She was only supposed to say, "That's okay." I don't know if the rest was a response added by her own father, but I do know she was never sent to sit in the Room with the Bathtub Full of Plastic Balls. Instead, the interventionist let Saskia add her own flair of grand sweeping forgiveness. For more than a year, while we practised this script, or other scripts like it, I was forgiven my sins. Therapy at Excalibur House was like a confessional.

I haven't confessed in ten years now.

31

I opened my eyes and I was seventeen. I was in the cafeteria, and there she was.

Saskia Stiles came back into my life in winter, early in the new year. I knew it was her the moment I saw her from across the cafeteria. There was no way I could have missed her. Locks of blond hair escaping from under her wool cap like refugees across the border. Her hands bursting with nervous activity, scribbling in her notebook, or rising in the air, fingers flexing, palms opening and closing. It was Saskia and I knew it, even though ten years had passed.

The cafeteria was a loud place, with eyes looking in every direction. At least one set of eyes was on me at any time, if only by chance. When I walked to my table, people glanced up at me. Especially girls. More girls looked at me than boys. Perhaps they looked at other boys as much as they did at me. I was never preoccupied enough with it to find out, and the threads seemed to have no problem with it.

Boom chicka wow, the threads said.

I don't know what that means, I answered.

Whether it was with a girl or a boy, I worked to avoid eye contact, but it wasn't always easy to do in a way that didn't call attention to myself. Looking down didn't work. Oscar Tolstoy, for instance, never looked up, and he engendered all sorts of remarks and comments. He couldn't get through a single day at Templeton without someone pushing him into a locker, it seemed.

My strategy to avoid eye contact was different. I looked straight ahead, eyes fixed on a point on the horizon. I remained resolute and refused to let my eyes dart about the room.

Pick a spot on the wall at the end of the cafeteria, the threads advised. *Don't stop looking at it.*

Done, I said. Now what?

Walk toward it.

And when I get there?

Probably you should stop.

My spot on the wall was straight up the aisle, on the wall behind my lunch table, three feet below the ceiling. With just enough room to picture my clock.

4:32, the clock called out each time.

That's so weird, said the threads.

The day Saskia returned, I walked up the middle of the aisle, eyes locked on the red clock. Still, I could see a girl, sitting at my table. Directly in my line of sight. Her head immediately below the spot on the wall at which I stare every time. So I looked at her.

Things happen for a reason. No they don't.

Saskia.

The last time I saw her, it was ten years ago. On that day, she did especially well, was extra attentive, and earned six stickers, enough for a Fun Break. She sat with her interventionist and wrote a poem, while I fumbled to get my coat on as my father waited to take me for ice cream. She shouted out each line as she wrote it.

"ONCE upon a very merry time," she said loudly as she wrote the words. "Once. Once upon a VERY! MERRY! TIME!" and she wrote some more.

I never saw Saskia again.

A decade later, here she was, at lunch hour, sitting at the seventh table in the third row. *My* table.

That's when I noticed the others at the table. She wasn't alone. The metal shop boys with greasy fingernails and scuffed boots were there, clustered beside her. She was leaning slightly away from them. I don't think she welcomed their presence.

No one ever sat at this table except me, which was why I chose it in the first place. The door to the janitors' lunchroom was only a few feet away, always open, with janitors inside, having lunch, talking or playing cards. So no one sat here. I think people don't like to be this close because janitors are not people. Janitors should not have lunchrooms. Janitors are not supposed to eat lunches.

They are supposed to *mop*.

I approached my table, then stopped. There was Saskia. There

33

also sat the three loud boys from shop class, and they laughed loudly, talked loudly, and threw Tater Tots at each other. Loudly.

One of the boys leaned over to look at Saskia's sketch pad. He was tall, with a wide frame and closely cropped red hair. "Whatcha drawing?" he asked and moved closer to her along the bench. She didn't acknowledge him. She didn't answer. She adjusted her headphones instead.

All the better to hear you with. Or not.

"Leave her alone, she's busy," said the boy with a gold earring in his left ear and shoulder-length blond hair. I knew him. His name was Danny Hardwick, and we shared the same homeroom class. He bounced a Tater Tot at his friend; the chunk of potato hit Saskia in the shoulder and fell to her lap. All three boys laughed. Saskia did not.

"Whoops," Danny said. "Sorry."

I don't think he meant it.

Saskia wiped the Tater Tot to the floor. It rolled to the lip of the janitors' lunchroom. Inside, Mr. Earle and Mr. Bryce argued baseball, unconcerned with the Tater Tot. I was suddenly annoyed at them. They weren't supposed to be having lunch. Janitors are supposed to clean up floors and bathrooms; they are not supposed to eat. In particular, they shouldn't eat sandwiches, because they eat sandwiches with their hands. Although they *may* wash their hands, I can't be certain that they actually *do*. Not all of them. Not all of the time. By the law of averages, janitors periodically eat sandwiches with the same unwashed hands that just scrubbed a toilet.

A *toilet*.

Listen: On December 18, 2010, I read a study by Dr. Charles Gerba that found that a flushing toilet sends a plume of aerosols into the air. These aerosols, contaminated with fecal matter, bacteria, and viruses, can dissipate about the room for hours, settling on everything exposed: doorknobs, sink fixtures, and any person who walks into the bathroom.

I told my father about the aerosols. It was the first thing at the top of my mental stack when he asked me to tell him something I had done that day.

"How was your day at school?" he asked.

"Good," I replied, a mouth full of mashed potatoes.

"Tell me three things about your day," he said.

I chewed slowly. He stared at me, expressionless. Waiting.

So I told him about the fecal aerosols. I was reluctant to do it: I expected he would want a discussion about proper hygiene. This had the hallmarks of an *opportunity to learn*. Instead, he laughed loudly, slapped the kitchen table with his palm, and called it a shitstorm.

"*That* should have been the title of the article," he guffawed to himself.

These were the thoughts that stomped about my mind, like tenants looking for the super. When I surfaced, when I opened my eyes, all three boys were looking at me.

This happens far more frequently than is safe. Time skips on me. I become lost in thought; I'm pulled into a vortex of exploding ideas and questions. One pediatrician suggested that much of my behaviour could be attributed to sleep deprivation.

"He could be having microsleeps," he told my father, as I stared blankly at the wall. "He's probably having one right now."

"Jesus," my father said. "That's just great."

I wasn't microsleeping this time. I stared at the three boys with stains on their jeans, and they stared back at me with expressions mute, uncertain of who I was, what I was doing, why I was standing in the middle of the aisle, holding a lunch tray, staring back at them.

"What are you looking at, sport?" Danny Hardwick said, and the air in the room seemed to disappear. I tried to reply: What was I looking at? I was looking at *them*. My throat constricted and I felt my chest tighten. "What are you looking at, sport?" and I was thinking something I hadn't thought for a long time.

I walked into the next room of my mind.

Years before, I wasn't sure when, I had heard those same words. Now the threads howled at me to connect it to the moment. But I couldn't make the bridge, which was a problem. I don't have difficulty

35

connecting to older memories. I don't forget things. To know someone had said *What are you looking at, sport?* but not know *who* said it was highly unusual. It was even concerning.

It was distressing.

In my mind, a picture rose before me, a fragment of a memory. This is what I saw: low clouds reflecting the light of a darkening day straight above me, rain falling on my face. A light shining in my eye.

What are you looking at, sport? said the voice behind the light.

But the voice was buried down in my mind.

Here, now, the hubbub of the cafeteria all around me, I stood, digging back to connect the voice to a face. I heard Danny Hardwick snicker, then his friends did the same. He started to say something but stopped. He reached into his pants pocket and took out his vibrating phone.

"Dave just got home," he said to his friends. "He's got some stuff."

"Let's go then," said the boy with the red hair, and they all stood up.

As they walked by me, Danny Hardwick gave me a light slap on the cheek.

"Take it easy, Silent Sam," he said, and his friends laughed.

I didn't say anything. My throat was too dry.

What are you looking at, sport?

Listen: Someone said that to me before. Someone looked at me and said, *What are you looking at, sport?* and they didn't really care what I was looking at.

When Danny Hardwick said it to me, I felt a surge of adrenalin, a spike of fear exploding below my lungs. My pulse quickened, my breathing became ragged, and I turned inward, chasing the thread. In a flicker, I was lost to the moment.

Who *said* that?

My mind jumped back in time. I think the principal of Templeton College said it. He said it to me as I stared out the window.

But that's not right. He said, *What are you looking at, Mr. Wyland?* And then he expelled me.

I think Chad Kennedy said it. Outside my locker at Templeton College, he pushed me, I pushed him, and it was all because he said, *What are you looking at, sport?*

But that's not right. He said, *What are you looking at, you dick?* and I didn't know how to reply. It's always safest to repeat the same sentence back if you don't know how to reply.

What are you *looking at?* I said, and he pushed me.

I couldn't remember who called me "sport." Now a thread fixed firmly in my mind, an unanswered question to which I would have to return until it was resolved.

For now, I *niced* the thought, sent it to the bottom of the stack. The threads didn't complain.

What is Saskia Stiles doing here? they asked me.

Saskia remained at my table, no change in posture or expression, as if the three boys had never been crowding her. She continued to write in her journal. I hoped it was a poem.

Ten years ago, the last time I said goodbye to Saskia Stiles, she was writing a poem. The last words I said to her were "Goodbye, Saskia," and I waved. "I'll see you later."

She put down her pencil. "GoodBYE, Freddy!" she shouted, infused with an excitement reserved for the vessels of seven-year-olds. She shouted, "I forgive you!" Then she went back to her poem. "ONCE upon a very merry time," she said loudly as she wrote the words. "Once. Once upon a VERY! MERRY! TIME!" and she wrote some more.

A poem now, a poem then. Poetry bookended her absence from my life.

I put my tray down on the table. She didn't notice, or at least didn't acknowledge me. She scribbled furiously. The words came in short sprints, bursting from her, pulsing out like blood from a ruptured artery. Once it was complete, she tore whatever she wrote from her notebook, crumpled it, and tossed it aside.

In between poems, she ate carrot sticks and stared at the table, ignoring the random hubble and bubble of everyone else in the cafeteria. Blond hair hung around her face. She rocked back and forth in time to her music.

She didn't look up at me, and gave no indication she knew who I was. So I ate my lunch. In the lunchroom to my right, the janitors ate sandwiches and disagreed with each other's insights. I tried not to think about their hands. I had no success.

Saskia wrote aggressively, as if she were late for a bus. She didn't look at me, and she neither nodded nor said hi, hello, or how are you. But she was excited about something. After a minute, she put down her pencil and lifted her hands in the air, like she was being robbed. She rapidly opened and closed—open and *clenched*—her hands. She picked up her poem, looked at it, put it down, and froze, staring at it for a moment. Then she began writing again. A minute later, she ripped the paper from her pad, crushed it into a ball, and let it fall to the table.

Then she squeaked.

I'd never heard anyone squeak before. I had heard people make sounds that were intended to mimic a squeak, but those were not squeaks. Squeaks are shrill piercing sounds emitted by small animals with tiny voice boxes. Humans can't squeak.

Nevertheless, Saskia Stiles *squeaked.*

After a few minutes, in which I ignored Saskia and she ignored me, she stopped writing altogether, and her hands dropped, relaxed. She opened her backpack and pulled out an iPhone. After turning it over in her hands a few times, she began typing in bursts, replacing pen with keyboard.

Perhaps she was nervous or intimidated. I understand that ignoring one another is a standard ritual between teenage boys and girls. I'm not sure of its purpose, but I'm good at it. I've never had a girlfriend, yet I've still mastered the art of ignoring other people. It's been hard work.

As I ate, I stared at the wall in front of me. It was blank, except for a poster in the far right corner—an image of a chimpanzee holding both its hands in the air in the appearance of victory. The poster read: YOU CAN DO IT! It offered no clue as to what *it* actually was. I think *it* may have been bananas. That would interest a chimp.

On the table, equidistant between us, her balled-up poem lay. I saw a single word, peeking out.

hello.

Her pen rolled off the table and she bent under the table to pick it up. I reached out, took the crumpled scrap of paper, and put it in my pocket. She straightened back up, and we continued our silence together.

While I ate, I stared at the wall, and a red digital clock counted the time. My mind kept returning to the ball of paper in my pocket.

Why did you take it? the threads asked.

39

I don't know, I replied.
What is it?
I don't know.

I only glanced at Saskia twice. Enough to remember a girl from ten years ago, hold a snapshot of the past firmly in my mind's eye, then map it over a picture of the girl in front of me. She was the same, she was different.

She had more freckles. Her hair was longer. She was thinner. She was older. Taller.

Prettier.

She was the same. She wore a white wool cap like the one she wore then. She was different. She wore grey Bose headphones overtop of the cap. Her jacket was pink, which was her favourite colour then. But her shirt was white with red polka dots; she never wore polka dots at group therapy. Ten years ago, she didn't have a journal. Now, she leaned over one and made quick short drawings and wrote patches of words.

The Saskia of today wasn't smiling. The Saskia Stiles of my memory smiled. Although the Saskia before me seemed so much like the Saskia in my memory, she was also strikingly different.

At once, a new thread began in my mind: *Why? Why is she different? Why isn't she smiling?*

Why do these questions seem so important?

I sat, silently, and absorbed her. She was the same, she was different.

She wore no makeup, no jewellery.

Her eyes were—

She hadn't looked at me, but I didn't have to look at her to know how blue her eyes were. I remembered their colour from the last time I said goodbye to Saskia Stiles. Back then, she looked up at me from the table where she was writing a poem. Back then, she looked up at me and smiled, and I saw her eyes. The colour of blue ice, shed from a glacier and spilled into the bay.

I've never forgotten.

I don't forget *anything*. I'm not supposed to.

I finished eating and stood up.

This is what I said to Saskia, the first words I said to her in ten years, the same words I said to her the last time I saw her: I said, "Goodbye, Saskia, I'll see you later."

She didn't reply. I saw the barest flicker of her eyes, the slightest lifting of her head. Like a flash of lightning, I saw the blue, then it was gone, and she was looking at her phone again.

Outside the cafeteria, I took out the balled-up piece of paper and unwrapped it.

hello

is there anybody in there

I didn't know if it was a good poem or not—I am not a poet. But I knew it was a *short* poem, and I think that reduced the probability it was bad.

Ten years ago, she worked on a poem as I left, and I never knew what it was about, because it was unfinished when I put on my coat and left. Although she insisted on reading out every poem in a loud voice, she zealously guarded its secrets until it was complete.

I said goodbye and that I would see her later. It wasn't much, but she loved hearing those words from me, because she knew exactly how to reply. She treated it like an epiphany. Laying down her poem, she stood up and followed me to the door, then stopped, hopping up and down. Her hands opened and closed on either side of her head. My father always said that it looked like she was quoting herself.

Ten years ago, she hopped up and down, her eyes wide, trembling, barely able to contain her excitement. "GoodBYE, Freddy!" she shouted at me. "I'll see you LATER."

On that last day, we parted like it was any other day, the only difference being that I had shown her where I lost my front tooth, and she tried to touch the gap between my teeth.

"Your TOOTH!" she shouted. "What happened to your TOOTH!"

That was the only thing different. There was no final reckoning.

She didn't know that she would not see me later. She hadn't heard her mother talking to my father earlier, like I had, and she didn't see that they both acted angry. Speaking in low sharp whispers, that rose louder and louder. Saskia didn't see when her mother said goodbye to my father, and my father said good riddance to her, and then she said he needed to go somewhere and cool off. And he said she needed to go somewhere and fuck off, and neither of them said, "I'll see you later."

Instead, Saskia Stiles stood at the door, hopping up and down, waving as she quoted her forehead, and said "GoodBYE, Freddy!"

Ten years later, Saskia didn't say goodbye to me when I left the lunch table.

I folded the paper carefully and put it in my pocket. Then I stopped thinking about it. It was now time to have a discussion with Jim Worley and agree that his chair had magic powers. Then it was time to read my book.

Then it was time for chemistry class.

Mr. Pringle, my chemistry teacher, looked at me for more than ten seconds. My cut-off point is five seconds. He looked at me for twice as long as he should have. Then he looked away and said nothing, and I was left to wonder why he was looking at me. And argue with the threads that burst into my mind.

Are you about to be expelled again?

No. There has to be a compelling reason to expel me.

Did you insult him?

I don't talk to him.

Like that makes any difference. You find ways to insult silently.

Ignore. I am going to ignore this.

No, you aren't.

Everyone refers to Mr. Pringle as Mr. Chips behind his back. He is a grumpy man who doesn't like talking to students. As a result, we usually got along fine. I sat at the back; I did my homework, took notes, and didn't ask questions. In return, he left me alone. That was the unspoken deal.

But at 1:35 PM, halfway through my chemistry class, Mr. Pringle looked up from his desk and stared at me. People do this to me often, and I am adept at ignoring them. But it wasn't to be the case this time. My mind was already troubled. Threads already elbowed through the door, asking questions, making guesses, explaining themselves.

I found myself reading the same page in my textbook over and over again. I wanted to lose myself in the monotony of balancing equations, but the threads were too loud.

Whither Saskia? they said, in summary.

Why didn't she smile?

Does she remember you?

In the maelstrom of these questions, Mr. Pringle chose to look at me, and I was perturbed. His face was inscrutable. There were no telltale signs of anger, fear, happiness. His expression was unreadable.

You're not an expert on interpreting facial expressions.

I'm observing that I can't interpret his facial expression. If I could, this would be a less notable incident. Should we forget what happened the last time we ignored facial expressions we didn't recognize?

We don't forget those things.

Therefore—

Therefore, you're talking about an incident where there was a specific look on their faces. You're referring to an incident where they had expressions and you didn't interpret them.

How is this different?

Mr. Pringle had an expression that you recognized. It's an expression you've seen over and over again.

Where?

Every time you look in the mirror.

Possibly.

Indifference. You saw indifference.

I *may* have seen indifference. I may have seen something else.

You're not observant.

I am.

Says someone who stares at a clock that isn't there.

I only look at it to stop you from talking to me.

Not true. You only look at the clock because you don't want to look at anything else.

Because you won't give me peace.

Because you won't say anything otherwise.

How about I say this? Shut up.

Not productive.

I will talk to you later.

Yes. You will talk later. You will talk to all of us later.

"Freddy?" said Mr. Pringle, seemingly from the end of a long hallway.

I pulled myself up from the depths of my own mind to see him staring at me from his desk, with a puzzled expression.

I looked around. Everyone else was doing their homework. My pen was in my hand, but my pad was empty. I looked back at Mr. Pringle.

"Did you have a question?" he asked me.

"No."

Don't call him Mr. Chips.

Stop it.

Really. Mr. Chips. Don't say it.

"You were looking at me," Mr. Pringle said.

"You were looking at me," I said and put my head down, beginning my exercises.

"Because *you* were looking at *me*."

Mr. Chips. Mr. Chips.

I bit the inside of my cheek. Focus on the bite. Focus on the bite.

Mr. Chips.

"Well?" he asked.

"What?"

"Were you looking at me?"

"Yes."

"Why?"

I clenched my teeth together. "I don't know."

"If you don't know why you're looking at me, don't look at me."

He *was looking at* you!

"Okay," I said.

Mr. Chips.

"Look at your homework, okay?"

I started writing quickly. Avogadro's constant. Moles. Equilibrium.

"Okay?" he asked again.

"Mr. Chips," I said softly.

I told you not to call him that.

Mr. Pringle stood up. "*What* did you say?"

"You looked at *me*," I said.

This time, he stared at me with a little more than indifference. But he said nothing. He shook his head and returned to his work.

One of these days, the threads said, *you will fail to dodge the bullet.*

AN ACCOUNTING OF MY
DAY IN THREE PARTS

The evening of the day Saskia returned, Bill and I walked the trails behind the house, and he requested an accounting of my time.

"Tell me three things you did today," he said as we walked single file up a path made rough by granite knobs, made stubborn by hemlock roots, some as thick as an arm, lacing up the path underneath.

As we walked, I took my water bottle from my belt. Bill led, at a steady pace, not looking back, waiting for my reply. He didn't wait long. He never did.

"Three things, Freddy," he said, and his voice was irritated.

"I ate my lunch," I said and shook my bottle, listening to the water splash about.

"You can do better than that," he told me and turned back to look at me directly, still walking, paying no attention to the broken ground beneath him. I broke from his gaze, and he turned back to watch his footing. The forest was silent, except for the dropping of our feet, and the sloshing of the water.

"What else did you do?" he asked again. "Lunch is no longer an allowed answer."

"I sat at the cafeteria table with someone."

He stopped walking. His eyebrows went up. "With someone?" he said, as if he were contemplating a new postulate of science. "What kind of someone?"

At that moment, I felt my stomach tighten. I didn't want to tell him about Saskia Stiles but I didn't know why. Not knowing my own motivation is unusual and causes me alarm. But I was even more alarmed that there were no threads appearing in my head, asking *why* I didn't want to tell him.

Zero threads.

None.

Apparently, the threads in my head were quite okay with it.

"Who did you have lunch with, Freddy?" my father asked again.

"With a janitor," I said, and I wondered if I said it too quickly and was now acting suspicious.

My father didn't answer. I held my breath for a moment but realized it was not a good long-term strategy. I exhaled in a burst and took a quick swig from my water bottle.

"A janitor?" he said, frowning. "You had lunch with a janitor?"

I didn't answer. I sloshed my water.

"Well," he said, then closed his mouth and pursed his lips. He opened his mouth again and began to speak, but stopped. He frowned.

"What in the world did you talk about?" he asked me, at last.

"Fecal aerosols," I replied, and flecks of water flew from my lips to land between us.

Somewhere the mountain trolls were watching, chuckling.

You pulled that *one out of the fire*, they probably said.

THE THREE THINGS

Listen: Eleven years ago, my parents started asking me to tell them three things I did during the day. Notwithstanding the few times someone was sick or the few times we were out, or the times Bill sat in the living room and watched my mother dance, one of them asked me for an accounting every single day. They thought it was good for my memory.

It's not.

I remember conversations I had weeks ago, to the word. I remember the date and time when I saw a dog with only three legs. *Three* legs. I remember the commercials that appeared in the first quarter of last year's Super Bowl, and I remember their order.

So I certainly remember what I did today. I did *many* things, and therein lies the problem. I do many things *every* day. I get out of bed. I put my feet in the slippers at the foot of my night table. I walk to the bathroom and pee. I run cold water over my hands. I wash my face. I brush my teeth. After I brush my teeth, I fart. Every time.

I put on grey underwear on even days of the week. I put on black underwear on odd days of the week. I won't wear white underpants because they get dirty too fast. My father used to yell at me when I wore white underwear.

"Jesus Harold *Christ*, Freddy!" he shouted, sorting the laundry. "Did you wipe your ass at all this week?"

"Yes," I said.

"With what? Your underwear?"

By the time I am asked *What did you do today?* I have done literally hundreds of things. I don't have difficulty remembering what I did. I have difficulty deciding what's noteworthy enough to talk about.

When they first introduced this exercise, my parents had trouble getting more than a single unique thing dredged up from my memory.

49

"Tell me one thing about your day," my mother said, long ago, and I didn't like the new game. I stuffed my mouth full of whatever food was available. It was my most successful avoidance tactic to dodge questions, just ahead of closing my eyes and screaming at the top of my voice.

My mother touched my hand, her most successful compliance tactic. "Try and remember," she said.

"I don't know." I looked to her face for approval.

"You must remember something," she said.

"I ate breakfast," I offered.

"Everyone has breakfast, Freddy. Tell me something interesting."

"Breakfast is interesting," I replied.

My mother took my chin in her hand. "It's not interesting enough," she told me. "Do you understand interesting?"

"What," I said, not as a question, but a half-hearted attempt to dodge the original question. Often, such a response stopped them asking questions and started them explaining things, at which point I could stop listening. I hoped it would work this time.

It didn't.

"The word *interesting*," Mom said. "Do you understand what it means?"

"Yes."

She smiled. "What happened to you today that you really found interesting? But not breakfast."

"I ate lunch," I said.

As I grew older, I grew better at knowing which things were interesting and which things weren't. I was seven when I finally grasped that there were certain things during the day that merited remembering for the pop quiz later that evening. Infrequent occurrences were always good candidates.

"I had a spelling test," I said.

"Did you!" My mother's eyebrows went up. She finished cutting my meat. "How did you do on it?"

"Yes!" I said, excited.

"And how did you do on the test?"

"I had a spelling test," I agreed.

"Did you get them all right?"

50

"Yes!"

"You didn't get any wrong?"

At this point, I began to panic. The questions were becoming increasingly specific, and I was beginning to get confused.

My mom tried again. "I'm so happy to hear you got all the answers right! What words were on it?"

"Well, that's just GREAT!" I shouted, threw my fork into my mashed potatoes, and crossed my arms in frustration.

The worst thing about the Three Things You Did Today game is the prize. If I successfully guess three things that were interesting, then I will have to guess several more answers to the follow-up questions. It's mentally exhausting. It's frustrating to know that my reward for answering questions is more questions.

———

When I was eight, we began the tradition of walking the trails in the early evening. In the winter months, we raced the shortening day to see if we could escape the forest before night fell. Half the year, we shortened the trip to only the midway point, turning around at the first fork, fifteen minutes into the bush.

Sometimes the dwindling light made me afraid, and our walk slowed as I stared up the side of the mountain, watching for mountain trolls. To take my mind off of this, Bill would ask me about the three things. I answered as reluctantly as I did at the kitchen table, but it kept us occupied, and perhaps the trolls were interested enough to hear my answers: they never bothered us on those walks.

The three questions became a regular outdoor sport when Bill became too preoccupied with his other nightly activities. He began to ask them on every walk behind the house, and stopped asking at the kitchen table altogether. I was fine with that. At least, the game was shorter on our walks. All the more reason to like the walks.

Favourite thing number 3.

THE DAY I LEARNED WHO
LIVED UP BY THE CLIFFS

I opened my eyes and I was six years old. The wind blew through the trees, and I held my father's hand as he walked with me on the trails behind our house. They wind along the bottom of the mountain, over steep gullies and through fir forests plump with mossy bedding. The trails were dug into the hillside, shored up with logs and gravel. They zigzag up the side of the mountain, spread out like a web, splitting and joining, and some go to the summit, thousands of metres up the ribs of the Coast Mountains. Always, we watched for trolls.

I learned there were mountain trolls in the hills behind our house earlier that year. We went for a walk through the forest, from a path that begins just up the road on the west side of our house and shoots straight into the trees.

"It's time you knew the truth," Bill told me as we walked between two giant firs, the sentinels at the path entrance.

Our home is at the edge of town, high up on Westwood Plateau, where the rainforest tumbles down the steep mountain walls and spills into a steep gully. It's a beautiful neighbourhood, with a wide view of the valley. On clear nights, the city lights spread out away into the deep distance. On other nights, the lights are lost in the low-hanging mist. When the rain falls, the gully echoes loudly, angrily, with runoff. When I was younger, my father took me to the edge of the creek where we threw rocks into the tumbling water.

The trail follows the creek, through salmonberry and devil's club. It climbs out of patches of alder and dogwood, with blackberry bushes so thick a mouse would get trapped on their thorns. After it crosses a bridge, it winds up the side of the mountain and joins an old logging road reclaimed by alder and cherry wood.

We like to take walks along this path, and I'm happy to do so. We rarely speak, and, when I was younger he let me run ahead, or lag behind. He called to me to hurry up and called to me to slow down, depending on his mood and my energy level. But he gave me my freedom on those walks.

They are good memories. Favourite memories.

One day, I ventured off the path and climbed straight up the mountainside to the rocks above me, the tumbling cliffs where the sunlight burst through the canopy of hemlock and fir, where the moss-covered cliff glowed like gold.

That day, my father called me back in a tone of voice I had never heard before. When I came back to him, he got down on one knee, put a hand on my shoulder, and said, "There's something you need to know about these woods. I'm going to share it with you, but you have to promise to keep it a secret. Do you promise?"

I nodded.

"Do you know what a secret is?"

"What?" I said.

He adjusted the hood of my rain jacket. "A secret is something that you only tell to one person. Okay?"

"Okay."

"And who is the one person you can tell it to?"

"You."

He nodded. "So, you can't tell anyone else. Right?"

"Right."

"You can't tell anyone at Excalibur House, right?"

"Right."

"You can't tell the bus driver, or the cashier at the grocery store, or the person who stops traffic at the school at the end of our street. Right?"

"Right."

"And you can't tell your mom. Right?"

I hesitated. He sighed. "Okay, *fine*, you can tell your mother, but only if I'm with you. Right?"

I nodded.

He looked around to see if anyone was listening. He pulled me closer to him, put his arm around me, and pointed to the cliffs above the path. "This forest is alive, Freddy," he said. "With things you don't want to come across."

Listen: There are mountain trolls just beyond my backyard. They come out at night. If I went into the backyard by myself, they might come down from the cliffs, with thundering steps, with arms as thick as garbage cans, feet shellacked with calluses, toes growing out at every angle. Noses long and drooping, eyebrows hung like eaves.

If I went into the backyard alone, if they heard me, if they came down, they would eat me. If they didn't eat me, they might make a raucous noise and wake the neighbourhood. Then I would be responsible for disturbing everyone's sleep. I would probably have to answer a *lot* of questions.

So I stayed out of the backyard.

If I went into the forest alone, the trolls would see me and come stomping, guttural, growling, a stench of decayed flesh under their claws and between their teeth. If I went into the forest alone, they would sit on me, crush my bones into jelly, take me back to their caves in the cliffs, and hang me over a fire, slow cooking me for days. They would eat me like turkey dinner.

So I didn't go into the forest alone.

"You can't *ever* go by yourself, Freddy," my father told me. "Trolls are not creatures to be made friends with. They are stupid and angry, and always want to look you straight in the eye."

"Will they eat *you*?" It was a fair question. He'd walked in the forest alone plenty of times.

He fished a rock from his pocket. It was green, no bigger than my thumb, and polished. I ran my finger over its top, back and forth, back and forth. When I tried to take it, he closed his fingers and pulled back his hand, smiling.

"This is my talisman," he told me. "So long as I have it, no trolls ever bother me. It's a sign that we have come to an understanding."

"The trolls understand you?"

Nodding, he pointed to the forest. "I let them keep the forest as theirs. They let me keep this house as mine. They let me walk in the forest, and take whomever I want with me. And they leave us alone."

He pointed to the sky. "You know how the clouds come over the mountain and it rains? That's the trolls, sending it our way. When there's thunder, that's the trolls. Sometimes, they're dancing. Other times, they're arguing. Thunder and rain are a part of their life, and it's a part of ours, and they have to keep sending it our way. So I let them."

The cliffs loomed higher up the slopes, deep with cracks and fissures.

"Up there," he said. "That's where the trolls live. That's their land, and up there, they have a legal right to sit on you and squish you into jelly." He knelt down and looked me straight in the eye. "Do you want to be made into jelly?"

I shook my head.

"Good," he said. "All you have to do is stay away from the cliffs."

"Those cliffs up there." I pointed.

My father nodded.

"The thunder is trolls dancing."

"Right."

"Like Mom dances."

He shrugged. "Kind of, I guess."

"Is Mom a troll?" I asked.

"Sometimes, Freddy." My father sighed and patted me gently on the shoulder. "Sometimes we all are."

When I was younger, thunder at night terrified me. When the winter storms arrived, my father came to my bedroom, sat at the windowsill, and talked with me.

"It's the trolls," he said. "Just the trolls arguing."

"They're loud," I complained. "Why are they loud?"

He shrugged and stood up. His hands in his pockets, he was calm, while the wind howled and rain fell like the first wave of an invasion.

"Sometimes trolls argue for no good reason," he said at last. "Sometimes they're just bored."

There were some good thunder days, though. They were joyous occasions, because when the trolls grumbled in the hills, my mother danced. Sometimes she went out and bought orchids, white ones, for the living room. After she shook off her umbrella and hung up her raincoat, she hurried into the living room and found a spot for them on the coffee table or the end table against the sofa chair by the window.

The TV was off, the laundry folded, the dishwasher finished. Everything became quiet, except sometimes when the thunder rumbled. I ran into the living room and hid behind the curtains, my hands popping my ears or slapping at my thighs, just to make noise.

Still, I knew it was going to be okay, because soon the music would start. My mother stood at the stereo, smiling at me.

"I know just the song," she told me and slowly turned up the music until it was pounding off the walls and I couldn't hear the thunder anymore. She gave me a book, and I sat and stopped moving, fidgeting, stopped clapping my hands. My mother closed her eyes and danced. This was one of my Favourite Things. I'm sure it was one of hers, too.

She danced with the blinds open, and sometimes people slowed as they walked by, standing under their umbrellas. The heat of their stares never bothered her. They were strangers she would never see again, or they were people who saw her dance often enough to not be surprised by it. My mother liked to dance a lot.

When Dad came home from work, he opened a Bud Light and sat back on the couch, to watch her. Relaxed, I sat in the living room with them and stared at the wall.

My first memory of my mother is of the thing she said to me, the same thing she said when she danced.

"*Look* at me, Freddy," she said, and I remember her.

She doesn't say it anymore. If she asked I would look.

If she asked.

When I was seven years old, my mother drove me to the train station. "Look at me, Freddy," she said. Then she kissed me on my cheek and was gone. I sat on a bench, lay on my back, and it rained.

I never saw her again.

At suppertime, our third chair is always empty, and my father fills the vacant space with questions, while I fill the vacant space with abridged answers.

The next day, Saskia Stiles sat at my lunch table in the cafeteria again.

She wore the same pink coat, the same knitted wool cap, the same Bose headphones. But she didn't have her notepad in front of her. She had her iPhone, and she clutched it to her chest like it was trying to leap from her grasp. She bent over, praying into it; her thumbs tapping away in bursts of frantic activity, then frozen in moments of thought assembly. She worked feverishly.

I didn't expect her to be at my table. I expected her to find somewhere else to eat. Somewhere less crowded. Somewhere uncrowded. That's what I would have done.

But there she was.

I sat down, at the opposite end. She squeaked.

We ate in silence, the only thing between us the empty space of a lunch table.

When Saskia Stiles squeaked for a second time, she put her sandwich down, brought her hands up, and flapped them.

Just then, a Tater bomb fell.

"Heads up, fucknuts!" Danny Hardwick called out to me.

Six days after I arrived at Hampton Park, Jim Worley asked me how I was getting by.

"Getting by what?" I asked him. His nostrils flared. Our relationship had progressed to the point where he was no longer certain I was as simple as he thought, and he suspected that I often baited him. His smile tightened a little more each time we talked. Although I understood what it means to "get by," I also knew that with Jim Worley a literal response was the best response, because it annoyed him. The more annoyed he was with me, the fewer questions he asked.

"I see you're eating lunch in the cafeteria," he said after my first month at Hampton Park. "Have you made any friends?"

"No," I replied.

"You don't talk to anyone at the lunch table?"

I shook my head. "No one sits at my table."

"Why do you think that is?" he asked.

"People throw Tater Tots at this table."

Jim Worley paused to absorb this. "Do you mean," he said after a moment, "that they throw Tater Tots at you?"

Don't tell him, a thread advised. *He'll just ask more questions.*

"No," I said.

Jim Worley waited for more. *Told you*, shrugged the thread.

"Sometimes they throw them at the janitors' lunchroom. I think they're trying to annoy the janitors."

Jim Worley nodded his head thoughtfully. "That stands to reason, I guess."

He leaned back and put his feet up on his desk. "It seems odd that they sell Tater Tots in the cafeteria. People buy them to throw them. Not to eat them, you know. Little Tater Bombs, we called them when I was a student here." He looked at me and smiled, as if he was sharing an inside secret. "Yes, Frederick," he said. "I was once a student, too. And they had invented Tater Tots by then, too."

"That's not what I was wondering," I told him.

"No?"

"No," I said. "I was wondering if they threw them at you or if you threw Tater Tots at them."

His smile tightened.

In the cafeteria, Tater Tots fell.

I sat, eating my lunch in silence, and wondered if I should advise Saskia Stiles to eat somewhere else, not because I didn't want her at my table, but because I believed that eating at my table may cause her distress.

Another Tater Tot arced across the cafeteria and bounced off our table. I gave no reaction. She jumped slightly, and I found myself

59

compelled to say something reassuring. Which I have never felt compelled to do before.

"It's a stochastic event," I said and looked down at the table like it was the most interesting surface I'd ever seen.

Saskia stopped mid-chew, staring down at her phone. Then she put it down and reached into her backpack. She took out her notepad and a pen, and began scribbling.

"A stochastic event," I said again, "is an event that happens at random intervals but is expected to occur on a dependable frequency. The Tater Tots are a stochastic event."

The first time a Tater Tot landed near me, I was startled and looked around for an explanation. Why were little bits of deep-fried potato plummeting out of the air onto my table? The second time it happened, one landed on my plate, and Danny Hardwick laughed with his friends. Then they high-fived each other, and I knew the explanation for why little bits of deep-fried potato were plummeting out of the air was me. I was the target.

After that, the Tater Tots came periodically, and I paid them no attention. When one hit me on the shoulder, I hardly noticed it. When Danny Hardwick and his friends cheered, I stared at the wall and ate my cheeseburger.

After a while, Danny Hardwick realized I was a target that would not react. He became bored with me. Periodically, he fired a test shot, to see if I was ready to say something, but I never did.

To be clear: my lack of response wasn't a strategy. It wasn't a plan at all. It was a realization that Tater Tot bombs would rain on me at random, unpredictable intervals. It was a realization that Tater Tots and thunder weren't too different. Both were distressing. There was nothing I could do about either. That was enough to put me at peace with incoming Tater bombs.

A second Tater Tot fell on the table near Saskia.

"Ninety-five percent of the time," I said to her, while still staring at the wall, "two or less Tater Tots are thrown at the table." My cheeseburger was finished. It was time for me to go. But I sat. "They've only thrown three or more Tater Tots on four occasions."

A third Tater Tot bounced between us.

"Five occasions," I corrected.

She glanced at the Tater Tot sideways and started typing on her iPhone again.

A fourth bounced off my left ear. Danny Hardwick cheered.

We were now outside the standard deviation.

I didn't know Danny Hardwick or his friends personally, but I knew who they were, because they made it their business to make sure everyone in school knew who they were. They were the boys who sat at the seventh table on the first row of the cafeteria. No one else sat at the seventh table on the first row, except those who were invited.

No one was invited.

It was a loud table. Each lunch hour, they told loud stories and laughed at loud jokes. They ate popcorn and threw Tater Tots.

Danny Hardwick's friends deferred to him. When he threw kernels, they threw kernels. When he was quiet, they were quiet. He was the Alpha Tater. He wore a leather jacket and his hands were always stained black with grease and oil from the auto mechanics shop at the end of the school. He was large, with thick dark eyebrows and a face pocked with acne scars. His hair was blond with a thick dyed stripe of black running up the middle, like an etched mohawk. He only smiled when he threw Tater bombs.

We went to different classes in different ends of the school. Although his locker was on the same bank of lockers as mine, we never talked. We only interacted in the cafeteria. It was our Jerusalem.

Once, we bumped shoulders walking down the hall, but I didn't turn to see what his reaction was. I had not bumped his shoulder; he had bumped mine, and I know he bumped it deliberately. At school, if you're new, you will have your shoulder bumped. That's residual instinct at work. Young men have been bumping each other's shoulders for tens of thousands of years. That's just the way it is. Danny Hardwick likes to bump shoulders. He wins at it a lot.

Sometimes, out of the corner of my eye, I saw him staring at me.

Sometimes I sat, eating my lunch, and I knew Danny Hardwick wanted to bump my shoulder. But we were never in the same class together, and we walked different hallways.

I think that made him angry. The corridors we walked defined, at a basic level, how much more intelligent I am than he is. That's just the way it is.

Now that Saskia sat at my table, he seemed angrier. Tater bombs rained down.

They rained down on the third day we ate lunch together.

They rained on the fourth. And the fifth. I hardly noticed them.

—————

On the sixth day, I stared at the wall across from the table. She drew pictures in her notebook for the first half of her lunch, then wrote text messages for the remaining half.

My right hand stayed in my jacket pocket and played with a folded-up piece of paper. It was the now *un*crumpled poem I took from the table on the first day I saw her.

This is what she wrote on the paper:

hello

is there anybody in there

I didn't know what she meant by it, but it didn't rest well with me, and the threads wondered about it.

Is anybody in where? they asked.

I gave up trying to figure out what she wanted to say. Google was helpful, and I discovered that they were lyrics by the band Pink Floyd. So I added, beneath her words:

Just nod if you can hear me.

Is there anyone at home?

As I got up to leave, I took the poem from my pocket, unfolded it, and lay it before her.

"Goodbye, Saskia," I said. "I'll see you later."

—————

On the seventh day, she arrived to lunch late and sat down at the opposite end of the table. She pulled the poem from her pocket and uncrumpled it. She read it, then crumpled it up, then opened it again. Putting it down, she took her iPhone out of her pocket. She turned off her music, then scrolled through her selection, and started a new song.

I could hear her listening to Pink Floyd.

Relax, the song continued, *I'll need some information first.*

I listened to its tinny quality seeping out of her headphones, as the band broke into the main riff.

I have become, they sang.

At lunch on the eighth day, she was agitated and turned her music up, then down, then up again. She tried to eat, but kept putting her food down, flapping her hands at shoulder level.

She took a pencil from her backpack and opened the poem I had given her two days before. She scrawled on it, crumpled it back up, and lobbed the paper toward me. Then she got up and walked away, leaning forward, her hands clasped to her chest.

There is no pain, you are receding, she wrote.

I opened my eyes and I was sitting in the duck sauce chair, with Jim Worley staring at me. My status was yellow, but it had been green before this moment, turning yellow only when Jim Worley pressed the conversation forward.

"I saw you in the cafeteria today," he said, making a temple with his fingers. "You were sitting with a girl."

I didn't reply.

"Did you mind it when she came and sat at your table?"

"No," I replied.

He waited for more.

"She was already sitting at my table when I got there."

He nodded, placing his index fingers, in the shape of a church steeple, under his chin. "And yet you sat beside her. This isn't such a bad thing, I think." He nodded. "Yes," he continued. "Real progress."

"Maybe it's because of this chair," I offered. He frowned.

"Probably not," he answered after considering it for a moment. He tapped his desk with a pencil. "Did you talk to her?"

"I said goodbye," I confirmed.

He nodded. "Well, that's a start." He opened his laptop and typed quickly. He smiled. "Ah. There she is. Her name is Saskia Stile."

"Stiles," I corrected.

His eyebrows went up. "You know her?"

"Yes."

"How?"

"When I was seven, we attended the same therapy sessions."

He tapped at his computer and went through various screens. "I see," he said. "So you know she's autistic."

"She has PDD-NOS," I said.

He squinted at his computer screen. "No, no," he corrected me. "She's autistic."

"Saskia Stiles is on the spectrum," I agreed. "But her diagnosis is Pervasive Development Disorder, Not Otherwise Specified. PDD-NOS."

He pointed at his computer screen. "It says here she has—"

"No," I said. "She has PDD-NOS."

He closed his laptop. "Potato, potahto," he allowed. "So, she's your friend, then?"

I didn't reply.

No one says potahto.

———

Listen: Here is how I knew Saskia Stiles had this diagnosis. She told me, eleven years ago. She was excited about it.

"I have Puh-DID-noss!" she shouted, jumping up and down. I didn't understand what she was saying.

Nine days later, I overheard my mother and father talking about Saskia, and my mother said, "She has PDD-NOS."

I realized then that Saskia knew that she was diagnosed with PDD-NOS because she had *read* it. And she pronounced it PuhDiDNoSs.

The things you remember.

THE TRANSFER OF SASKIA STILES
TO MY CHEMISTRY CLASS

Jim Worley was not a man who let ideas linger, good or bad. Saskia Stiles was an idea.

"I think we can build on this," he said and looked at me. I continued to stare at the wall. He didn't say anything more and I realized I was expected to answer a question he hadn't asked. Those are the *worst* kinds of questions.

"What?" I said.

"I said we can build on this."

"What?" I said.

"We can build on sitting at the same table as Saskia Stiles."

"Yes," I agreed.

He nodded and made a temple out of his fingers. "Excellent," he explained.

"What," I agreed.

"It's fortuitous that the two of you met." He said the words slowly, with a serious expression. "Do you understand what 'fortuitous' means?"

"Yes."

"Tell me, then."

"To be fortuitous is to have the characteristic of experiencing good fortune."

"I suppose, I suppose." He opened a folder on his desk and lifted a sheet of paper. "Saskia Stiles is in your grade. Takes the same classes as you. She's also—" He stopped and looked at me. Paused. "—a loner. Like you."

"I'm not a loner. I'm an anthropophobe."

He blinked. "A what?"

"I suffer from anthropophobia."

He opened a second folder and rifled through the papers. "I don't—" he said, distracted. "It doesn't say anything here about—"

"I have a condition where I don't enjoy interacting with others. At times it's an irrational feeling and, therefore, a phobia."

He leaned forward. "When were you diagnosed with that?"

"I'm self-diagnosed," I explained.

"Oh," he said and looked at a sheet in his folder again. He looked at another. Picked up another sheet. Put it down. "I see," he said.

He didn't.

"This is a nice chair," I offered.

———

Saskia Stiles was transferred to my chemistry class the next day.

Jim Worley seemed pleased that we got along. He believed it was synchronous. She was non-verbal, and I didn't like talking to people. It seemed to him, I expect, an ideal match. From that perspective, Jim Worley was a very insightful man.

Saskia Stiles walked into my class only a few minutes after I took my seat at the back of the room. Her headphones ever over her wool cap. Her notebook ever present. She clutched it and her textbook to her chest like a breastplate. Hunched over, she looked down and moved with short quick steps, as if she were scrubbing the floor with her feet.

She sat at the empty table next to mine. Like every other table, it seated four, on tall stools. At the centre of the table was a sink and a natural gas outlet for the Bunsen burners. She laid her books down, took off her backpack, and opened her notebook.

I also sat by myself. When I first came to this class, people tried to engage me, or become lab partners with me. Usually, it was a girl who sat with me. While this may sound amenable to a typical teenage boy, it was annoying to me. Girls like to *talk*.

I had endured several lab partners. Now, people rarely sat with me; it didn't take long for the others to learn I was a poor conversationalist. I said things that weren't in the proper context of the conversation. I said things that weren't in the proper context of the silence. I said things that sometimes startled them. So now, I sat alone.

Saskia and I sat silently, each at our own table, waiting for the class to begin, looking at the blackboard. It was the sensible thing to do.

And then she began testing the taps. On. Off. On again.

When the chemistry teacher walked into the classroom, he put down his notes and looked directly at Saskia.

"Young lady," he said. "Stop playing with the water."

She ignored him. Perhaps she didn't hear him, but I think she did.

"Young lady!" His palm slammed the desktop. "Hey!"

The end to this was not going to be happy, I could see, especially if he did the thing he appeared about to do: walk up and grab her, or even try to take her headphones off. At best, there would be a confrontation. At worst, there would be a one-person riot.

A deer in the city, said the threads.

Shut up, I explained.

Mr. Pringle stepped away from his desk, his jaw tight, his brow furrowed. He breathed through his nose.

"Mr. Chips," I said, softly, but clearly, crisply, as if I were speaking from the ranks at reveille.

Seriously? asked the threads.

Mr. Pringle stopped, mid-step, frozen. His eyes snapped to mine, then his head slowly followed suit.

"What," he said, his lips parted, his teeth clamped together, "did you just say?"

I stared at my textbook and turned pages slowly. "She can't hear you," I said. "She has her headphones on." I flipped the pages of my textbook back and forth.

He looked at me, then back at her. "Well, she'd better bloody well take them off," he said. "Tell her to take them off."

"But she won't take them off."

"The hell she won't."

"The hell she *will*," I replied, then turned the pages faster.

I could feel his glare. He stared at me for ten seconds. My mouth dried, I began to sweat, and I felt a pressing need to swallow. Then he went back to his desk and shuffled through his papers. Seeing a red manila folder on his desk, he picked it up and opened it. As he read it, he glanced up at Saskia three times.

"Autistic," he said. "Great."

Heads turned. Eyes fell on Saskia, the newest artifact of interest in the class.

"P.D.D.N.O.S." I said.

Mr. Pringle looked at me. "Christ, Wyland, now what?"

"I don't know," I hastily responded. I had meant to say nothing at all. I wasn't interested in a conversation. Not another one. I'd already had one, earlier in the day, with Jim Worley. That was enough.

"Okay," said Mr. Pringle. He slammed his folder shut and put it down on the desk. "Do you know her?"

"Yes."

He considered her as she ran a pencil back and forth under the water. Slight squeaks, barely audible above the sound of the central air coming from the ceiling above her, popped from her lips.

Mr. Pringle nodded. "Congratulations, professor, she's now your lab partner, and your responsibility. Go sit beside her. And, for God's sake, get her to stop playing with the water taps."

I picked up my binder and carried it to her table. Moving the stool until it was as far away from her as it could be, I sat down. I slowly reached out and tapped her pencil with a single finger. She glanced at me, looked away quickly, then turned off the water faucet. She put the pencil down, sat back, and folded her hands in her lap, looking at the desktop.

Mr. Pringle, after observing this, sighed and shook his head. "What idiot decided she was ready to use an open flame?"

Saskia turned down her headphones and copied the notes that the teacher wrote on the chalkboard. She opened her book to the correct page. She read the text and turned the pages. She did her work in silence. Slightly, just slightly, the corner of her mouth turned up in the hint of a smile. And then it was gone. She turned her pages.

As she did this, I began to feel a growing sense of alarm, because I was not supposed to find this as enjoyable as I did.

The inquisition began, as per normal, Sunday morning, halfway through our patrol in the mountains behind the house.

"Tell me three things that you're excited about," Bill said as we trudged forward, single file, at a slow enough pace to comfortably talk in short sentences, just fast enough that neither of us could sing. We had tried singing years before. It wasn't satisfying. That is why we walk at this pace.

Every week, I am asked to look forward to the upcoming week. Every week, Bill has to ask twice, because the pace is just fast enough that his patience for a response is abbreviated.

"Three things, Freddy," he said.

We reached the crest of a hill and paused for a rest. There was a break in the trees and we could see the valley stretching below, until it disappeared in distant rain bursts.

Tell him you're excited about telling him three things you're excited about, the threads urged.

It won't work, I told the threads. It never does.

Maybe this time.

"I'm excited about telling you three things," I said and tried to look nonchalant.

Bill frowned and stared at me, waiting.

The jig is up! howled the threads.

"Tell me the *next* two things you're excited to tell me about," Bill said.

"Apples."

"You're excited about apples?"

"No," I said. "Yes. Sometimes. Not now."

"Then why did you say 'apples'?"

"It was the first thing that came to mind."

The wind shivered the tops of the trees. "Freddy, do we have to go through this every time?"

Say no, warned the smarter half of my mind.

Just tell him yes, shouted the threads.

"Not every time," I said, which I thought was a happy medium.

We don't know what that means, said the threads.

Bill rubbed his eyes. He sighed. He fiddled with the Velcro holding his water bottle to his belt.

"Freddy," he began.

"Chemistry class," I said quickly, and everyone in my head was surprised.

We did not *see that coming*, said the threads.

I didn't realize I was going to say it before I said it. It just came out. I blurted.

I never blurt.

Sometimes I stammer. Sometimes I pause mid-sentence because the threads have led me down a rabbit hole, and I have forgotten the last half of what I was going to say. And sometimes I stare because I have nothing to say. I can't pull anything relevant from my queue of answers. The threads are silent. The smarter half is thinking about something else. I have been abandoned in my own mind, and I have nothing. So I just pick the nearest approximation. Usually, it's something from a movie that I've seen recently.

When I was younger and Bill asked me "How was school today?" I would answer with something relatively appropriate, perhaps from *Finding Nemo*.

"Just keep swimming," I'd chime. "Just keep swimming."

"Ah!" Bill would say and wonder if we'd Made a Breakthrough.

That was then.

Today, if he asked me, I would be more likely to answer with something from an Ed Norton movie.

"How was school today?"

"Welcome to Fight Club," I would reply. "The first rule of Fight Club is: you do not talk about Fight Club. The second rule of Fight Club is: you *do not* talk about Fight Club!"

He doesn't ask how school went all that often.

This time, I just led him into it. I didn't know it was something I was looking forward to.

Bill tilted his head. "Chemistry class," he said slowly. "That's good, isn't it?"

I braced myself, for I knew that there were more questions coming. I had opened the door. Would I not expect that Bill would just walk right in?

Change the subject!

"Frogs," I said. And I began walking.

That did it. Bill pursed his lips and pondered the new revelation as he fell in behind me and we began our descent. "What about frogs?"

"I'm excited about frogs. Frogs is the third thing I'm excited about."

"Why on God's green earth would you be excited about frogs today?"

"I'm excited about them every day."

He said, "Let's go back to chemistry class. Why—"

"Just keep swimming!" I shouted quickly. "Just keep swimming!"

Down the valley, a low crack of thunder. Rain began falling on my hood.

"Let's get going," Bill said, and I was all too ready to agree.

———

Despite the Three Things I Did or the Three Things I Look Forward To or the Three Things I'm Excited About, the trails behind my house remain a Favourite Thing. They have been a constant in my life.

After my mother left, Bill and I walked the hills like soldiers to the front. Our heads down, single file, a strong march, with little time to look around. I thought a lot. One of the things I thought about was Saskia. I wondered where she was. I wondered if she still went to Excalibur House. And I wondered why, even years later, I still wondered these things.

Saskia was one of my Favourite Things when we were friends. Even after I stopped seeing her, she remained a Favourite Thing. Over the years, new memories began to erode the spot she held in my mind, and I gradually thought about her less on my walks until, more than five years after I last saw her, I stopped wondering. She sat down in her seat at the back of my mind and rarely crossed my thoughts.

I don't know why she remained such a Favourite Thing for so long, but she did. While she was on my list, I thought of it as rational. She was my friend, my only friend, and her absence didn't seem a reason for her to stop being my friend. So, every week, for years after I left Excalibur House, she came with me on my walks.

Hello, Freddy, she called out. *Did you have a good day?*

I did. I had a good day.

I had a good day too!

I marched behind my father, while the winds played the trees like cellos and the trolls glowered down at me from the cliffs above.

I opened my eyes and I was seven years old. The rain made a *tat-tat-tat* noise on my hood. I sat with my back against the cliff and listened to the wind shaking the trees, the rain like applause, and I waited for the trolls to come down and meet with me.

Not long before that, I stood in the kitchen, staring out the window into the forest. The rain was our constant companion; it had been pouring for weeks. I wondered if there was something I could do about it. I went to my father's room and searched through his desk until I found his jade talisman, the one he kept in his pocket when walking in the forest.

I put on my raincoat and walked out the back door, through the yard, and past the gate. I didn't stand or pause, but stepped between the two giant firs that stood like sentinels at the entrance to the forest. I went in. Among the trees, it was dark, and the water drops grew thicker, slapping on my hood like birds pecking at my brow.

In my pocket, I nervously caressed the talisman.

————

Although I had heard the back door slam when I shut it behind me, I didn't see it pop back out of its latch. When my father came home, the house was as cold as a tomb. I was, by then, too far away to hear his calls.

He went upstairs to check my bedroom. When he found it empty, he went to his bedroom to phone the police. There, the dresser drawers were open, the contents astray; he saw how I had rifled through his things.

The bottom drawer of his desk was open. His talisman was gone. He knew where I went.

————

Deep in the forest, I sat with my back against a lichen-strafed cliff wall. Across the valley, I saw mountains poking out from the mist.

A hundred yards down the steep slope, my father, in a heavy green fisherman's coat, grunted and cursed as he made his way over salal and deadfall, up to the base of the cliff, where I sat.

He arrived, out of breath, and took a moment to compose himself.

"Dammit, Freddy," he said, "what are you *doing* here?"

"Where's Mom?" I asked, looking out into the disappearing mountains.

His shoulders sagged. He sat beside me, and we didn't speak for a half hour as night slipped overhead.

———

Ten years ago, the rain came like the locusts and stayed for three months. During its visit, there were only four days that staggered the downpour.

On weekends, I stared out the window of the living room and watched the sidewalks, empty of neighbours. No one casually walked by anymore to see if my mother was dancing. They stayed out of the downpour, which was just as well, because my mother didn't dance anymore. After the first few weeks of the rainfall, she shuffled about the living room in a housecoat and slippers, with a cup of coffee and a head full of morning hair. Sometimes she didn't dress until dinner.

When someone is feeling sad, you're supposed to rub their backs and empathize. You are supposed to do kind things for them. But I didn't know how to do any of that, I didn't know what to say.

I knew I was *supposed* to say, "What's wrong?" but I wasn't going to pretend. I already knew what was wrong: she was unhappy. At night, I sometimes sat in bed and stared at the wall, and listened to her crying in the living room. At other times, I awoke to the sound of my parents arguing. Sometimes, they shouted until my father stormed out of the house.

Often, my name was one of the words shouted back and forth.

On the fourth week of the downpour, she shuffled less about the living room and sat more in the sofa chair, staring at the rain, a glass of wine always in her hand. On the fifth week, she sat there for large parts of the day and would still be there when my father came

75

home from work at night. He sometimes sat with her and drank his Bud Light in silence. On the sixth week, Bill began working overtime shifts and came home only after Mom had gone to bed.

On the seventh week, she came early for me at Excalibur House. "Where's Dad?" I asked, and she didn't answer.

I got in the car. "Where's my booster seat?"

The last thing we talked about was the location of my booster seat. It was a substantial conversation, lasting the entirety of the ride.

She drove me to the station and held me tightly until I finally pushed her away. "It's time for you to be a man now," she said. "Get up and get on with your life." Then she sat me on the bench, made me lie down and close my eyes, and she left. That's just the way it is.

I don't remember how I got home. It's one of the few things in my life I don't remember. Instead, I remember lying on my back, looking at the dark night sky, as the rain fell on my face. I remember feeling cold, listening to the sound of people around me, the sounds of the train station, the ticking of cooling metal, the hiss of air being released from brakes.

I remember someone standing over me, as I lay staring up at the sky.

"What are you looking at, sport?" he said.

THE CANDLES THAT RESTED
ON MY TWIN BROTHER

I opened my eyes and I was fourteen years old, in my bed, and my father was drinking in the kitchen. I couldn't sleep, and the house was cold. I got up from bed and walked downstairs. I found him at the kitchen table.

The kitchen table is my brother, my father often told me. When I was a child, he liked to tease me about it. It made no sense to me, but I liked it, because he played with me when he said it.

"You're the two funniest looking twins I've ever seen," he told me, putting down his beer and chasing me to the living room, where my mother was dancing.

The table and I are non identical twins, so that makes us fraternal. We were both delivered on the same day. Me, at 9 pounds, 12 ounces. The table, at 158 pounds. I don't know how many ounces. Me, with a slight swirl of blond hair. It, with oak stained cherry red.

Both the kitchen table and I were difficult deliveries.

The table was too large to easily fit through the front hall and had to go into the house through a more circuitous route, lifted up to the balcony, through the sliding door into the living room. Then to the nook in the kitchen.

Similarly, I was too large to easily fit through a birth canal and had to go out through a more circuitous route. The womb from which I was ripped grieved petulantly. It mourned its loss, crying eleven units of blood over the next two hours. Until the surgeons finally stopped the flow of blood, it wasn't known whether I would be born to a one- or two-parent family.

The table was my father's present to his beloved wife, to my mother, for the work she had done, for the sacrifice she gave. She could never have children again. I destroyed her womb. I blew shut the door from which I came, and no one could follow after me. I made my mother into a one-act play, and I was the plot.

And now, fourteen years later, my father sat alone in the dark with his scotch and his candles.

"Where's Mom?" I asked him, and the candles danced.

"You keep asking that," he sighed.

Outside, a flash of lightning turned the night to day, and I saw the alder at the window, tapping.

"You know where she is," he said. He motioned to the chair across from him. "Sit," he said. "Just sit for a bit."

I sat down.

"Have you asked me where Mom is before?" he said.

"Yes."

"Have I told you the answer before?" he asked.

"Yes."

"Tell me what the answer is."

"She left us."

He nodded.

"When did she leave us?" he asked.

I paused. "Seven years ago."

"How many days?"

"Two thousand, seven hundred, and forty-three days."

He nodded again. "Two thousand, seven hundred, and forty-three days," he said and took a sip of his scotch. "That's a long time for you to keep asking, you know."

The refrigerator turned on. I listened to its chatter for a moment and it calmed my mind. I watched the candles flicker. They were a characteristic of our home. My father preferred them to a lamp. He claimed it made the evening more important.

"A candle at the table means there are secrets, Freddy. A candle is *intimate.* On a night where there is only a candle for light, you are probably about to enter into a dialogue with your own soul."

He leaned toward me. "Tonight, boy," he pointed his dying cigarette at me, "we can talk about questions of the soul."

"Why did she leave?" I asked.

"Some people can't handle it." He shrugged.

I stared out the window.

"Listen," he said. "There were stages we went through. I think they're the same stages every parent like us goes through. Some of the stages overlap." He held up his glass. "Like the drinking stage.

"But the first stages are the same for everyone. First there's shock, and you sit around waiting for someone to pull out the accidentally misplaced file and tell you it was all a mix-up. Then there's the stage where you don't believe it, what if the diagnosis was wrong, what if Freddy was just having a bad day?" He shook his head. "But deep down you know none of that is going to happen, because you've suspected for too long, you've lived with it for too long. You know it's true. And you move on to the next stage.

"You go through each phase and it's tough," he muttered as he stubbed out his cigarette. "Because nothing happens. You get angry, but there's no one to be angry at. You sit in denial and hope that your kid will spontaneously get better. You do nothing and watch it get worse. After that, and for the rest of your life, you live with the guilt that you didn't start soon enough."

He looked at me. "Betty had a tough time getting past that stage."

I waited.

"There was the stage where we believed that it would come to an end soon. And there was the stage where we decided that by the time you were fifteen or sixteen you'd be cured."

"Cured of what?" I asked.

He nodded and pointed a finger at me. "Exactly," he said. He sat back, his shoulders relaxed like a great truth had been spoken. "Exactly."

Clink, clink.

"Then there was the stage where we stopped pretending that some things were getting better. Because some things weren't. That's the stage where we knew it would be like this forever. This isn't like the flu. Autism isn't acute." He looked me directly in the eye as he said this, then he was quiet for a while.

"And when you realize something like that," he said at last, "your world collapses like a mud hut. It drops down on you, and there's no more lying about it. Your son has autism. He has it and he'll have it the rest of his life." He pulled out another cigarette, his fingers shaking. "That's the worst stage because the question becomes: how far will your son make it in life? And the answer is now back in your court." He pointed a finger at me. "Where *you* end up depends on what *I* do right here, right *now*. This is the stage where I realize that your future is in my hands, and it scares me to death. For the past ten years, I've been afraid that I don't have what it takes."

Not good enough, the threads said.

"Why did Mom leave?"

He sighed and dropped his head. "I don't know. I don't know if she realized she wasn't up to the challenge, or if she thought that I wasn't up for the challenge. Either way, she left."

He took a long drag of his cigarette and looked at me as he drank the last of his scotch, then set his glass on the table. "And she didn't take you."

THIS, MY MOTHER

That night my father told me that my mother left me behind was
an inflection point in my life. It marked the end of seven years of
wondering why she left. Now I finally knew: she left because of me.

So began the three years since, wondering what to do about it.

This is what I remember of my mother: her hair was blond and
it hung two inches past her shoulders. Her eyes were blue. She was
three inches shorter than my father. She wore dresses. Her favourite
flowers were orchids. She smelled like strawberries off a knife. She
liked to wear red lipstick. Her housecoat was pink and came down
to just above her knees. On weekends, she liked to make a morning
pot of coffee and sit with my father in the living room for an hour,
looking out the window, talking about the years ahead and what
would be. I was not allowed to take part. Until the last cup of coffee
was finished, I was not supposed to interrupt. My mother called it
their Special Morning Time.

My father called it his Time Out from Me.

I remember my mother liked to dance in the living room, or
fuss with her orchids, ignoring my father's complaints about the
expense. I remember she liked to hop up and down with me when
I got excited or agitated, and it ended up calming me. Sometimes,
we clapped our hands for twenty minutes until I stopped bouncing
on the couch. I remember when we did it on our feet and my father
walked in and took a bow because he said he thought we were giving
him a standing ovation.

"No, we're NOT!" I shouted, jumping up and down.

I remember at night, sometimes, I would sit in my bed and stare
at the wall and listen to my mother crying. At the time, I didn't
understand what she was crying about. On the night my father told

me why my mother left, I realized she was crying about me. I realized that when they yelled, they were yelling about me.

For days after I realized this, the thread consumed me, this question of what I did to make her leave. It appropriated my time until it became my Most Favourite Thing. I still stared at the giant clock, and still watched the time pass, but my mind was no longer empty. It was filled with questions and thoughts and logical rabbit holes.

Over those days, I withdrew. When outdoors, I was especially unresponsive to others. My head went down when I walked. My eyes went distant when I stood. I thought about my mother and watched the time tick away.

A week after our conversation over the candle, as I sat at the bus stop and turned the pages of my book, a group of boys chatted among themselves, pushing at each other and laughing. I stared at a grey wall in the distance, watching the clock tick time. 4:32, 4:33, 4:34. But it was difficult to stay focused because one of the four boys was directly in my line of sight.

"Could you not stand there?" I asked him.

That was how it began.

I opened my eyes and I was fourteen years old. I lay on my back and looked straight up into the sky. Rain fell on my face. The wheels of my stretcher rattled, and two paramedics rolled me to the ambulance, put me inside, closed the doors, and took me to Eagle Ridge Hospital.

It was unusual that I went willingly on a stretcher. I'm not fond of things with small wheels, like shopping carts, or skateboards, or ottomans. I don't feel the same way about Hot Wheels cars, which also have small wheels. The wheels aren't small in proportion to the rest of the toy car. Small wheels are disconcerting when the chassis is disproportionately larger than the wheels. I don't like large airplanes for that reason.

It took the paramedics a small amount of coercing and shepherding to get me on the stretcher. They didn't know I was autistic, and thought I was just injured. So they went slow. They put a collar around my neck. They slid a board under me.

"What are you looking at, sport?" the paramedic first asked me, then shone a light in my right eye.

What happened? a thread finally asked.

It may have been a troll that did this to me. Perhaps there's a subspecies of troll, shaped like teenage boys, with rings and baseball caps and thick green coats. If so, it was trolls that did this to me.

On the way to the hospital, they asked too many questions.

"Can you understand me?"

When I tried to reply, they interrupted me with a different question.

"Can you tell me what day it is?"

I didn't reply. Fool me twice, and all that.

I was disoriented and frightened, but mostly I was annoyed at the two paramedics for asking questions that didn't require immediate answers. I could tell them the date later. It wasn't the most pressing question.

The most pressing question was: *why did this happen?*

I lay on the stretcher, even though I wanted to stand, and I remember they put an oxygen mask over my mouth, even though I wasn't having trouble breathing. Their actions kept spawning new questions in my mind, and I was overwhelmed. I lay back, closed my eyes.

"Okay, he's shutting down," said the first paramedic, alarmed.

"Stay with me, sport," said the second.

"Stop talking, please," I said.

I closed threads:

The stretcher has small wheels, said a thread.

I knew that the gurney was tall relative to its wheels, probably unstable, and therefore dangerous. But I was inside the back of an ambulance, in a confined space. Further, the paramedics collapsed the gurney so that it was only inches off the floor. There was little chance that the gurney could tip over.

Okay, said the thread.

However, the ambulance door could open at a stoplight, the ambulance could accelerate, and I could spill into traffic, strapped to the stretcher. I did a memory search for any examples of a patient accidentally sliding out the back door of an ambulance at a traffic light and found nothing. *Okay*, said another thread.

A thread remembered a news story I read, two years, three months, and four days ago, about an enraged mob blocking an ambulance carrying a suspected rapist. The mob dragged him from the back of the ambulance and beat him to death.

But I wasn't suspected of rape. In fact, I was the victim of violence, not the suspect of violence. It was unlikely that an enraged mob would attack the ambulance and beat me. *Works for me*, said the thread.

One thread remained: the four boys could pull me from the ambulance and complete my beating. They had motivation and had indicated they weren't done. The one in the thick green coat warned me that the beating was incomplete.

"If they ask you who did this," he said, picking me up by the scruff of my shirt, "you tell them you don't know nuthin'. Otherwise, we'll find you and finish the job."

"This isn't a job," I said weakly, and he hit me again with my book before throwing it to the pavement.

––––––––

In the emergency room, a nurse examined me and concluded I wasn't so special that she could spare me any more attention. She left me sitting on the gurney in the hall. I sat for two hours. The bleeding from my nose stopped, then congealed, then crusted. A front tooth wiggled but didn't come out. My left eye swelled shut. I wondered if it would stay shut forever.

I don't like to wonder about things. I am not good at it. If you were to ask me why my eye was swollen shut, I could tell you that it was because the other boy's right fist hit me there. If you asked me why he hit me, I could tell you that it was because the other boy was angry with me. If you asked me why the other boy was angry with me, I wouldn't be able to answer.

I'm not good at subjective questions.

––––––––

Years ago, at Excalibur House, they had warned me about this: that people may often misinterpret the things I say. But I'll never understand why people get angry with *me* when *they* fail to understand what I say. They could be angry with me if I deliberately told them a lie, but I rarely tell lies. Although I'm capable of telling them, I'm not good at it. And I'm not good at identifying lies. This makes sarcasm a minefield of misinterpretation.

If someone said, "Well, that's just great," I used to believe the person was satisfied with the thing that was Just Great. It turns out that it can mean the opposite. This phrase gets me into trouble, especially with my father. He says "That's just great" often. It's usually not.

Once, when I was five years old, I knew I needed to go to the bathroom, but I was watching *Dora the Explorer*, and I wanted to hear her say what her Favourite Part was. I could never guess the reason beforehand. It frustrated me to no end.

"What was *your* favourite part?" Dora the Explorer asked and I became frantic.

"Crossing the Foggy Ocean!" I shouted.

"I liked that part, too," she replied, after considering my reply. "*My* favourite part was when the Rocky Rocks sang to me!"

"Son of a BITCH!" I shouted in frustration. I learned that phrase from my father.

I peed in my pants because I was waiting for her answer, and my father got angry. He saw the wet stain on my pants and said, "Well, that's just great."

"It's not great," I said.

"I *know*," he said.

I tried to spread my legs while standing, so the pants would hang from me. "I'm uncomfortable."

"Good for you," he answered.

"Peeing pants is not good," I said.

"Then why the Christ did you do it?"

"I wanted to watch *Dora the Explorer*."

He closed his eyes and his jaw muscles clenched, unclenched, clenched again. "It's a DVD, kid. A goddamn DVD. You could have asked me to pause it."

He saw my sopping wet socks. "Look at that, it's all over the rug now. Well, that's just great."

"It's not great," I said. "You will have to clean it up with soap."

"Shut the fuck up, will you?" he said.

———

At the hospital, a doctor with thick black glasses and red hair tied back in a ponytail examined me. She lifted my chin and shone a small flashlight in my eyes. "Do you know your name?"

"Yes," I answered.

She waited for me to say more. I stared past her at the wall.

"Do you know your name?"

"Yes," I said. "I still do."

The doctor clicked off her flashlight and straightened up, frowning at me.

"He's not showing any symptoms," she said to a nurse. "I think he's just a smartass." She looked at me. "Tell me your name."

"Freddy Wyland," I said. "I'm here against my will."

"Aren't we all?" she said, leaning forward and feeling under my jaw.

"Am I going to need glasses?" I asked her.

"Why would you need glasses?"

"If my eye can't be repaired, will I need to wear glasses as a result?" She looked in my ear.

"Freddy," she said, "you won't need to wear glasses. Do you hear a ringing?"

"I don't hear a ringing," I said. "Not right now."

"Did you hear a ringing before?"

"I heard it six times," I explained. "I also heard nine sirens and two car horns."

"In your head?"

"No," I said.

"How old are you, Freddy?"

"I'm fourteen years old. I'm closer to fifteen years old than fourteen years old, but I'm not supposed to tell people I am fourteen-point-six years old."

She smiled wryly. "Most people can't do math," she said. "Do your parents know where you are?"

"If you asked, Bill would say yes, but he's wrong because he thinks I'm at home."

"Why aren't you at home?"

"Because I'm in the emergency room of Eagle Ridge Hospital."

"Hah, hah, you are quite the sarcastic teenie, aren't you? Okay, Danny—"

"My name is Freddy," I corrected.

"Can you tell us your parents' phone number?"

"Yes," I said.

She waited. I looked at the wall. Annoyed, the doctor waved a hand at me and said to the nurse, "I'll be back in a bit. Get this kid's parents, okay?"

As the doctor moved to the next patient in the hall, the nurse frowned. "Do you know where you are?" she asked.

"Yes," I said.

"Can you tell me your phone number?"

"Yes," I said.

She gritted her teeth. "Tell me your phone number, Freddy Wyland."

"393-3200," I said.

I don't know why they made it so hard.

Two hours, seven minutes after I arrived at the emergency room, they moved me to a bed and pulled the curtain around it. Two hours and nine minutes later, I heard the doctor say, "He's fine. A little bit beat up is all."

She opened the curtain, and there was my father, unsmiling.

"Maybe a little bit of a smartass," the doctor said, with a small smile.

Bill nodded. "That's Freddy, all right." He quickly walked over to me, slowing as he reached out. He looked me over and lightly touched the side of my head.

"Champ," he said.

"I'm not a champion," I told him.

The nurses had cleaned the blood from my face. The eye that was swollen shut had a red and purple bruise underneath. A patch of hair was shaved away above my right ear, and the doctor sewed seven stitches. She also used three stitches to sew a tear in my lip.

"Oh, Christ," my father said. "This is great. This is just great."

I began to reply that it wasn't great, but stopped myself. "You know what's great?" I said instead. "These stitches are great."

My father blinked. At first, he cocked his head sideways, as if I had spoken in a different language. "What? The stitches are *great*?"

"No," I answered. "They're not. I was being *sarcastic*."

For moment, he didn't speak. Having never heard me say anything sarcastic before, it took a moment before he realized I was doing it now.

He turned his head slowly to the doctor. "How bad did he hit his head?" he asked.

My mother left because of me. My father never said those words exactly, but he said all the words around them.

"Where's Mom?" I asked, the day after she was gone.

"She's out," he told me, swirling ice cubes in his drink, with a stare focused a thousand yards away. "She needs some time alone for a bit, Freddy. Do you understand?"

"Yes," I replied. "Where's Mom?"

He didn't answer.

On the second day, I asked again.

"She left us, Freddy," he said, and I asked again the next day. Then again the next day, and for days on end, weeks on end.

"Where's Mom?" I asked, every morning, when I came downstairs and walked into the kitchen.

Every morning, he was up first, waiting for me, sitting at the breakfast table, drinking a cup of coffee, reading a book. Every morning, he waited until I sat at the table.

"She's gone, Freddy."

"Where did she go?"

He said, "She left us, Freddy, and I don't know where she went. I don't know when she's coming back."

I said, "Will she bring me a present when she does?"

He nodded. "Of course," he said. "Of course."

His eyes were red.

The orchids in the living room wilted, and the soil became desiccated. One day, the orchids in the living room were gone.

I no longer went to Excalibur House. My father sold our home, and I was glad to be out of it. The place echoed like a crypt, and my father moved through it like a grave keeper.

We moved to Heritage Mountain, down the road, to a townhouse complex, still on the edge of the forest. I went to Templeton College.

Saskia Stiles was gone from my life.

"It's just too far away," my father said of Excalibur House. "I can't get you there anymore."

"I can walk," I said and went to the hall to get my coat.

"It's night, Freddy," he said. "Besides, it would take you hours to get there."

"Mom can drive me," I offered.

"No, she can't," he sighed. He took my hand and led me upstairs. It was time for a bath.

———

Seven years after she left, I finally understood that the reason my mother left me was that I was not one of her Favourite Things. It wasn't that I was autistic. She didn't leave because of what I *was*. She left because of what I *did*. The things I did were driven, to some extent, by my autism, but that was just an accounting entry in the ledger of my life. In the end, it was *me* that did them. It wasn't the autism. My mother was sure of that.

"Don't say he's autistic," she told my father weeks before she left. She yelled it, actually, loud enough that I heard them from my bedroom.

"Balls to that," he replied, and he had been drinking. His tone was rougher, the hard consonants harder, the soft consonants softer. "He's autistic."

"No, he is someone *with* autism," she said. "*He* is Freddy. Dammit, Bill, it's about how people see him. Do they see him as autistic first, or as someone first?"

He slammed his glass on the kitchen table. "Holy Christ, we're the ones in control of how other people see things? All we have to do is make a couple of grammatical backflips with our sentences, and *whammo*, they see Freddy different?"

"It's about how you frame it."

"I don't want to frame it," he yelled. "Why do I have to accommodate the world? Why can't it accommodate me?"

"It's not about you!" she yelled back.

90

There are inflection points in my life. The slope of my personal arc changes direction, and things begin to get better, or things begin to get worse.

Arcs rule my life. The first arc was ten years ago, when the slope became negative, the day my mother left me on the train platform and was gone from my world. My life didn't get much better after that. I moved schools, I left Excalibur House, and I left Saskia Stiles.

The second arc began when four boys in thick winter jackets put me in the hospital. My life had been in descent until that moment, a litany of misspoken words, misinterpreted intents, and conversations that exploded in my face.

But the beating was the trough of my arc. It was the lowest point, the final culmination of everything I had done wrong and continued to do wrong. It was the beating that began the change, the point where things started getting better. A new arc began.

It went like this:

I opened my eyes and I was fourteen. A cold wind blew. Four boys stood looking at me. Each one at least two inches taller than me. One, in a red hoodie under a green jacket, stepped forward, for I had been looking at him—trying to look *through* him—for almost a minute.

"Could you not stand there," I said to him, and they stopped what they were doing. They came over. I watched the one with the hoodie.

"What are you looking at?" he said and pushed me.

"I was looking at the wall, but you were standing in the way," I said.

"So what?" he said.

"Your jacket is fat." I tried to step around him and stand on the other side of the bus stop.

"What is wrong with you?" He blocked my path.

There were more than a few answers to that question, but I settled for the most immediate problem.

"I'm here against my will," I said.

"What the fuck does that mean?"

"I'm not comfortable right now."

"That's why you want me to move?"

I nodded.

"Because I make you uncomfortable?"

I nodded again.

"Because I'm *black*?"

"You're not black," I said.

His hands dropped to his side. His eyes widened slightly. "What are you talking about *now*?"

"You're not black," I said and immediately realized that he heard me already and therefore didn't understand what I had said. So I rephrased. "Your skin is not coloured black and your jacket is green." I looked at his hands, then at his face. "Your skin is a shade of brown. HTML Colour Code #663300."

He pushed me on my shoulder. I tried to walk around him, but he blocked my way again. "Are you serious?" He pointed to his friend, who also had a thick green jacket, but a black ball cap. "What about him? What is he?"

I was about to answer that he was a teenage male, but stopped, realizing he was asking if I knew his name. I was momentarily confused, because I had never met this boy before, and quickly searched my memory for any occurrence of a meeting with him in the past.

The other boy pushed me hard on my shoulder again.

"Well?" he demanded. "I'm asking you a question, kid."

Whenever my father spoke in that tone of voice it was because I wasn't answering a question quickly enough, and the situation was about to change to a Time Out for Not Listening. The solution: answer quickly, without spending any more time analyzing for the correct response. So I answered and told him what his friend was.

"Nigger," I said, and both of the boys took a step backward, their jaws dropped, eyebrows raised. That was evidence that I had surprised them.

I hoped that it was because I was correct in my guess.

———

92

I called his friend Nigger because that was the thread I was resolving at the moment the first boy urged me to answer. Earlier, I had observed the first boy call the second boy "Nigger."

He said, "Nigger, just shut up. You don't know a thing about football."

When someone addresses someone else, they may begin the sentence with the name of the other person. My father often says, "Freddy, did you remember to brush your teeth?" and then he will say, "Freddy, go brush your goddamn teeth," and sometimes he will say, "Freddy, either you brush your teeth now or I will brush them for you and believe me, you don't want that."

It is also common that some people who share the same relative skin colour will speak to each other and preface their comments with "Nigger," for instance in the movie *Mississippi Burning*.

This was the state of my thread when it was interrupted. If allowed to continue, I would have reasoned that people preface remarks with other common words, such as "Jesus Christ," but I shouldn't infer that the person *is* Jesus. Proof of this is that my father frequently addresses me as Jesus Christ, but we both understand that my name is Freddy. "Jesus *Christ!*" he will shout. "I swear, the next time you spit toothpaste all over your shirt, I'm going to make you wear the damned thing all day!"

If the boy had not alarmed me, my thoughts would have taken their normal course and closed the thread as illogical, and I would have answered, "I don't know his name." Instead, the first boy interrupted me, and I said the first answer that was at the top of my stack of possible answers.

"Nigger."

It turns out that neither of the two boys in green coats were named Nigger. One of them stepped forward and pushed me hard. Another boy pushed me from behind.

"Who the fuck do you think you are?" the boy with the black cap said.

"I'm Freddy," I said. "My last—"

"Shut up," explained the first boy and he punched me in the jaw.

"Stop that," I said.

"I said *shut up*," he repeated and punched me in the eye. He punched me hard, and I realized that he was not trying to correct me.

Sometimes my father corrects me by hitting me. The difference between these boys and my father is that my father slaps me on the top of my head with an open palm. Both of these boys closed their hands into fists.

Another difference is that my father never asked me what I thought of his performance while he struck me.

"What do you think of this," said the boy in the black cap, and then he hit me across the nose with *The Twentieth Century in Review*.

The nose is made of cartilage. Shark bones are made of cartilage as well. The nose makes up eleven percent of the front of your face. The front of my face is eleven percent shark material.

It didn't make a difference.

I opened my eyes and I was lying on my back. Rain fell on my face. Blood streamed from my nose. A gash, from the fall to the sidewalk, lay open on my head. My left eye was swelling, closing. My ribs ached and, when I breathed too deep, a sharp piercing pain ran up my side.

I tried to speak and closed my eyes again.

A man shuffled by, pushing a shopping cart full of empty beer cans. "It's time for you to be a man now," he said and kept pushing the cart. "Get up and get moving on with your life, son."

I stayed at the hospital until the next morning for observation. All night, I sat straight up in my hospital bed, green blankets bunched into a ball in my lap, staring at a blank TV screen that hung above the end of my bed. I stared into the screen and saw a movie of myself, moving through time. I narrated dispassionately the events of my life.

I told the moments when things went wrong, or when they did not go as expected. I told the mornings when the quote-headmaster-unquote demanded I hurry up. I told the afternoons when the gym teacher called me an idiot. I told the evenings when my father yelled at me. Sometimes, those were also mornings. And on weekends, there would also be afternoons.

I thought about these things, and the threads asked me the same thing over and over again.

What's the same with these pictures? they demanded.

I don't know. I don't know. I stared at the wall, but the clock never came.

———

The next day, we drove home from the hospital. The four boys still clattered and clammered around my mind. "I don't understand why they hit me," I said to my father. He glanced at me, then turned the radio off.

"What did you say to them?" His voice was less steady than it usually is. It carried the tenor and cadence of a person who is trying to control what they are saying because they are concerned that they are unable to say it effectively. I had observed this with my mother, who sometimes spoke like this before she began to cry.

"I said many things to them," I replied.

"Did you make them angry?"

"One of them was angry. He hit me because he was angry. He wasn't angry when I first saw him. He was laughing with his friends."

"How many of them were there?"

"There were four. They were laughing. The one that hit me the hardest wore a green coat over a hoodie. He had the hood over his head, so he couldn't see to the side effectively. I think he may have been angry that he couldn't see to the side effectively."

Bill turned the radio back on. "I don't think so, Freddy," he said and changed stations. "I don't think so."

MY FATHER AS AN
OBJECTIVELY GOOD MAN

Over the years, my father has risen to and fallen from my list of Favourite Things, depending on my mood and circumstance. I don't think I've been on his list of Favourite Things for a long time.

My father doesn't like me. He swears at me a lot. When a person swears, it's at people they don't like. This doesn't alarm me; why should life alarm me? I live it every day. He dislikes me for the correct reasons. They're the same reasons every father dislikes his teenage son who keeps dropping hand grenades into his life. That's how he often explains it.

"Teenagers are idiot kids who do stupid things," he tells me. "Glad to see you're fitting in."

"You're welcome," I always reply.

My father is, objectively, a good man. I know that because I have googled "what is a good man," and an argument can be made that my father meets sufficient criteria.

My old behaviour interventionist said that all of this was true, but not quite. "It's not just criteria," she told me. "You need to feel it in your heart."

"I don't want to feel it in my heart," I replied. "I don't want to visit a doctor."

"Soon, Freddy," she sighed. "Soon, we'll work on metaphors."

"I don't want to work on metaphors," I said.

Later, I googled "feeling something in your heart." I learned that it's a metaphor for feeling something significant. A feeling in your heart is synonymous with a heart attack, which is a life-threatening event. I concluded that the act of feeling love is also a life-threatening event.

I told my interventionist this, and she said that love doesn't threaten your life like a heart attack does. Love can only change your life, but sometimes the pain associated with it feels like a heart attack, and the change in life feels like a death. Three days later, she quit her job and moved to a town in Indiana. I know this because I heard two staff members at Excalibur House talking about it.

"It was a painful divorce," the first receptionist said to the other.

———

My father has goodness with statistical significance. He is not cruel, although he has hit me. He slaps the back of my head, but only to encourage me when I'm going too slow at home. My father says it's to remind me I'm being stupid.

But fitting in, right? say the threads.

He's a good man because he taught me how to brush my teeth. This is an example of a larger set of things he has taught me, and the act of mentorship is an act of goodness.

He taught me how to wipe my bum. This indicates he is willing to instruct me in areas he finds distasteful. The last time my father wiped my bum was when I was seven years old, on May 9, 2005. He instructed me that, from now on, I was to wipe it myself, for he had Had Enough of My Shit.

Later that same evening, just before I went to bed, my father told me his statement was a double entendre, and I would appreciate its depth when I was older. I am older now and still don't understand its depth. I will review it again in a year.

He tells me that I am a good person. He is consistent with this: he never tells me that I am a bad person, although he has frequently told me I am an idiot. But idiots can be good people, too.

He's the first person I see in the morning, the last person I see at night. In the hospital room, he sat in the chair all night and kept vigil while I slept. My sleep was fitful, and I awoke many times. Each time, I saw him slumped in his chair, eyelids drooping, but still awake. Sometimes, he saw me awake and drummed up a weak smile.

After the day the four boys left me on the street, I began to walk the trails alone each day. On the day of my liberation, it was raining, and I was on patrol.

Halfway through my walk, I stopped below the cliffs and stared up at them. I stood for ten minutes, while the rain came down, and my mind wandered across a dozen different things, hopping from thread to thread. I was oblivious to the outside world, as I stared up the hill and thought about everything and nothing.

At the eleven-minute mark of being motionless, I surfaced, because I was shivering. The rain had changed from a drizzle to a downpour. The temperature dropped, and the icy cold water found its way through a tear on the right shoulder of my jacket.

A noise. I heard a noise, and that is what pulled me out of my own mind, back to the tapping of the rain on my hood, and cold breeze blowing. I suddenly realized how cold I was.

What was that sound? the threads asked. But I couldn't tell. I stood still for another full minute, but I heard nothing else.

I began the walk back home. As I walked, I saw how much of a slave I was. I had stared up at the cliffs until I was almost frozen stiff, because staring up at the cliffs was one of my Favourite Things. I held no control over my life. But my list did. It always called, relentlessly demanding, altogether irresistible. And I always answered, enslaved by my Favourite Things.

I realized this and knew that there was nothing I could do to change it. But in this defeat I saw that there was a way back again. There was a way out. True, my body decides which Favourite Thing it will pursue. But I always control what's on the list. It's *my* list of Favourite Things. I'm the one who places an item on the list, and I'm the one who moves if off the list.

A thing never randomly appears. I always make a conscious choice to connect with it. I always make a conscious choice to say *This is now a Favourite Thing.*

That was my moment of clarity. This was my liberation. I couldn't control my impulses, but I could control the things I was impulsive about.

I could control my list of Favourite Things.

I opened my eyes and I was fourteen, standing on the lip of my life.

I stood inside my bedroom, the door open before me, and I was uncertain. In my hands, I held *The Twentieth Century in Review*. I gripped it as if it might suddenly spring away from me and dart down the hall.

"Freddy!" my father called from the bottom of the stairs. "Let's go! You'll be late."

I didn't know what to do. *Let's go*, said some of the threads, *we'll be late*. And other threads said, *You can't leave*.

I've got to think.

Listen: I finally knew the source of my difficulties. Me. The problem was how I was viewed by everyone else. I wasn't on anyone's list of Favourite Things. It was because of things I did.

And this book was one of the things that kept me off their list. I had to stop carrying it around, I knew.

I can't change, I thought.

The better half of me said I didn't have to. That I only needed to change who other people *thought* I was. That much, at least, was within my control. I could at least appear to be like everyone else.

I needed to stop flipping pages back and forth when I sat on a bus. In fact, I had to stop a lot more than that. I had to stop repeating—over and over—lines from a movie I saw last night. I would have to listen to more than the one song over and over and over again in a month. Stop talking about non-parallel lines, bad parking jobs. In fact, it might be best to stop talking about anything at all.

I didn't know *why* these were the things I needed to stop doing. I didn't *want* to stop doing these things. The world, however, wanted me to stop.

So I stopped.

I put the book down and never took it out of the bedroom again.

———————

"Quitting isn't as difficult as you think," my father often told me. "It can be easy. I did it. The first time I quit smoking"—he snapped his fingers—"just like that. And I didn't pick up a cigarette for ten years."

"And then what?" I asked with anticipation. He'd told me this story on more than one occasion. I knew my lines.

He held a cigarette in his hand as he told me this.

"And then you came along, Freddy." He smiled and took a drag. He exhaled slowly. "And then you came along."

"And then what?" I asked.

My father sighed and rubbed his temples. "And then nothing, Freddy. That's the end of the joke." He sighed. "Jesus, you wreck it every single time."

Well, there was another thing. I had to stop wrecking jokes.

———————

I put *The Twentieth Century in Review* down. Its pages were ripped and crumpled, the binding shredded and held together by layers of packing tape. For years, I carried that thick hardcover with me everywhere I went. But the day I was liberated, when I came home from my walk in the forest, I put the book on my night table and never took it outside my bedroom again.

Solitary confinement. No exercise yard privileges.

———————

Inside my bedroom, everything was fair game. I allowed me to be who I used to be. I allowed myself to stim—to chant, to sing, to practise words. I allowed myself to rock to my music. I flipped pages. I listened to the gossiping birds, the tapping nervous tree, the leaves giving their applause, and the silence of the flat olive wall.

I left that part of me in the bedroom every morning. Outside, I was careful.

I was a deer.

I made it a goal to never engage in conversation except when absolutely necessary. Becoming a mute was desirable, but impractical. I needed to talk, because never talking would end with more people trying to get me to talk. So I answered questions as politely as I could, but scrupulously avoided the game of small talk. Light discourse was a minefield that had blown my leg off on multiple occasions. And trying to hold a conversation with four boys almost killed me.

That day in the forest, I found an answer to the question *how do I move forward?* But it didn't answer the second question. *How do I stop this from happening again?*

It didn't take me long to answer and close the thread. I realized I will never always know when I am about to get in trouble. Adrift in conversation, I always hope that the next reply will be the one that ends the conversation, so I throw up responses as quickly as I can, in my haste to retreat from words.

This realization of my true self led to a final confusion: because of who I am, some people were going to try to hurt me. There was nothing I could do about it. That opened a new thread: *how do I avoid being sent to the emergency room again?*

The answer: I had to learn what to do when four boys came after me again.

I had no idea how I would do it.

But I found out.

THE CHEM CLASS REVELATION

After three weeks of chemistry classes with Saskia, after sharing the same textbook, and writing notes, I realized something. This was also the third week without a conversation in chemistry class. It was the third week of wordless, uninterrupted study and experimentation. I felt calmer than I had in a long time. Chemistry class had somehow become a new Favourite Thing.

Knowing that Saskia was not going to attempt conversation brought peace to me. Our table was silent, almost sacred, and we were two monks of our own order.

With Saskia at my table, there was no need to concentrate on mundane banter. There was no need to try to anticipate questions, or analyze comments for non-literal meanings. So I relaxed and became the person I wanted to be. Saskia and I sat in our two solitudes, together enough that we could let each other be safely alone.

Saskia was the perfect lab partner. She never asked to copy my notes, not like every other lab partner before her. She made her own set, rudimentary and scattered. Sometimes, I took her notebook from her and added my own notes. When I did this, she straightened up, her arms at shoulder level, quoting her forehead. I knew she was grateful. None of my previous partners were grateful when I did that for them. Often, it was the reason why they stopped sitting at my table.

The ones who had stayed at my table for a while lost track of where they were. They wondered out loud about random things. They didn't know which step we were on. They asked me what I was doing. "I'm answering your question," I said.

So there it was. It wasn't chemistry class. It was Saskia. She was my new Favourite Thing. When we were together, classmates left us alone. No one talked to her paternalistically, no one talked to her slowly in short sentences with small words, and no one talked to her with feigned enthusiasm. At the same time, people left me alone because they assumed I was otherwise occupied with her. They were often relieved they could carry on their normal lives without talking to me.

Saskia Stiles was my new Favourite Thing because, when she was around, my least favourite thing—other people—stayed away. She was a human antidote.

I realized that this could have application elsewhere. Strategies in chemistry class should also work in real life. I knew then that Saskia Stiles and I should stay close to each other. We would form our own herd, at table seven of the third row. We would be friends. And we wouldn't talk.

————

Jim Worley took little convincing.

"Frederick," he said, making a temple with his fingers. He put his feet up on his desk and looked to the ceiling. "Okay, okay," he said, still staring upward. "Let's think this through. You want me to get the school to move Saskia Stiles from her current homeroom to your homeroom."

"Yes," I said.

"And you want to change your schedule so that you and Saskia have the same study hour." He pursed his lips. "Because . . ."

"We can support each other," I said.

"I think I understand how you can support her," he said. "Act as her advocate or proxy, I get it, I get it. But how does she support *you*?"

"By taking on responsibility for a peer, I am taking gradual steps toward independent living." I said the words carefully, slowly, enunciating clearly, hoping that I wasn't obviously repeating verbatim something I had researched on Wikipedia.

Jim Worley, lips still fully pursed, looked at me skeptically. After a moment, his lips unpursed. "My gosh," he said. "That might just work."

My fingers barely flickered, but flicker they did, for I was surprised by his response. I hadn't anticipated it, even though I had carefully crafted my words to lead him to this point. My carefully crafted plans rarely succeed.

This one, it seems, succeeded on the first try.

————

Later that day, I sat with Saskia for lunch, and I stared at the ceiling with a single overpowering thread running through my mind.

What the hell just happened? the thread asked.

HOMEROOM

On the morning of the next day, a school aide brought Saskia Stiles to my homeroom. Huddled behind her armful of notebooks and pens, Saskia stood at the door looking in. Her eyes darted up and down rows, looking for a free chair. In the back corner, she saw the furthermost desk, with no one sitting at the adjacent desk.

"Take a seat, please," said Mrs. Brody, who was the homeroom teacher.

All eyes followed Saskia as she entered the room. No one spoke.

As she walked quickly to her seat, I stood from my regular seat and went to the desk beside her. We both sat down in silence. Putting her books on the table, and her backpack under her chair, she sat down. Her hands came up. She squeaked.

I opened my eyes. It was study hour and Saskia wasn't anywhere to be found. That is, she wasn't in the study hall or the library, and I found myself having difficulty doing my homework, for things were out of place. It wasn't that I missed her. It was that my study hour was now abnormal: Saskia was supposed to be here. But she wasn't. I closed my books, took them back to my locker, and walked the halls, an old habit I indulge in when my mind is cluttered with threads.

When I walked the halls, I did so without intrusion from teachers. Autism had few advantages, but this was one of them: other students weren't allowed to wander the halls. I had this freedom because teachers thought it was a form of stimming. Instead of flapping my hands, I paced the halls. They decided it was better to have me stim alone in the hall, than be a distraction in class. They convinced themselves that walking the halls was a form of therapy for me. Who was I to say otherwise?

Sometimes they asked me why I was walking in the halls or where I was going, but I had a ready answer: I was going to check my locker.

Jim Worley did it twice. "Where are you going?" he asked the first time he bumped into me in the hall.

"To check my locker," I replied.

"Isn't your locker the other way?" he asked.

"Yes," I agreed. We looked at each other in silence.

"Uh," Jim Worley said at last, then shrugged. "Okay." I knew he was disappointed. He was probably hoping for more small talk.

The second time, he found me on the other side of the school, near the gymnasium. "You checking your locker again?"

"Because I love to," I replied. He looked at me, and I hesitated. I thought he was going to say, "Look, I don't know where to go with that." So I tried another tack.

"Hot enough for ya?" I asked. He frowned. So I started flapping my hands.

Gets them every time.

———

The day Saskia wasn't in study hall, there was no teacher interference. I paced the halls in peace. As I was walking, I approached a group of girls who were giggling loudly, talking in high-pitched gossipy voices.

One of them said, "Honestly, a wool cap and a pink coat? It's ridiculous."

One of them said, "She doesn't even brush her hair. The way it sticks out like that? It's like she isn't even trying."

The three of them laughed loudly, because each was trying to show the other that they abhorred such an ensemble the most. When they saw me, the conversation stutter-stepped.

Small talk hates perturbations.

———

When I walk by groups of people in the hall, conversations fade. Oscillating arms dampen, laughter abates. It's not because my appearance is disturbing—in fact, it's the opposite: I have laboured to make myself as nondescript as I can, in order to avoid drawing attention and the random small talk it evokes.

But I can only blunt my appearance so far. Objectively speaking, I'm a good-looking young man. I'm fit, not too short or too tall, and I have no deformities. At worst, I'm average looking; at best, striking in my appearance. I have long eyelashes. My jaw is well defined. My hair is thick. My skin is unblemished by freckles or acne. My pores are not big. I understand that small pores are a measure of attractiveness, but I don't know why. I have no moles or warts, no goitres or deformities sticking out at odd angles. I don't have the qualities of a sideshow freak.

All of my deformities are on the inside.

Mine is a carefully constructed persona. This is who I worked to become. It has served me well because, in my presence, girls are intimidated into silence. My aloof and silent caricature keeps them shy and unlikely to initiate conversation with me.

Similarly, boys look at me with suspicion, and most keep their distance. I'm not only silent, but brooding, possibly seething, possibly coiling. Every girl's silent bad boy is every boy's silent gangster.

When I walk by boys, I quiet them like cold air blown into a room. They glance at me from the corners of their eyes, concerned about not looking concerned about the person walking by. But my aloofness is non-aggressive. It's just anti-social enough to keep other people at bay, but not so threatening that they become aggressive themselves.

When I walk by girls, I quiet them like snow falling on a field. This bundle of girls was no different than any other. My hands were in my pockets, and I walked with a carefully designed carelessness. I looked the picture of a brooding teenager, smouldering with intellect, cynically rejecting the world around him. I could have been part of a boy band.

I also had long bangs.

They subconsciously moved closer to one another, subconsciously tilted their heads down slightly, and subconsciously batted their eyelashes. One of them giggled nervously, but the laughter evaporated as I approached. The talk of bad hair, pink parkas, and knitted caps halted.

"Yeah, so," one of them began, but didn't continue.

Six lockers down stood Saskia Stiles, leaning against her locker. She wore Bose headphones. Over her knitted cap. She was tucked inside a pink parka.

I saw her backed against her locker, pressing her shoulders together. Danny Hardwick towered over her, one hand against the locker door, just to the right of her left shoulder. He talked to her, words I couldn't hear, and she looked away from him.

Her eyes caught mine.

She squeaked.

THE FUTILITY OF CONVERSATION
WITH DANNY HARDWICK

"Do you like listening to the Clash?" I heard Danny Hardwick ask Saskia as I approached. As she dropped her eyes from mine, she relaxed, and her shoulders came down, and she squeaked. When she did, the girls laughed.

Saskia looked down. She fumbled with her headphones.

I stopped before her, on the other side of the hall.

Seeing me, Danny Hardwick turned to face me. He was a couple of inches taller than me, and his shoulders were wide. The Alpha Tater.

"What do *you* want?" he said angrily.

At once, several feelings came upon me. The first was annoyance with Danny Hardwick, although I couldn't immediately identify why. But I felt it nonetheless. It filled my chest cavity like gel, and I started breathing faster.

A second feeling was surprise as, muscles tensed, I felt a rush of adrenalin course through my stomach.

"What do you want?" he asked again.

I searched my memory for a topic we could discuss, but nothing came to mind. Those things that interested me surely didn't interest him. Of those things in which I knew he was interested, I wasn't. I struggled for something neutral to say.

"How about them Cowboys?" I said, which caused him to open his mouth, but then pause and say nothing in response. He may not have been a sports fan.

At that moment, Saskia slipped under his arm and stepped away from him. She stood a little straighter and turned to me, looking down, as if she was waiting for direction.

My hands were sweating, and my heart was beating fast. I found myself wanting to look closer at her, but couldn't bring myself to do such an unexpected thing. Instead, I remained true to character. I searched for something to say and, finding nothing relevant, took the first thing from the top of the stack: I was getting hungry.

"Did you want to come to lunch with me?" I asked her.

She nodded, then took a short step closer to me. Her arms were tight against her sides.

Danny Hardwick started to move toward me but stopped, as if he was considering something other than his next statement. He said, "Enjoy your lunch, retard." Then he turned and walked away.

"I'm not retarded," I said.

Behind me, the girls whispered. I was unconcerned with what they were saying, although I could tell that we were the central topic of their conversation.

I reached out to Saskia and lightly touched her arm above the elbow.

"Let's go to the cafeteria," I said and turned. She followed. As we approached the cluster of girls, the whispering stopped. I lifted my head and looked directly at them as we walked, until they began to fidget and adjust their hair.

I asked Saskia to come to lunch, but it wasn't lunchtime yet. It wasn't even noon. It was too early, and I couldn't buy a hamburger.

I stopped at the hall junction and looked both ways. The cafeteria lay at the end of the left corridor. To the right, an exit to the school grounds. It wasn't raining outside. I turned and walked outside. She followed me without a word.

We passed the smoking pit where students stood around a five-gallon bucket filled with wet sand and cigarette butts, and walked to the crest of the hill overlooking the parking lot. The sky was overcast, but the clouds were breaking up. Sunlight shot through the gaps in the clouds, like pillars.

We stood and looked out over the town for several minutes. I was going to suggest that we go inside when I felt her arm brush mine. I suddenly became aware of how close Saskia was to me. There was a small breeze from my left and she stood on my right, edging closer to me for shelter. Her hands tucked deep into her coat pockets. She stared down the hill and leaned against me.

I didn't move. I barely breathed. Normally, if someone touched me for so long, I would hasten to move away. I would push their arm off of mine. I would suggest that they give me space. I didn't do this with Saskia. Instead, I leaned a little into her. I pushed back a little on her arm. To my surprise, she didn't pull away. She moved closer.

This is, said a thread. *I don't even—*

I grew uncomfortable and turned, just as she turned, and suddenly we were facing each other, my face inches from hers. She was shorter than me, and my lips were level with her eyes. She looked down but tilted her head forward.

I could smell her hair; the shampoo she used had a scent of lavender. It washed over me, wrapping me like a quilt. I half closed my eyes and felt myself lowering my head toward her, until my lips were nearly resting on her eyebrows. We were so close that the random movements of our bodies brought us into brief contact, the feel of her eyelashes touching my lips, the feel of her rapid breath on my neck. The feel of her fingers against mine for a fleeting instant. They lightly brushed the back of my hand, the tips tracing down to my knuckles.

We stood that way.

Why don't you say something? the threads asked.

What should I say? I asked back.

We got nothing, the threads admitted.

The lunch bell rang. So I knew what to say.

"Let's go get lunch."

She nodded and we walked to the cafeteria in silence. On the way there, the threads kept asking the same question.

Why is your heart beating so fast?

We sat at the lunch table. I sat directly across from her. It made it harder to look at the wall, but I did it anyway.

For the first few minutes, we said nothing. I chewed my cheese-burger, and she ate her sandwich. When she finished it, she pulled out her journal and began to draw spiralling circles, triangles nested inside each other, zigzag lines.

"Danny Hardwick called me a retard," I said. "But I'm not a retard."

She paused, then began sketching again.

A moment later, my phone vibrated.

I'll be late tonight, my father texted. *Thaw out some chili.*

Okay, I replied.

Then two things, two unexpected behaviours, happened in rapid succession.

The first unexpected behaviour was that Saskia lunged across the table and snatched my phone out of my hands. It happened so quickly that I flinched only a split second after she had pulled it from me.

That was the second unexpected behaviour: I flinched. I am rarely surprised. I am rarely alarmed. My dad stopped shouting Boo! at me when I was five years old because it never startled me.

But Saskia startled me.

She sat back and I leaned forward, mouth open, staring at the phone in her hands. She tapped away, swiped left, then right. Her thumbs flying, she typed something. Then she stopped. For a second she regarded the phone, *my* phone, tapped and swiped the screen two more times, then put it on the table. She pushed the phone toward me even as her free hand began to draw in her journal.

I reached over and took back my phone.

She had entered herself as a contact.

I lay my phone on the lunch table in front of me. I didn't touch it. I stared at it as if it were nearly dead but could leap up at any moment. I was at a loss for what to do, and the threads were of little help.

Could you just delete her from your contact list? they suggested.

I could.

She stole your phone. Should you report her?

I could do that, too.

You could text her.

I hadn't considered that.

I've had a phone in my pocket for the last four years. It's rung nineteen times. Each time, except once, it was Bill, and each time our conversation was short. But I haven't had a phone call from him for nine months. He learned to text message me. *Where the hell are you?* he usually texts.

Few others have messaged me. I made the mistake of giving my number to Oscar Tolstoy and he had bombarded me with text messages on the hour.

The newest edition of the Beckett price guide is in bookstores today, he texted.

I didn't reply.

A rookie card is the first licensed issue from a major manufacturer, he texted, *and not the first card on which an athlete appears.*

I didn't reply.

Ken Griffey Jr.'s rookie card was not included in the Topps base set of baseball cards, he texted.

I changed my phone number.

Now my phone lies dormant, save for the messages from Bill that seep through. I like the sudden slight surprise when my phone vibrates, informing me that a rare new text has arrived. I like the special moment in between picking up the phone and looking at the message. I like the momentary stuttering of the threads, as they shoulder each other to the side.

Who's calling? the threads demand.

Well, let's find out.

And then I see it's Bill. So I put the phone back in my pocket.

Oh well, the threads shrug. *False alarm.*

But now there was a new name that could potentially appear on my phone. My list of contact was now my list of contacts.

I stared at the phone. I considered sending a text to Saskia. It merited consideration: I had never texted someone except in response.

Why would you text her? the threads asked.

We could communicate about chemistry class.

What is there to communicate about?

Nothing.

Try again.

I could have texted her to come to lunch instead of having to find her.

But she may not have answered. She was with Danny Hardwick.

But she didn't want to be with him.

She needed your help.

She can text me when she needs help.

That works.

I typed, *This is a test text message* and sent it to her.

Very nice, said the threads. *Smooth.*

Three minutes later, my phone vibrated. I looked at the message.

this guns for higher

Two minutes after that, she sent me another message.

even if your just dancing in the dark

A minute later, she texted me again.

hey baby

117

She did this three more times over the next fifteen minutes. I looked at each message but did nothing more. She was simply typing words, sending them to me. She was listening to Bruce Springsteen's "Dancing in the Dark." I could hear it playing on her headphones.

Later that day, near the end of chemistry class, she texted me as I read from my textbook.

> what are you doing

"I'm studying chemistry," I said to her.
A minute later, she texted me again.

> what are you doing

"I'm studying chemistry," I said, annoyed.
The third time she texted me to ask what I was doing, I opened my mouth to reply but stopped. Instead, I texted back:

> **I'm studying chemistry. Do your work.**
> all right
> goodbye

Five minutes later:

> why
> **Why what?**
> why did you send me a test text
> **You may need to text me, and I wanted you to have my number.**
> why
> **Because you may need my help.**
> **If you need help, type h.**
> h
> **Do you need help?**
> no
> **Only type h when you need help.**
> only wen I need elp
> **You can use h in words.**

it was a joke
Okay.

Five minutes later:

say saskia do you want to try it
Saskia, do you want to try it?
h

"Do you need help?" I asked.

She put the phone down and lifted her hands, clasping them open and shut quickly. She picked up the phone.

no thanks
goodbye

We continued our studies.

I don't remember what I was studying. Just that it was with my friend.

JACK SWEAT

In my life, I've had four true friends, although I am not counting Gordon, my hamster. My parents were the first two. Saskia Stiles was and is the third.

The fourth was Jack Sweat, and we became friends because he was a brute of a young man, plain in form and function. His eyes were intense, his tone deep, and his words sparse. He preferred the language of motion and that was why we were friends.

He attended a nondescript school three blocks from his home and was the captain of the wrestling team. He could have gone to any number of schools. Everyone wanted him, but a public school got him. He needed to be close to home: on weekends and some evenings, he worked at his father's store, the Butcher's Shop.

Jack Sweat was one of the few people who still stayed around after I told him I was autistic. He said he didn't hold it against me. And then he hit me.

But I hit him back, so we were even.

....

Behind the Butcher's Shop was a boxing club called the Butcher's Gym. Both were owned by Jack's father, Leonard Sweat. In his prime, before he became a butcher by trade, he was known as one by name. He was the Butcher in the simplest of ways: a relentless fighter, he never quit, was never knocked down, and never failed to finish a fight. At the end of twelve rounds, he sometimes looked like a slab of meat.

In the end, his career battled itself to a draw and he hung up his gloves. The Butcher turned his nickname into a name when he bought a meat shop at the edge of downtown. After that, he opened a gym and trained others for a different kind of meat processing. That was where I met Jack Sweat for the first time.

I opened my eyes and I was fourteen, standing outside the Butcher's Gym. Bill drove me down, dropped me off, and drove away, all at my request. "You don't want your dad walking you in to get boxing lessons, do you?" he said, and then he nodded. "Fair enough. Who *would* want that?"

The front of the Butcher's Gym is painted yellow and black. Plate glass runs across most of it, floor to ceiling. When people look inside, they see a boxing ring and an octagon and someone training in at least one of them. From seven in the morning to ten at night, the gym is never empty.

Except on Sundays, when the gym is closed. Nobody gets to beat anyone up on the Sabbath.

I walked in the front door of the Butcher's Gym and stood at the edge of the carpet. The place was hot; it smelled like wet socks. A compressor ran in the corner, cooling the meat in the freezer of the Butcher's Shop next door. It made an overriding background noise so consistent in tone and tremor that, within thirty seconds of being in the room, the sound was forgotten.

An athlete methodically punched the third heavy bag in a row of five. A man with a white towel on his shoulder held the bag. When he saw me, he let go and walked over.

He was short with a thick brow, feral eyes, hairy arms and hands. His face bore the history of someone who had boxed all his life. His nose skewed at arguing angles, his ears cauliflowered, and thick scar tissue made his forehead look armour plated.

"Help you?" he asked.

"I'm here against my will," I said. The man looked at me, frowning.

No, that's not right, a thread said. *Try again.*

I said, "I want to talk to the Butcher."

"Well, I guess you're talking to him. What do you want?"

"I want to fight."

When he got close enough, he could see the fading bruises on my face. "I'd say you've done enough fighting already."

"No," I said. "The other boys fought. I was what they fought. But I didn't fight them."

"Why not?"

"I don't know how."

"So you're looking to get some revenge."

"I don't want revenge."

"What do you want?"

Even before the words finished coming out of my mouth, I knew that I was saying things wrong. "I don't want to end up looking like you," I said.

I estimated that I had angered him, because he said, "Are you fucking with me, kid?"

"No," I answered. "If I don't learn how to fight, I will get beat up, and I will end up with damage to my face that may become permanent, and it may resemble the permanent damage that you have on your face."

"Holy ratshit, you don't filter the things out of your mouth, do you?" His jaw was tense. I saw the muscles flexing rapidly. "How old are you?"

"Fourteen years, seven months, and nine days. I was born at 12:35 AM, at Eagle Ridge Hospital, which is the same place that the ambulance took me—"

He held up his hand. "Shut up," he explained. "No wonder you got shitkicked."

"I wasn't kicked," I said. "I was punched. I was punched twenty-one times."

"Can't say I am surprised. You got a mouth."

"I have autism."

The Butcher frowned. "You have a what-ism?"

"I'm autistic."

"You mean pencils and paints and such?"

"I am not *artistic*," I said. "I have Autistic Spectrum Disorder. It is a neurological condition that affects one in every one hundred and eight people."

He paused. Then his eyebrows raised with enlightenment. "Like *Rain Man*."

"The character in *Rain Main* was a stereotype of someone with autism."

"Can you count cards, then?"

"I don't know."

"But you're lippy."

"I have difficulty understanding subtleties in conversation. I interpret things literally. I reply literally."

The Butcher scratched the grey stubble on his chin and nodded. "And so you pissed someone off. Maybe more than one someone?"

I didn't answer.

A boxer walked over and stood beside the Butcher. He was sweating profusely. His hands were wrapped with brown bandaging. He appeared a little older than me. He looked first at the Butcher, then at me. He nodded. It was Jack. Jack Sweat.

"How did you hurt your hands?" I asked him.

Looking down at his wrapped hands, he said, "Seriously? Are you a retard?"

"No," I said. "I'm not retarded."

"He's artistic," the Butcher said.

"Artistic?" asked Jack.

"I'm autistic," I corrected.

"So what?"

"He wants to fight," said the Butcher.

Jack looked at me, at my fading bruises. "Looks like you got your wish."

The Butcher shook his head. "If you've got a mental thing, then maybe this ain't the right thing for you."

"Autism isn't brain damage. It's a neurological disorder. Depression is a neurological disorder. You would let depressed people box."

The Butcher laughed. I believe he inferred that I was making a joke. "They'd be awful slow fighters if they were depressed," he said and laughed again. Jack laughed.

I turned my lips up and smiled along. This was going well, I thought. At that moment, I realized I should say something humorous.

Which is typically how my conversations implode.

———

I am unable to crack a joke. I am not a humorous person. Bill tells me it's because of my autism, but I know many non-autistic people who are not humorous. Therefore, I suspect it is a condition of my character. I am not funny. Not deliberately, anyway.

I have a large mental repository of riddles and jokes, but they're filed according to their facts, and according to the humour within. If I tell a joke, it will be based on physical similarities with the present.

For instance, on June 2, 2009, Bill put down his newspaper at the breakfast table and shook his head. "Goddamn Christ," he said. "An Air France plane went down. Two hundred and twenty-eight people were killed."

He looked directly at me, and I suspected I was supposed to say something. I think I was wrong. I should have said nothing. But I didn't.

I did a search of my memory and returned several things:

1. Once when browsing through Wikipedia, I had ended up on the Air France page.
2. I had arrived there by a long, convoluted route that began with "pop music." On this route, I had travelled through Rihanna's Wikipedia page.
3. Rihanna dated a man named Chris Brown, who was charged with assault after he hit her.

The most important relations were then tied together, and the strongest correlation to these three items was a joke that I read two years previous.

"Why do so many husbands hit their wives?" I asked.

"Huh?" My father stared at me. "What are you talking about?"

"Many husbands hit their wives for a reason. Do you know what the reason is?"

"What does that—" my father started, then he stopped. "I don't know. Tell me what the reason is, Freddy," he said.

"Because they just won't listen," I responded.

My father did not reply. He shook his head slowly and returned to reading his newspaper. At the time, I thought he had obtained the information he was looking for and was satisfied with my answer.

Being unable to make spontaneous humour, I try not tell jokes. But sometimes, when I judge the situation as appropriate, I attempt to make a joke.

"They'd be awful slow fighters, if they were depressed," the Butcher said to Jack, and chuckled.

I said, "What do you call a boxer about to graduate tenth grade?"

He continued smiling. "I give up," he said.

"Eighteen," I told him.

His smile froze, then dropped. He stared at me and did not say anything.

I had read several web articles about comedians on stage who have had their jokes greeted by silence. I had an appropriate response at hand.

"Is this mic on?" I said.

I opened my eyes and I was six. It was midday. My mother, father, and I sat at the kitchen table. I stared at my hands, folded on the table.

"Are we going to have a snack?" I asked hopefully.

"No, Freddy," my mother said. "We aren't. Instead, you are going to sit with us and we're going to have a conversation."

"Okay," I said.

"I want you to tell me a joke."

Outside, a dog barked. Down the street, I could hear the laughter of playing children.

"I know a lot of jokes," I said.

"I know," my mother said.

"I've read books of jokes."

"Tell us one of those jokes, then," she said. She brushed some loose hair away from my face.

A joke instantly sprang to mind; I was reminded of it because my mom had brushed away the same loose hair four weeks earlier, while I was watching a news item about complaints that the smell of a pig farm was ruining the pleasure of the people who used a nearby jogging path.

"What's the difference between a woman jogger and Wilbur the Pig?" I asked.

"I don't know, Freddy," my mother said. She smiled at me, her eyes eager and excited that I was about to tell her a joke. "What's the difference between a woman jogger and Wilbur the Pig?"

"One is a cunning runt," I replied.

Six seconds passed.

My father burst into laughter and hit the top of the table with his hand. His laughter subsided to a chuckle, and he rubbed his eye. "That was a *doozy!*" he said, chortling.

"I don't know what a doozy is," I replied.

My mother stared at me. The look of hope was not there anymore.

This particular joke has been an unfinished thread in my mind ever since I heard it. I didn't—and still don't—understand the punchline. The only reason I said the joke was because it was the first one I found when conducting an internal search.

I'd overheard it the week before my mother asked me to tell her a joke, on a Saturday, when I was at the mall with her, shopping for underwear. Two boys sat on a bench outside the store, and I heard them exchanging jokes and laughing at each.

I didn't understand the point of the joke, but what caught my attention was less the woman jogger and more Wilbur the Pig. After I googled "Wilbur the Pig" and subsequently read *Charlotte's Web*, I understood the joke even less. It was tautological. Wilbur the Pig was the smallest in his litter and, by virtue of being able to speak to spiders, was cunning. Wilbur the Pig was, therefore, a cunning runt. But a jogger wasn't necessary to make this statement true. The question "What's the difference between Friedrich Nietzsche and Wilbur the Pig?" is also answered, "One is a cunning runt."

This joke remains in my queue of threads. I have not yet understood why it is considered humorous when it is neither sarcastic nor true.

After I told it, my mother stared at me and then, when she understood the joke, she looked away. I have never forgotten the exactness of the moment. It unfolded two things that I eventually came to realize are intrinsic about me.

First, it unfolded how abruptly different I am from other people. It's a joke that I don't understand, whereas everyone I know does. By extension, everyone but me knows why it is (or is not) funny. It outlined just how much my view of the world is at a right angle to everyone else's view of the world.

Second, it unfolded the reason why my mother left. I was a faded hope. I was the look on a face after one realizes all is lost. I was the participation ribbon that never gets hung up but never gets thrown out.

Two weeks after I told this joke, the long rain began. Eight weeks after that, my mother left.

Maybe if I had told a different joke.

I opened my eyes and I was fourteen. Jack Sweat and the Butcher stared at me, as my joke lay gasping on the floor between us.

At last, the Butcher said, "So you want to fight?"

I said that I did.

"Okay." He nodded. "Let's see about that." He turned and walked into the gym, stopped, and motioned for me to follow. "Jimmy, get this kid some gloves!" he called out, and a man brought me white gloves.

I followed the Butcher to where he was taking headgear down from the wall. When he turned and raised it to place on my head, I shrunk back.

"You'll want to wear this for protection," he said.

I considered it for a moment, then lowered my head and allowed him to put it on.

"Too tight?" he asked me as he did up the chinstrap.

"I don't know," I said.

He tugged on the strap. "You're good to go. Get in the ring."

"It's not a ring. It's a square."

"Get in the square, smartass," he said.

My gloves were damp with someone else's sweat. This bothered me, but I didn't protest, which surprised me. There were no threads, no questions asking why I was dipping my hands in someone else's sweat.

Meh, said the threads.

There I was. I had the sweat of one boxer covering my hands, and my head was covered with the sweat of another boxer. Not a thread to be found.

I stepped into the ring, and the Butcher shoved a white mouthguard between my lips. So now I had the sweat of two boxers on my hands and head, and the dried saliva of yet another boxer in my mouth.

"Bite down on it," he said. "Don't let it go."

"Whutdoo eyedoo iffeyehafta eeddasamwich?" I said, the mouth-guard gripped firmly between my teeth.

"No idea what you said, kid," said the Butcher. He lifted my left hand and placed it six inches in front of my left cheek. He placed my right hand six inches in front of my right cheek.

"Hold your hands here," he said. "When the other guy throws a punch, block it with your hands. Then punch back."

He knelt down and adjusted my stance. My left foot came forward. My right foot went back and out three inches. He said, "Bend your knees," and I bent my knees. He said, "Not so much," and I straightened until he said, "Good. Now keep them bent."

He pointed to my feet. "Keep your front foot pointing to where you're going to punch. When you punch with your left, move your left foot forward. Got it?"

"Yes," I said.

He held up his hand. "Punch."

I punched his hand. Then he took my arm and extended it. He turned my fist until the knuckles were parallel with the floor. He pulled my shoulder forward.

"Punch with your shoulder, not your forearm. Lean into it. Twist your wrist as you extend. And punch through your opponent. Don't try to punch the front of his head. Punch the back of his head."

"Eye can't see the back of hizzhead," I spat.

He tapped his temple. "See it with your mind, kid. Punch to where the back of his head should be. If his face gets in the way, keep punching through. Now hit my hand."

I hit his hand again.

"Harder."

I hit it harder.

"Harder!" he yelled.

I hit it again, with all I had, and knocked him back a step. He lost his balance for a moment, recovered, and looked at me, frowning. "That's good," he said quietly.

He turned around and stepped out of the ring. "Okay, kid, it's time to go in the deep end of the pool."

I looked around. "Therez no shwimming pool," I said.

———

The Butcher rang the bell and pushed me into the centre of the ring. I laboured to consider his instructions and simultaneously implement them. Mostly, I looked at my feet, ensuring they were the correct distance from each other.

Jack stepped forward to within arm's reach and jabbed me in the cheek. He stepped forward again and jabbed me in the nose. I tried to step back, but my head was already leaning back, and I was off balance, so my foot went back slower than expected. I suspect this resulted in my feet no longer being the correct distance apart. When Jack Sweat hit me again, I lost my balance, falling to the canvas.

I lay on my back and processed what had just happened.

No threads.

"Well, I guess that's that," said the Butcher and turned away.

I stood up. In fact, I leapt to my feet. It was twenty-two seconds into the round. I spit my mouthguard into my hand and said, "Best two out of three."

The Butcher stopped. He paused before turning back to look at me.

"Best two out of three," I said again.

The Butcher shook his head. "Kid, you ain't got it."

I turned to Jack Sweat. "You can knock me down once, but you cannot knock me down two times before I can knock you down two times." I understood this was the correct literal method of appealing a loss.

Jack shook his head and smiled. "Your funeral."

The Butcher shrugged. "Back to your corners, then."

I went to my corner and stood there, facing the centre of the ring. The Butcher, standing beside the bell, stared at me for a moment, scratched his nose, then came over to me.

"I was keeping my feet the correct distance apart," I said.

He placed a hand on my shoulder. "Worry about keeping your hands up. Don't let him hit you in the face. You got that?"

I nodded.

"Okay," he said and began to step down from the ropes. He stopped and stood back up. He leaned over and said quietly, "When he jabs at you, you block both punches, 'cause there's gonna be two, got it?"

I nodded again.

"His hands are too low. After he punches twice, he'll pause just a second before stepping forward with his right. When he pauses, you jab. Got it?"

I nodded. "With which hand?"

"With this one." He grabbed my right glove and shook it.

He stepped down and rang the bell again.

I stepped forward.

———

Jack and I met in the middle of the ring, and I stopped just out of his arm's reach. My feet were the correct distance apart, my gloves were in front of my face, close together. Jack jabbed. I blocked with my gloves. He jabbed again, and I blocked again. He slipped to my right. Leaning across, he tucked his shoulder and swung a left hook into my rib cage. I said something about it.

I said, "Oomph."

My hand dropped to protect my rib; he straightened up and delivered a left hook to my jaw. The mouthguard flew out of my mouth, and I lost my balance again. He punched me straight in the nose and my knees no longer responded to orders. Toppling to the floor, I lay on my back, staring straight up.

"Okay," said the Butcher, "that about wraps it up."

I lay on my back. My eyes traced the ductwork that ran across the ceiling like subway tunnels.

"Best three out of five," I said, grinning.

I try not to smile. It's better for all concerned.

I smiled the day my father told me that my mother would not be coming home again. He, on the other hand, wasn't smiling. I had heard him the night before, and deep into the morning, his banging around in the kitchen, his watching television in the living room.

His eyes were puffy and red, and I knew he needed to be comforted. I recalled relevant scenes in literature and concluded that a good way to comfort an unhappy person is to try to cheer them up. Relevant examples also included affirming the individual by overly praising them.

I smiled as broadly as I could. "Well, that's fantastic," I said to my father and did not break the smile. "You should be very proud."

Perhaps my smile was too wide—I couldn't tell.

I am, at the age of seventeen, a veteran of this war, this battle to communicate with the outside world before it communicates with me. I have lost many battles where I smiled when I shouldn't have smiled.

A neutral demeanour resonates with my character. It isn't hostile, so others aren't threatened. It isn't happy, so others aren't chatty. It's so perfect a display of no opinion, that few people think I have an opinion. As a result, few people ask for one.

When I don't offer an opinion, when I don't offer a response, when I don't display easily misinterpreted emotions, I don't get into trouble.

I used to think my solution to life was to understand how to talk to other people. In reality, the solution to my life is to understand how to *avoid* talking to other people.

And that's why I never smile.

Yet that day in the Butcher's Gym I lay on my back—my mouth-guard on the canvas beside me, a sinew of spittle stretching back to my mouth—I lay there and I smiled.

"Best three out of five," I said loudly, with gusto.

The Butcher looked at me and said, "Kid, you ain't got it."

I sat up. Still smiling. My nose ached, and my left ribs ached, but I was suddenly and inexplicably happy. This sparked a thread that asked, *Why are you happy? You just got punched.*

The thread didn't take long to close. I was happy because I was enjoying this.

But a new thread appeared. *What are you enjoying?*

Shut up, silly thread, I thought.

I stood up. "Best three out of five," I said, and the Butcher shook his head.

"Get out of the ring, kid," he said. "Go take up power walking or something to get in shape."

I walked to my corner and turned around to face the centre of the ring. "Best three out of five," I repeated.

Jack snorted and smiled with one side of his mouth.

"Laugh it up, fuzzball," I said to him.

His smile disappeared.

There is a scene in *The Empire Strikes Back* where Han Solo turns to his best friend Chewbacca, who is laughing at him, and says, "Laugh it up, fuzzball." I said it to Jack because he was laughing at me and I was certain that Jack was my best friend.

Friends play games together. Boxing was a game. We agreed upon the rules and tested each other in friendly competition. Which is just what Excalibur House always told me would happen. I was playing a game with Jack, he was my friend, and because I had no other friends, he was *de facto* my best friend.

Jack, however, hadn't discovered this yet.

"What did you just call me?" Jack demanded and walked over. He stood inches from me and was not acting like my friend. All the evidence indicated that I had angered him.

"Best three out of five," I said.

He pushed me back into the corner ropes and I bounced back up at him. "Stop grinning," he said.

I stopped smiling. Looked to the side, away from his glare. And started grinning again.

"Best three out of five," he agreed and went back to his corner.

"Kid, you're a frickin' stubborn idiot," the Butcher said.

"He hit me in the ribs," I said to the Butcher. "You didn't say he would hit me in the ribs."

"Keep your elbows tucked in. They'll protect your rib cage. Make your punches come out quicker. You almost caught him. Keep your hands up." He stepped down, then looked back up at me. "This is your last chance. Got it?"

"Got it," I said.

He raised his hand to ring the bell, and I told him to wait a moment.

There were several threads in my head.

How do I stop him from hitting my face?

I can move my head.

How do I stop him from hitting my ribs?

Keep my elbows tucked in at my sides.

Where else can he hit me?

He can hit me on the side of my head.

How do I stop him from hitting me?

He can't hit me if I hit him first.

I reviewed the moments before he had hit me. Both times, he bobbed before he threw his right hand. Just before he slipped my punch to come in with a right hook, he moved his head to the right slightly, and then to the left.

He had tells. I just found two of his tells.

I turned to the Butcher. "I'm ready," I said, staring straight into his eyes.

Let's do this thing, the threads said and went silent.

I opened my eyes and I was fourteen. Jack Sweat met me in the middle of the ring.

He jabbed and I blocked. I jabbed and he blocked. We circled, and he tested me, looking for the perfect opening. He stepped in, jabbed twice, paused, and bobbed his head. As he was throwing his right hand, I jabbed with my left. I caught him square in the jaw, and his punch pawed the air. He stepped back, his brow furrowed.

Jab, block. Jab, block.

I tucked my elbows in as he came at me with a hard right hook that hit me in the arm; he followed with a left hook that caught me high on the shoulder. But I stepped back as he shot out the left cross, the one that was supposed to knock me down. It missed me completely. I saw him about to come in with a right hook.

I threw one of my own.

I didn't aim for his face. I aimed for the spot where his head would be after he tried to slip my hook. I hit him hard on his forehead. Both of his feet came together and he was off balance as he tried to straighten up. He appeared to be uncertain of what was happening. His eyes were unfocused, and his hands waved slightly as if they were no longer under his control.

As he straightened, I followed with a right cross to his jaw and he spun to his right, staggered away from me, then tumbled face first onto the canvas.

It was a knockdown. I knocked him down.

When I sent Jack Sweat to the canvas, I thought I was going to be yelled at by the Butcher, but he didn't speak. He stood by the bell, not moving, watching his son, who was immediately back on his feet, brushing his gloves on the front of his shirt.

"I slipped," said Jack. He looked earnestly at his father. "I slipped."

"Of course you did, Nancy," said the Butcher.

Jack Sweat grimaced. He raised his hands and faced me. "Let's go!" he said.

I stepped forward. I didn't step forward because he told me to. I didn't step forward because I was afraid of disobeying him. I didn't step forward because I was confused and uncertain about what to do.

I stepped forward because I wanted to fight some more.

We met at the centre of the ring.

Friendship gets forged by shared trauma. So it was that the second friend I ever made was a boxer, for we shared an experience that required no verbalization.

Because I was willing to let him hit me, and he was willing to let me hit him, we came to see each other as equals.

Because we endured being hit by each other without complaint, we came to respect each other.

People with autism often have a refined skill, such as a photographic memory, the ability to play music, or a talent at advanced math.

I have boxing.

From the first day I put on gloves, I knew boxing was something that I was good at. Within a few weeks of training at the Butcher's Gym every Tuesday and Thursday evening, I became Jack Sweat's sparring partner.

During the first few weeks after picking up gloves, I was consistently out-boxed and beaten by Jack, but I consistently gave him a challenge, and I improved with every match.

For his part, the Butcher was happy that he had a quiet, obedient, and even-tempered sparring partner for his son. In the evenings, Jack and I duelled for an hour. Most rounds were light, but sometimes they grew heated and competitive. On those occasions, I lost, but I held my ground enough that I saw a look on Jack's face that I had never seen before. At least not directed toward me.

It took me another few weeks to understand that the look was one of respect.

Because there was no need to talk about any of this, we enjoyed each other's company. Unlike the rest of humanity, Jack Sweat had no constant throbbing need to say something to fill empty spaces.

Jack preferred to avoid useless conversation. In his case, I think there was a secondary motivation: Jack Sweat truly didn't like people. He strove to be outside the centre of attention. When he spoke, he preferred to speak of things with purpose, with a point.

Our friendship began soon after the Butcher agreed to teach me to box. Two weeks into my training, he took me upstairs to his apartment and showed me DVDs of famous boxing matches.

The three of us sat in the living room while the Butcher played key rounds from Ali–Foreman, Leonard–Hagler, and Tyson–Lewis. Jack's father, and sometimes Jack, talked throughout, but it didn't bother me, because I knew no one expected a response from me. They were instructing me, and I liked being instructed. I could listen without having to construct responses.

This became a regular occurrence. We would review old fights, with the Butcher pointing out subtleties in the stances, the shifts of momentum, the ebbing moments. He talked throughout each round and even as he got up, walked to the kitchen, and took three Heinekens from the fridge. He talked as he came back and gave us each a bottle of beer.

The first time he did this, I held the beer in front of me and stared at it.

Jack noticed my reticence. "Have you ever had a beer before?" he asked. I shook my head. He reached over and twisted off the cap.

"Just sip it slowly," he said. I did. It tasted terrible, but I said nothing, for it was apparent that drinking beer with Jack and the Butcher was a required activity.

I didn't mind. That day the Butcher sat on the couch, and both Jack and I remained silent, for over an hour, as he talked rapidly and non-stop about each fight.

He was like Oscar Tolstoy, except with less data and more visual aids.

I would sit in a sofa chair, and Jack would sit with his father on the couch, and we'd watch the fights, while Jack and the Butcher talked. To me. To the television. To each other.

We sat, we three, and I never had to speak, yet I was still a part of the group. It made me want to stay. It made me want to watch more old fights.

It made me happy.

A TEXT CONVERSATION

Saskia sent text messages frequently. They came in randomly, with no connection to anything either of us was doing. They were usually jumbled words from songs she was listening to. Sometimes, they were words from books she was reading. None of them required a reply.

But on the fifth day after she added herself to my contacts, at study hour, I found her sitting in the library at a round table. An Asian girl with a short blue skirt and a shock of red in her black hair also sat at the table. Saskia wasn't pleased about it. She rocked. The Asian girl pretended not to notice, but it was clear she was annoyed by the stimming.

For a moment, I wondered if I had made a mistake switching my schedule. Saskia's study hour was significantly more crowded than my study hour had been. Every table had at least one person sitting at it. But, having made the choice, I now had to live with it.

I sat across from Saskia, who immediately stopped rocking. The Asian girl glanced up, but otherwise ignored me.

I began to do my homework.

Five minutes later, Saskia texted me.

> say, are you having a good day
> **Are you having a good day?**
> yes
> good night
> **It's not night.**
> good notnight
> **Good notnight.**

I opened my chemistry textbook and read for a few minutes, and she texted me again.

> i don't like the cafeteria

I stared at my phone for a few moments, then replied.

Why?
it makes my brain ache
Why do you go to the cafeteria?
to eat
why do you go to the cafeteria
To eat.
i wear my headphones
my ears hurt in the cafeteria
it's loud
You should take an aspirin.
i'm not allowed to have aspirin
it's medicine
are you allowed to take an aspirin
Yes.
what does it taste like
It tastes like ink.
i'm not allowed to have ink

I opened my eyes and I was seventeen again, waiting out the night. I sat on my bed, stared at the clock on the wall, and waited to fall asleep. The night was quiet.

A soft buzzing noise began. It took me a moment to recognize that it was my phone vibrating with a text message alert.

Up until last week, any text messages I received had come from Bill. Beginning last week, Saskia peppered me with mostly nonsense texts. Up until this moment, I had only received text messages from either of them during the day. No one texted me when I was at home.

My phone vibrated again.

This was an entirely unexpected event. I handled it well. I stared at my desk with suspicion. And then I picked up the phone.

The message was from Saskia.

> what are you doing
> **I'm sitting on my bed.**
> do you like sitting on your bed
> **Yes.**
> say, what are you doing Saskia
> **What are you doing, Saskia?**
> i'm sitting on my bed
> **Okay.**
> I wrote a poem on the bus
> **Did you wash it off?**
> no no no no
> I wrote a poem
> I was on the bus
> **It was a joke.**
> say, did you like my joke saskia
> **Did you like my joke, Saskia?**

no
now say tell me your poem saskia
Tell me your poem, Saskia.
A bead is a bead
But only with other beads
A bead is bound to beads
Forever
Is that the poem?
YES
It's a short poem.
say, I like your poem saskia
I like your poem, Saskia.
say, what are you wearing saskia
What are you wearing, Saskia?
a blue night gown
goodnight
Goodnight.

———

I changed into my pyjamas and sat back on my bed, flipping pages in my book. After a few minutes, my phone vibrated again.

write me a poem
I'm not a poet.
you are a poet
No.
your heart is a poet
My heart is an internal organ.
write me a poem
I don't know how.
say, I can try
I can try.
good notnight
Good notnight

Listen: On March 3, 2010, I read a poem:

I wonder why.
I wonder why I wonder why,
I wonder why I wonder why I wonder.
Why, I wonder.
Why?

Its simplicity trapped me. It paused me. It made me stare at it for thirteen minutes, reading it over and over again. I wrote it down. Then I wrote it down again. I got up from my desk, left my bedroom, went downstairs, ate a bowl of Cap'n Crunch cereal (I did it silently because it was two in the morning). I went back upstairs. I sat at my desk, I read the poem again.

It bothered me. It elated me. It braced me and forced my eyes to stare at it.

I realized I was wondering about a poem that was wondering about itself. I realized that I was staring at a written rabbit hole.

I was staring at a thread embodied.

Could we please *not look at this anymore*, the threads wailed.

I wrote the poem down again. This time, I tried to vary it.

I wonder why.
I wonder why I wonder why.
I wonder why I wonder why I wonder why.
I wonder why I wonder why I wonder why I wonder why.
I wonder why I wonder why I wonder why I wonder why
I wonder why.
I wonder why I wonder why I wonder why I wonder why I
wonder why I wonder why.

143

I sat for the next half hour, expanding the poem. Each sentence grew in length. The meaning of each sentence changed slightly as it grew. Each sentence was self-contained, yet it depended on the sentence before it. It only made sense in the context that the writer was actually wondering about the previous sentence. Wondering why he wrote it.

I stayed up until four in the morning, staring at the poem, writing it down, writing it down, writing it down again. By the time I put my pen down and crawled under the covers, I had written twenty-eight pages. The final sentence was half a page long.

I was still wondering.

————

I still have the poem. I thought about giving it to Saskia, but decided it wasn't one to send to her. I suspected she would understand it, perhaps even enjoy it. But it would take too long to type into a phone.

Then one of the threads argued that it was a private poem, and that Saskia needed a public poem. Something less about me. Something more about her.

Something more about us, the threads advised.

When I was four, my mother tried to teach me to draw. She bought forty-eight pencil crayons and we sharpened them together. She bought a drawing pad and we made drawings together. She wanted to make a record of my progress as an artist, so she made me draw in the drawing pad and nowhere else.

We sat side by side. She would draw a scene on the left-hand side of the open pad. I would copy the scene onto the right-hand side of the pad. If Mom drew a circle, I drew a circle. If Mom drew a straight line, I drew a straight line. In that manner, we drew trucks and cows and houses and Imperial Walkers from the movie *The Empire Strikes Back*.

Every time I completed a rendition of my mother's drawing, she praised it. She pointed out the lines that were the straightest. She showed me which circles were the roundest. She told me I was a Fine Artist. Then she took my sheet from the pad and put it on the fridge. She left her own drawing on the pad, because there was no need to put it on the fridge.

I was an artist for six months, and then my mother stopped teaching me. We completed the sketch pad. My drawings were on the fridge, on walls, or just lost to recycling. The sketch pad itself didn't have a single drawing by me. Every drawing that remained was by my mother.

Her progression in ability over the six months was noticeable.

I am not an artist. Nor am I a poet.

If I were a poet, I would be able to Immortalize in Words the day I first met Saskia Stiles for the second time. I could capture in a metaphor the moment when I first recognized her as I walked toward my lunch table.

I don't understand poetry.

I don't understand how to compose sentences that, by themselves, have no significance, but together create narratives that write on the pages of someone's heart. I don't understand any of this because I don't have those sorts of feelings. I can't be a poet because I don't feel love.

I have never felt love. I can't say that this saddens me. I can't say it concerns me. I carry on fine without it: when my father tells me he loves me, for instance, I tell him back, "I love you too," and he appears satisfied. I don't love him, but he's none the wiser.

I may have loved my hamster, Gordon, because I liked to spend hours watching him run on his wheel. But I felt no grief when he died. Only curiosity.

"What did he die of?" I asked as I held his lifeless body.

"Probably old age," Bill said, and I was skeptical.

"It could have been cancer," I ventured.

"Perhaps," said Bill. "I guess we'll never know."

"We could do an autopsy," I said and started toward the kitchen.

Recently, I have wondered about love. Mostly, I have wondered why it's been on my mind at all. I wondered if it was because Saskia Stiles one day sat down at the seventh table in the third row of the cafeteria.

I considered the question, then concluded that Saskia wasn't the reason I thought about love. After all, we never talked. We never exchanged glances. That couldn't be love. The weeks in between when we first met again and the first night of texting didn't offer any evidence that proved otherwise.

I was thinking about this now only because it struck me that a poet would want to immortalize the moment in the cafeteria when I first saw Saskia Stiles, due to its serendipity. That the planks on which we were floating drifted together one more time.

I have an analytical mind. I don't subscribe to beliefs of destined coincidences or divinely placed chess pieces. I don't feel love, and I don't feel guidance. What is, is. Who is, is. And it's all very curious.

Yet, here I was, ten years later, and Saskia and I sat together and helped each other get through the day. We did it for each other, because it was the rational thing to do. We did it for mutual benefit.

Now she wanted me to write a poem. I wasn't sure how the benefit was mutual. I didn't see any clear benefit to writing a poem, but I suspected I could attempt something without it exploding in my face.

For the first hour of my attempt, I stared at an empty notepad, my pencil poised to strike.

In the second hour, I did research using Wikipedia.

I reviewed the more popular forms of poetry and settled on a limerick. The poem was short. The structure was rigid, probably easier to work with. Knowing that a poem had to come from the heart, and my heart was a foreign land, I didn't pause to consider the poem deeply. I plunged into it without giving it any thought:

> There once was a lady from Nantucket
> Her name was Saskia and she had a bucket
> She was in the lunchroom
> I was in the lunchroom
> And then she ate her lunch so just fucket

I regarded it afterwards for a half hour, reading it over and over again.

I'm not sure what any of that means, said a thread.

I'm trying.

Try again.

I opened my eyes and a poem came to me. I sat up in bed and turned on the light. Outside, the alder branches tapped at the window, asking to be let in. I reached for *The Twentieth Century in Review*, then stopped. For a full two minutes, I stared at nothing, not the wall, not the window, not my book, listening to a dim voice, straining to hear its words.

I climbed out of bed and took a pad of paper and a pen from my desk drawer. Slowly, carefully, I wrote out the words. They came effortlessly, as if I was simply taking dictation.

Ten lines.

Then I stopped, folded the paper in half, and stared at it for another minute.

My mind was empty. No threads speaking to me.

I climbed back into bed and went to sleep immediately.

———

Listen: Three years ago, I read a blog post by Susanne Olcrofft. The About Me page of her website stated that she was an autistic poet. The post was titled "What is it like to be an autistic poet?" I remembered a section of her blog and I heard pieces of it when I awoke. This is what Susanne Olcrofft's paragraph said, originally:

> You rest in the belfry of your mind, at the top of
> your tower, the same tower as mine, which we all
> visit, at times; the same tower in which you gaze
> across the land. The world sits outside the window
> and beckons, and you will only so long in the belfry
> stand, before you stand at the window. But I have
> stayed to read from the book of my soul.

This is what I wrote for Saskia:

> She rests in the belfry of her mind,
> At the top of her tower.
> The same tower as yours and mine,
> The same tower that we visit,
> The same tower in which we gaze across the land.
> The world sits outside the window and beckons,
> And we will only so long in the belfry stand,
> Before we stand at the window.
> But Saskia Stiles has stayed to read,
> From the book of my soul.

This is not plagiarism, I must argue. It's artistic licence.

———————

The next morning, I read the poem. I surprised myself: I changed the possessives. It was no longer the top of *your* tower, but the top of *our* tower. I don't know why I wrote it, but I wrote it, and I felt pleased with it. I understand that it is okay to be pleased with a poem even if you don't know its meaning. I can honestly say I am pleased by many poems whose meaning I don't understand. Almost all of them, actually.

In my poem, I didn't convert one of the possessives correctly. I wrote, "But Saskia Stiles has stayed to read, from the book of my soul." I meant to write, "But Saskia Stiles has stayed to read, from the book of *her* soul."

I was about to erase the mistake when it created a new thread in my mind. *Why did you write that?* it asked.

People sometimes write incorrect things. It's nice to be normal.

But, the thread asked, *how can the poem be correct if you wrote it wrong?*

Because grammatical errors are acceptable in a poem if they further the meaning of the poem.

What is the meaning of the poem?

I wish that Saskia would read the book of my soul.

Oh, the thread answered. *Oh my.*

I realized this was not a poem I was going to share. I needed a new one.

Well, that's just great, said the threads.

H

I opened my eyes and the Hampton Park cafeteria was out of white buns.

My day was difficult enough as I wrestled poetry from the rusty creative engines of my mind. The threads were backed up, clamouring, arguing, and I was ignoring them.

I had no poem for Saskia. I stood in line and tried to think of a Plan B. My breathing quickened, as if a panic attack was encroaching.

A poem, they said. *All we need is a poem.*

But not just any poem, I told them.

That's a problem.

So the day was already a mess. Now there were no white buns. I was feeling increasingly anxious.

I have been told that anxiety is a consequence of being autistic— my desire for white buns is an inflexible adherence to non-functional routine. I was told this by a behaviour interventionist whose desk was perfectly organized. The writing pad was parallel with a binder of notes, which was itself parallel to the pencil beside, and perpendicular to a pen above. None of them were touching.

Adherence.

The lady at the lunch counter gave me a cheeseburger on a whole wheat bun.

"That's not my lunch," I told her.

"It's what you ordered," she said. "Do you want fries?"

"No," I answered and stared at the burger. "I want a white hamburger bun."

She chewed her gum and stared at me with no expression on her face. "We're all out of white buns, sweetheart. Do you want fries?"

"I want a white hamburger bun."

Turning away to serve the next person in line, she said, "I want a Porsche. Sometimes we gotta drive a Volkswagen."

"I don't want a Porsche. I want a white hamburger bun."

"Sorry, kid." She dished a plate of fries. "Maybe you can run to the store and buy some buns, 'cause here at school we don't got none."

I considered what she said. "I don't think I'll go to the store," I said and took my hamburger to the till.

My phone vibrated and I checked it as I stood in line to pay. It was a message from Saskia.

h, it said.

And so it began.

Listen: This is how it happened.

I opened my eyes and the smell of the Hampton Park cafeteria washed over me like the smell from a meat grill at a carnival. My phone, in my hand, was vibrating.

h

"Are you going to take your money, or what?" said the cashier, and I looked up. She held out my change. I didn't know how long I had been staring at my phone. I was now at the front of a lineup.

The phone vibrated again.

h

I started to text her back.

"Can you not do that right now?" said the girl behind me. I stepped out of line, leaving my change and my lunch tray at the counter.

"Dork," muttered the girl.

I texted Saskia. *Where are you?* I asked.

here

I looked across the cafeteria. She sat at our table, huddled over her phone, turned away from the three boys sitting close to her. One of them was sitting very close to her.

h

I put my phone in my pocket and went back to my tray. It was time to have lunch at my table.

At *our* table.

When Danny Hardwick and his two friends came into the cafeteria, they should have sat at their own table. But four girls were already sitting there, so they were sitting with Saskia.

Danny Hardwick sat beside her. I watched, standing in the aisle that led to my lunch table. I stood motionless, holding my tray. Danny Hardwick sat beside Saskia, his hands near her.

The boys were talking to her, all of them, at the same time, laughing. Her hands were pressed hard against her headphones. Her phone was on the table in front of her.

Danny Hardwick sat beside her and looked up at me. I didn't move.

A single thought was in my head, by itself. All other threads had niced themselves.

I thought, Saskia Stiles is *my* friend.

I stepped forward.

Jack Sweat would have approved.

Danny Hardwick stood up when I approached.

"What are you staring at?" he said. He said it angrily, although there was no reason for him to be angry with me.

He walked around the table and up to me. "I said, what are you staring at?"

I didn't answer, for I was noticing how fast my heart was beating. *What are you looking at, sport?*

Listen: Danny Hardwick stood up and walked over to me, and I had a flashback. I flashed back to being strapped to a gurney, voices all around, an oxygen mask over my face. I flashed back to staring at the emergency ward ceiling, rolling down a hallway. The fluorescent tubes streamed by like boxcars.

I flashed back to the swishing sound of the doors to the emergency room opening, and two paramedics, in thick green parkas, pushing the gurney I was on.

But that wasn't right. Paramedics don't wear green coats. They wear blue uniforms.

I flashed back to being pushed down the hall, past four boys in thick winter coats, who were looking directly at me. But that wasn't right either.

"Nothing happened," they said. "Nothing happened. Got it?"

Before I had a chance to remember what the nothing was that didn't happen, the paramedics were back in their blue uniforms, one of them shining a light in my eye, and I was sitting on the pavement, blood pouring from my temple.

None of this made sense.

"Can you hear me?" asked the paramedic. "What's your name?"

Somewhere in the distance, I heard my mother's voice. "Don't hurt him," she said.

———

I snapped back to the cafeteria. Danny Hardwick and his friends stood around me in a circle. Danny faced me directly.

My heart raced. I was afraid, but not of Danny Hardwick. I was afraid because I had been so submerged in my memory that I didn't know how long I'd been away, how long they had stood there, talking at me.

I was afraid of what I remembered, but I didn't know why.

And then it registered: Danny Hardwick was wearing a green coat.

He stood in front of me, inches from my face. Poking me in the chest, speaking each word distinctly, clearly, abruptly.

"I. Said. What. Are. You. Looking. At?"

"I'm looking at you," I said, because it was the first thing I could think of to say. "Before that, I was looking at Saskia Stiles."

"Who's Saskia Smile?"

"Stiles." I pointed to Saskia. "She's my chemistry partner."

"So fucking what?"

"That's how I know her. We sit together in chemistry class."

The boy to my right was taller than the other two, and his teeth were crooked, stained thick yellow. His face burst with pimples. He wore a Yankees baseball cap. He wore a school colours jacket.

"I think the retard's got a crush on her," he said to Danny.

"I'm not a retard," I replied, looking down. "You were sitting where I sit."

"I don't see your name on it," said the boy.

"Did you look?"

He blinked. "Huh?"

"Did you look? I don't think you looked."

Danny Hardwick pushed me on the shoulder. "You want this kind of trouble?"

I am not large, but I am not small, either. Danny was two inches taller than me, and weighed forty pounds more. By objective standards, he was a big man.

He pushed me, and my lunch tray clattered to the floor. My

hands went up slightly, elbows loose, but in tight to my sides. Wrists turned.

I raised my head slowly to stare at him, and that wasn't the reaction he expected. A frown flickered on his face, and his eyes darted to his friends, then back to me. He licked his lips.

"You knocked over my lunch," I said.

My eyes were fixed squarely on his. They didn't waver. They didn't blink.

Then I said something I had never said before in my life.

I said, "Woof."

If you stare at a dog, you will make it uncomfortable. If you keep staring, it will lick its lips and turn away from you.

I have difficulty looking people in the eye because it makes me uncomfortable. When someone is looking at me, I become frustrated. When I look someone in the eye, threads burst into my head like popcorn from a popper.

When someone looks at me, and I look back, the first thread will be, *Why is this person staring?* I will immediately answer, Because he's talking to me, and close the thread. But a second thread will appear: *Why is this person still staring? They've stopped talking.*

No matter how many times I close this thread, it will continue to burst into my thoughts, as long as the person and I are looking at each other. It makes my thought process stilted. It interrupts the chain of logic.

It makes my eyes uncomfortable. It makes me want to blink.

It makes me want to lick my lips.

At the moment Danny Hardwick knocked the tray out of my hand, I remembered something Jack Sweat said, not long after the four boys put me in the hospital.

"You got beat up because you didn't make eye contact," he told me. "When you look down at the ground, some kids are going to think you're afraid of them. Bullies like making you afraid."

According to Jack Sweat, there was only one way to react to a bully.

"Don't back down. Don't try and fight him, but make sure he knows you're not afraid. That's all it takes to get a bully to leave you alone."

Danny Hardwick was a bully. I knew I had to react to him; I knew I had to imply that I was not someone to be trifled with.

At the same time, I was uncomfortable. He was staring me in the eye and I wanted to lick my lips, check to see if my nose was dry. A thread opened.

Why not be a dog, then? the thread asked.

———

I looked Danny in the eye. I said, "Woof."

It startled him. He looked around quickly, unsure of himself.

I don't think anyone had said "woof" to him before. It's unlikely he ever had a goal to make someone bark at him. More likely, his goal was to make someone afraid of him.

But I wasn't afraid. My eyes stopped hurting. The tightness in my stomach lifted. The tenseness of my muscles eased. I was in a spot where I was comfortable, for I had decided to become a dog. Now I knew what was going to come next.

At that moment, though, the class bell rang, and people began to stand, doors began to open, and students began to spill into the halls.

Danny Hardwick glanced around. He looked at me and nodded slowly, as if he had reached a conclusion.

"You're a fucking freak," he growled. "And you're dead if you cross me. Got it?"

I didn't answer. I didn't move. I stared at him levelly. I didn't break eye contact.

He motioned to his friends. "Come on," he said to them. "This guy's not worth our time."

Before he walked away he leaned even closer and whispered something in my ear, and I knew that one of us wasn't going to walk out of the cafeteria.

THE EYES

There are only three circumstances in which I am comfortable looking into someone's eyes.

I could look my mother directly in the eye. Our bedtime ritual included several minutes of looking at each other. She sat at the edge of my bed, stroking my hair, talking softly. Most of the time, I paid no attention to her words, and she had to repeat them several times. But we both enjoyed the game, I think.

I looked up at her blue eyes and was riveted by them. With anyone else, I would squirm, but my mother was the opposite. I was drawn to her eyes. Once I saw them, it was difficult for me to stop looking at them.

She never seemed to mind.

The second circumstance in which I can look someone in the eye is when I am in danger. When I am about to be in a confrontation. I haven't always been like that, mostly because I've rarely been able to tell when I am about to get in a fight. I still have trouble recognizing the signs. I still walk in oblivious most of the time.

Yet, when I read my environment right, when I understand what the person in front of me intends to do, that there is about to be trouble, I know to look into his eyes, and it doesn't bother me. In fact, it calms me, something that surprised me, and continues to surprise me, from the moment it first happened three years ago.

Before that, life was much more difficult.

And much more painful.

The third time I can look someone in the eye without pain is when I look at Saskia. I think it might be because she doesn't look straight back at me.

It makes it easier.

This is what Danny Hardwick said as he walked by:

He looked at me and I looked back at him. I didn't drop my eyes, even as his friends walked by me close enough to clip my shoulder with theirs. I ignored them. Danny snorted and shook his head. When he came abreast of me, his left shoulder knocked against mine, and he stopped.

"She's all yours, sport," he said in a whisper, leaning in to me. "Then maybe tonight, I'll drop by her place and give her a non-retarded fucking."

He walked away.

Danny's comment spawned several new threads, and normally I would have frozen for a moment. But these threads instantly vanished. They came in like a flock of locusts, but they didn't stay.

Will he actually drop?

From how high?

What is a non-retarded fucking?

How will he give it to her? What if she doesn't want him to?

Will he hurt her?

When I got to that question, all of my thoughts short-circuited. It was suddenly the only thread that mattered.

Will he hurt her?

I turned and kicked him in the back of the foot. He stumbled, then spun to face me. Rage wrote itself across his face. He raised his hands to hit me.

But he didn't.

I hit him first.

His hands were slow. The hands of his friends were slow.

Danny Hardwick swung at me clumsily and I came back with a left hook to his jaw and a right cross to his nose. I heard the crack of shattering cartilage.

Eleven percent shark was of no use to him either.

His eyes lost focus and he dropped to the floor. His friends hesitated, then came at me. One of them acted angrily and quickly, the other behind him, reluctant. It didn't matter. They swung at me, intentions obvious, next movements telegraphed, trajectories mapped.

I was calm. There were no threads. I knew exactly what to do.

I stepped away and their fists jetted past me like darting sparrows. To the left, to the right. Their fists grazed by me, without contact, and I came down on them like Moses from the mountain.

And I was calm.

Listen: That's not what happened.

Wait. That *is* what happened. That's exactly how it happened. But that wasn't the thing that was so important. That wasn't the reason I was now happy, even though I was sitting in the principal's office.

This is the reason:

The three of them lay on the floor around me. The cafeteria was as quiet as a morgue. My hand was already throbbing. I was breathing rapidly, but I wasn't afraid. I no longer wanted to hit them. I just wanted to go to class. I picked up my lunch tray, and the remainder of my lunch, and started to walk away.

And *that's* when it happened.

Saskia Stiles looked at me. Directly at me, her eyes unblinking, her gaze unwavering. Her body, ever taut and strung together tight, was now unwound, relaxed. Peaceful.

Goodbye, Freddy, she mouthed.

I stopped, frozen. Then, after a moment, I spoke. "I'll see you later," I said and started walking.

I forgive you, she said silently.

All at once the room seemed to shrink. The clink of glasses from the cafeteria kitchen disappeared. The muddled tromping of feet outside in the hall faded away for me. I was suddenly back, ten years ago, at the door to our therapy room, once again saying goodbye to my friend, Saskia Stiles. *I forgive you*, she said. Time and time again.

"I forgive you too," I told her and I didn't say anything else because I didn't want that moment to disappear. I was enjoying it. But I found I couldn't meet her gaze anymore. If I did, I might drop my tray. I might buckle at the knees. I might try and sink back into the past and stay there.

So I was silent. But I was at peace.

There were no more open threads in my mind.

162

I opened my eyes and I was fourteen years old, lying on my back. A man in light-blue pyjamas stood over me, with something in his hand, and there were bright lights.

His hand fell on my shoulder and I reacted immediately. I knocked away his arm and tried to sit up. When he pushed me back down, I punched him in the jaw. He straightened up, then grabbed me one more time. I kicked and struggled to break free of his clutches. But someone else rushed in, a lady, whom I had never seen before. Together, they pushed me back down on to my back.

At last, I relaxed, but they didn't let go of me.

"Are you okay, sport?" the man asked me.

"No," I said. "I need to go to the hospital."

"That's where you are," he told me.

I opened my eyes and was lying in a hospital bed. My father sat in a chair beside the bed, flicking the channels of the television.

"Where did the car go?" I asked him, because it seemed to me to be the most appropriate question. When I last closed my eyes, I was sitting in the front seat of our car. I was discussing why four boys had beaten me. I concluded that it was because they were angry at me, and my father had concluded that This Was Just Great.

After that I closed my eyes.

Was in car. Closed eyes. Opened eyes. Now in bed. That's *unexpected.*

The logical thing to do was to ask what happened to the car. After that question was answered, the next appropriate question was *Where did this bed come from?*

I never asked the second question. I didn't need to. My father knew how I worked.

"You're in a hospital bed, Freddy," he said, still looking at the television.

"Where's the car?" I asked.

"You were in a car, and now you're here." He put down the remote and turned to look at me. "You had swelling around the brain. You've been in surgery all night, and now you're in a hospital bed."

"Which side of my head?" I asked.

He blinked. "What?"

"Which side of my head had the swelling?"

"Your right side."

"Did they shave off all my hair, or just the hair on my right side?"

"Just the hair on the right side."

"Will I have a scar?"

My father nodded. "Seven inches in length."

Exhausted from talking, I closed my eyes.

I was grateful to my father. He had explained a complicated set of events in a way that spawned the fewest number of unclosed threads. I was not overwhelmed by them.

I closed my eyes to rest. Sometime later, I opened them again. The news was on. My father was still in the chair, his head bobbing, as he fought to stay awake.

"Where's Mom?" I asked.

"Go to sleep, Freddy," he said, his voice slurred as he rubbed his eyes.

I peed the bed that night. But I'm remembering wrong.

I remember that I drove home with Dad after the four boys beat me. But I remember staying in a hospital bed that night. But the sun was shining. It was morning.

But they don't send you home the day after brain surgery.

I remember sitting in my bed afterwards, and not sleeping all night. I remember waking up, my father changing the channels, his eyelids dropping.

But I don't remember.

Or, I do remember, and I'm afraid.

None of this is right.

FROM JIM WORLEY TO
THE VICE PRINCIPAL

I opened my eyes and Jim Worley came into his office. This is where I had gone, immediately after the cafeteria.

"My status is green," I said, before Jim Worley said anything or even stopped walking. I turned pages and didn't look up.

"You need to come with me, Frederick," he said. I turned the pages of *The Twentieth Century in Review* and didn't reply.

"Put the book down," he said to me.

"But I'm getting to the best part," I said, and he closed the book for me, taking it away. With one hand lightly holding my upper arm, he bid me to stand. I did, and he escorted me to a meeting room beside the school office, and sat me down at the table.

"Just be quiet," he advised. "Just answer the questions. No sarcasm."

"I don't want to be sarcastic," I said.

Vice Principal Nelson came into the room and took a seat across from me. He opened the folder he carried, and leafed through it, his frown growing deeper.

"How was your lunch?" he asked.

"I didn't eat my lunch," I said. "It got knocked to the floor."

"Is that why you beat the snot out of those three kids?"

"There was no snot."

"Freddy," said Jim Worley quietly.

I paused, then said, "They were going to hit me."

"But they didn't."

"No."

"Do you understand what sort of position this puts us in?"

"No."

He folded his hands together and leaned toward me. "It puts us in a bad position, Freddy," he said. "A very bad position. Do you understand?"

"No."

He paused. His eyes narrowed. "Are you being deliberately confrontational?"

"No."

He clenched his teeth. "Do you know that we have your file from Templeton College?" He lay the folder on the table. "I know all about why you were expelled." He looked up at me. "Is it true?"

"No."

"You didn't viciously assault a student?"

"Not viciously."

"That's a matter of interpretation, isn't it?"

I didn't answer.

He sighed. "Suppose you tell me what happened in the lunchroom today."

"One of them was sitting in my seat."

Vice Principal Nelson didn't say anything. He stared at me for a few moments, then closed the folder.

"One of them was sitting in your seat," he said slowly.

"Yes."

He rubbed his eyes and let out another sigh. "What am I supposed to do with that, Freddy? How do you expect me to respond to that? Do you expect me to say that it's okay to beat people up because they're sitting where you want to sit?"

"No," I said.

"Is that why you beat them up? Because they were sitting at your table?"

"No."

"Then why—" he began. He took a deep breath. "Then why did you start a fight with these boys?"

"I didn't start a fight. I told one of them that he was sitting in my seat. He said he didn't see my name on it. I told him I didn't believe him, because he wasn't looking at the seat, so he couldn't know with certainty that my name wasn't on it. Then he knocked my lunch to the ground."

Vice Principal Nelson nodded. "Do you know these boys? Do you have any classes with them?"

I shook my head.

"Have you had run-ins with them before?"

"Yes. With Danny Hardwick. Two weeks ago. In the shop wing."

"Why?"

"I don't know."

"What do you mean, *you don't know*?"

"I watched him talking to Saskia Stiles and then he—"

"Who," interrupted Vice Principal Nelson, "is Saskia Stiles?"

"Saskia Stiles is my chemistry partner."

"Is she your friend?"

I didn't answer. I didn't want to answer.

A moment passed. He noticed my hand, swollen, the knuckles bleeding.

"You do that on Danny Hardwick?" he asked, his voice softening.

"No," I answered. "One of his friends."

Nelson snorted, softly, abruptly. "Okay, Freddy, get someone to look at that hand."

THE MENDING BEFORE
THE SCHOOL OFFICE

I opened my eyes and the school nurse wrapped my hand in a bandage, taped it, and gave me an aspirin. Jim Worley stood behind her and took deep breaths to show his displeasure, then, when the nurse was done, bade me follow him.

"You have to wait in the office now," he told me. "Okay?"

"Okay," I agreed and went to the school office. I sat in a chair facing the receptionist, who wore a blue blazer and white shirt, and made no eye contact. I was of no interest to her.

My phone vibrated.

are you there
Yes.
you went away
Yes.
you didn't come to class
No.
are you mad at me
No.
are you hurt
No.
Yes.
I hurt my hand.
are they hurt
I think so.
I hope so.
they don't like you
I don't like them.
they came to my locker yesterday
i could smell them

What did they smell like?
cigarettes
They smoke.
they talk to me
if they walk by me in the hall they touch
sometimes
They won't anymore.
i typed h
Yes.
you came
you said you would
Yes.
i was afraid
they kept looking at me
but then they stopped looking at me
they were not looking at me
say, what were they looking at
What were they looking at?
at you
they were looking at you
there you were
i was waiting
i said h
you came
Yes.
they stood up
they went to you
you didn't run
why didn't you run
I promised you.

I opened my eyes and I was back in my chair, waiting in the school
office. I stared at the wall and silently repeated to myself, *Do not
say Jesus fuck.*
     Do NOT say it.
     Just once.

No.

Just softly.

"Jesus fuck," I muttered.

The receptionist slowed her typing. She looked at me over her reading glasses. "Did you say something?" she asked.

I nodded but did not speak.

When I was younger, I sometimes sat in my room and said all the swearwords I knew. I said them slowly, trying to understand the quality that turns swearwords into words I'm not supposed to say.

"FFFFFuuuuuuuuck," I would say, and do a search of my memory for times when I said it in public. In all three cases, my father told me to never use that word, not ever. When I asked why, he said, "Because I goddamn well said so, that's why."

I hate circular reasoning. I can't close a thread when that happens.

I told my father that his reasoning was flawed. He sighed.

"We're not arguing on this one. You don't say certain words in public. You have to trust me on this."

"But listen: *you* say those words in public."

"I try not to. Just like the time you tried not to piss your pants and failed. Everyone knows that you shouldn't piss your pants. But you did it anyway. Does that make it right?"

"No."

"It's the same with swearwords. You don't say them in public."

"Can you say them alone?"

"I suppose you could."

"Can I say them in my room?"

"Sure. Whatever. Why not?"

After that, I sometimes sat in my room and said every swearword I knew. They were bad words, but I didn't understand why. I suspected my confusion might have been because I failed to master the correct intonation and emphasis. So I practised them, like a wizard practising a spell.

"Shhhhhhit," I said, then paused. "Cock*suck*er," I said.

Sometimes my father passed by in the hall and opened the door to look in.

"Did you say something?"

"I was swearing."

"Is something wrong?"

"No."

"Then why were you swearing?"

"I was practising."

"Practising what?"

"Swearing."

He shook his head. "Great," he said. "That's just great."

"No, it's not," I said.

"Shut the fuck up, will you," he said angrily and slammed the door. I listened to him go downstairs.

For a few moments I sat quietly on my bed.

"Shut the fuck *up*, will you," I said slowly. "Shut the *fuck* up, will *you*?"

I stopped repeating swearwords long ago, because they were ubiquitous. In the shows I watched, in the books I read, on the websites I visited. There were no swearwords I hadn't heard.

There were no combinations I hadn't heard. Until today.

"Jesus *fuck*," moaned Danny Hardwick as he lay on the ground.

"Jesus *fuck*," I said under my breath, and the receptionist lowered her glasses and looked at me suspiciously.

My phone vibrated.

> what are you doing
> **Waiting.**
> im waiting too
> **What are you waiting for?**
> i want to go home
> i miss home
> i miss you

I looked at the words on my phone for a full minute before I replied.

> **I wrote you a poem.**
> you wrote me a poem?

My chem partner is Saskia
Every day we eat lunch
inside the cafeteria
Together she and me make we
Say, i wrote this poem for you saskia
I wrote it for you, Saskia.
thank you
You're welcome.
squeak
Squeak.

Listen: They sent home two of the boys I beat up in the cafeteria. They sent Danny Hardwick to the hospital for stitches. They made me stay.

I sat on a chair in a room in the principal's office until 2:30, when my father came to the office. He entered the room and stood in front of me. For almost a full minute he looked down at me, without saying a word, breathing heavily through his nose. I stared at the second button on his shirt. Then he turned and walked back to the door.

"Let's go," he said. I stood up and followed.

"Can we stop for ice cream?" I asked as we walked out of the principal's office.

"Just shut up, Freddy," my father said.

In the truck, in the parking lot, my father started the engine, but instead of driving me home, he slumped back in his seat, his hands on the steering wheel. I sat in the passenger seat and stared straight ahead.

The heater was on, but it was blowing cool air. My father never turns the heater off. It has been running since the day he bought the car, three years, four months, and nine days ago.

It makes him comfortable.

"God*damn* it, Freddy!" my father shouted and slammed his fist on the dashboard. "What the bloody hell is *wrong* with you?"

I had many answers for that question. It was, after all, the main question that has consumed me for most of my life. But I didn't say anything because I was sure he didn't want to hear it.

He leaned forward and lay his head on his hands as they gripped the top of the steering wheel. "How many times is this going to happen?" He turned to me. "I suppose they were annoying you, these kids. Is that what happened this time?"

"No," I said.

"Do you know you've been suspended for the week?"

"Yes."

"Do you know you might get expelled? Beating up three people in the cafeteria isn't a small thing, Freddy. It's a big thing."

I stared straight ahead. Rain began to fall. I closed my eyes.

"Should never have let you go into boxing," he growled as he drove. "Should have just let you get shitkicked some more times. Maybe you'd have learned something for a change."

As we drove home from Hampton Park, my father asked me the same question he asked after I was expelled from Templeton.

"Why *did* you hit him?" he wanted to know.

My reply, both times, was the same. "Because he was trying to hit me."

Both times, the rain began, and the windshield wipers beat at a rate of forty cycles per minute. I counted the beats and listened to the whirr of the wiper motor. It went whirrrr. Thump. Whirrrr. Thump. This was the noise it made in one cycle.

"Why was he trying to hit you?" my father asked.

"Because I kicked him in the back of his foot."

"What the hell? Why did you do that?"

I didn't answer.

———

In at least one way, Hampton Park and Templeton College were similar: my shoulders were bumped at both schools.

Chad Kennedy liked to bump my shoulders at Templeton College, and Danny Hardwick liked to bump my shoulders at Hampton Park. But Chad was still the opposite of Danny Hardwick. Where Danny was bellicose and sullen, Chad was outgoing and loud. Where Danny was rebellion and subculture, Chad was mainstream and all-American. Danny was an outcast. Chad was the type of guy who created outcasts.

The two, although similar in behaviour, would not have liked each other.

Classically speaking, both Danny of Hampton and Chad of Templeton were bullies. Classically speaking, I was the person who got bullied. Having no friends to interfere or object, I have always been a target for people like Danny or Chad. Having never fought back, or resisted, I continued to be a target.

As it happens, never fighting back and never resisting is usually a good strategy, because I tend to bore my aggressors. A pigeon can only peck a button so long before it decides that no more pellets are going to fall. Like pigeons in a cage, Danny and Chad pecked at me, expecting that I would react, preferably with fear.

Anger would be fine, too, they assumed. They were wrong.

Listen: The similarities frighten me.

In November of last year, I was expelled from Templeton College for fighting. The expulsion came at the end of a hearing, the same kind of hearing I would now face at Hampton Park.

At Templeton, it was the conclusion of the quote-headmaster-unquote that I was a threat to the safety of the other students. It was his finding that I was not able to control my violent impulses.

There were many other circumstances that influenced the conclusion reached by the quote-headmaster-unquote, but they were not significant enough to be included in his written decision to expel me. I know they were not significant factors because he said so in his written report.

It was not considered that I had done irreparable harm to the student body as a whole. It was so not considered that McClintock mentioned the irreparable harm three times in his report.

Chad Kennedy was the high school football team's starting quarterback, and the team, if it won the last game of the season, would qualify for the state finals for the first time in seven years. It was expected, by alumni, that the team should reach the state finals. Chad's starting position was guaranteed because the second-string quarterback, Ed Laughlin, the son of the leading donor to the school, was fifty pounds overweight.

But, in the end, Chad didn't start the playoff game. Instead, he watched from the side of the field, his nose taped, a set of stitches in the back of his head. Ed Laughlin started and led the team to an 18–0 drubbing at the hands of their archrival, the Upper College Titans.

The Titans' mascot is a giant stuffed missile.

Templeton lost the game and was eliminated from the playoffs. This meant a significant loss in revenue from anticipated home games, and "constituted a blow to the morale of the school."

A *blow* to school morale.

"This was not," quote-Headmaster-unquote McClintock read aloud, "a factor that influenced my decision."

"Then why is it in your report?" I asked him.

He glowered. "It illustrates the impact your actions had on the student body. They may not recover."

"They may," I said.

"Irregardless—"

"Regardless."

He looked like he wanted to say something, but held himself back. "Regardless—" he tried.

"Many students don't like football," I added

"Freddy," my father said softly and put his hand on my arm. "Just shut up, will you?"

It was also not relevant that a parent-teacher meeting took place one night after the Templeton Ruggers were eliminated from the playoffs. Nor did it weigh in his decision that several parents voiced their opinion that the loss could be attributed to a team that was not managed well, used primarily to generate extra revenue from home game sales, and not properly supported by the administration.

It was not a factor that many parents wondered whether the school was not making sufficient money, and that perhaps the administration needed to review its policies, perhaps its staff.

None of this was a factor that merited consideration on the part of quote-Headmaster-unquote McClintock. His decision was determined solely by the facts of the incident. The facts were these: in the hallway of the Main Hall of Templeton College, at 1:05 PM, Chad Kennedy fell back and smashed through the plate-glass trophy cabinet. A very large trophy fell from the top shelf, and he was knocked unconscious.

The trophy was for the most outstanding student of the year.

Several witnesses indicated that Chad didn't just fall. He fell because I pushed him. I struck him four times, causing him to lose his balance. To McClintock, this was an act of violence of such an unacceptable level that I should be expelled from school.

I tried to explain that the punches were not relevant to why Chad fell unconscious. He fell into the glass only because he stepped on his own shoelace when I pushed him backward. I pushed him backward because he was falling on me when he lost his balance. He lost his balance because I struck him. I struck him because he was trying to strike me. He tried to strike me because I pushed him. I pushed him because he pushed me. How far back do I have to go?

This was not relevant to McClintock.

"I don't want to know *how* you did it," he said. "It's enough for me to know *that* you did it."

In fact, it was only significant that I shoved Chad Kennedy. McClintock called this the Initiating Incident, and, after that, Chad Kennedy was justifiably defending himself. It was not considered that I shoved Chad Kennedy only after Chad Kennedy shoved me, for Chad Kennedy later told Principal McClintock that he was Only Playing Around and Didn't Mean Anything by It.

Nor was it considered that Chad Kennedy was four inches taller than me, outweighed me by forty pounds, and could bench press three twenty. In the opinion of quote-Headmaster-unquote McClintock, larger people should be just as safe from violent outbursts as smaller people.

No one considered that Chad Kennedy used to sneak up behind me between classes and give me gonch pulls. No one considered that Chad Kennedy snapped wet towels at me in the boys' change room.

No one considered that my actions were reactions.

"This is my point, Frederick," said McClintock. "You have an excuse for everything you did. And every excuse blames Chad Kennedy."

It was, in the end, concluded that I was unable to tell the difference between a legitimate physical threat and a case when a friend was playing with another friend, which was the circumstances of the incident that occurred between me and Chad Kennedy. As Chad told quote-Headmaster-unquote McClintock, I was Chad's friend, or so he thought, and I was probably jealous of Chad's position on the football team.

I checked Wikipedia. I couldn't identify any characteristics of my relationship with Chad Kennedy that would be consistent with friendship.

————

In making his decision to expel me, quote-Headmaster-unquote McClintock explained that he did not consider at all that I am autistic. This was a medical condition, and not relevant, beyond that fact that there was no one at the school with Sufficient Training in Controlling the Behaviour of an Autistic Student.

"This incident is explainable without invoking medical minutiae," he said. "This was a simple act of poorly controlled aggressive behaviour."

It was finally noted that I am disrespectful of authority, as evidenced by my dogged disagreement with McClintock about his reasoned assessment of the circumstances of the fight. This was indicative of a Stubborn and Irrational Outlook. Normally, this sort of outlook is controllable and mouldable by school counsellors, but no one at Templeton College had the sufficient training to control my behaviour.

It was not considered a factor that my past behaviour was not violent, yet it was considered that past behaviour was consistently disrespectful. Because I was a Growing Young Man, my temperament was beginning to change.

"My non-violent past behaviour is not a significant factor in your decision," I said.

Quote-Headmaster-unquote McClintock nodded.

"But my anticipated future violent behaviour is."

"That's the challenge of being an administrator," McClintock said. "Anticipating the future in order to protect the present."

————

I left something else out of the conversation with my dad after I was expelled: I wasn't angry when I hit Chad. But I did feel *something*, something I was unable to identify. I had never felt it before, and I wasn't certain if it was an emotion or a gastrointestinal incident.

But I felt it. As I stood watching Chad Kennedy and Oscar Tolstoy, I noticed I was observing a fundamentally illogical situation. The

179

disagreement was over whether or not Oscar should go away. They both appeared to agree that he should go away. Yet he wasn't leaving. The person advising Oscar Tolstoy to go away was the same person preventing him from going away.

I was perplexed by this. It wasn't logical to have a disagreement over something on which they agreed. But they were having this disagreement in front of my locker, which was inconvenient for me.

To make it worse, I wasn't certain who should be addressed when instructing them to move. Oscar was blocking my locker, but asking him to move would likely have no effect, for it was Chad who was keeping him there. Therefore, in order to ask Oscar to move, I had to ask Chad to move first.

This is too confusing, said the threads. *Why not assign Chad Kennedy full responsibility for ensuring Oscar Tolstoy moves?*

Works for me, I thought.

"It is my decision, therefore," the quote-headmaster-unquote of Templeton College told me and my father, "that Frederick Wyland is considered a threat to the physical safety of our students and will be, therefore—"

"You already said therefore," I interrupted. He stopped talking and, without moving his head from over the paper he was reading, looked directly at me, unblinking.

"Therrrrrefore," he said, "in light of the fact that the accused student has shown no evidence of remorse, I feel it is my duty as headmaster—"

"Principal," I corrected.

"Freddy," my father said. "Shut up."

"—to permanently expel Freddy Wyland from Templeton College. This is effective immediately."

The room was silent. The principal continued to stare at me, even though I was no longer doing Annoying Things.

The morning after I was expelled from Templeton College, I returned to collect the contents of my locker, and Oscar Tolstoy was there, leaning against my locker. I wondered if he enjoyed blocking my locker door.

He stepped aside and said, "Did you know that Ty Cobb's 1911 baseball card is now considered the second-most valuable baseball card in the world?"

"No." I opened my locker and began placing my things into my backpack.

"It's worth two hundred and seventy-three thousand dollars." He swung his hands back and forth, watching me empty my locker into a bag, and asked, "Are you suspended?"

"I was expelled."

"Shoeless Joe Jackson was expelled from baseball. His 1910 T210 red border card is worth one hundred and ninety-nine thousand, seven hundred and fifty dollars."

Two boys walking by came over. I didn't know them.

"That was awesome, what you did," one of them said.

"No, it wasn't," I replied. My locker was now empty.

"Dude, it totally was," he said. "You made him your bitch. I don't think *anyone* has seen a slapdown like that before. Not in this school. And the trophy falling on his head! It was like *art*."

I closed my locker door. "Chad Kennedy was standing in front of my locker."

The boy laughed. "Holy cow! *That's* the reason you told McClintock?"

I closed my gym bag.

"But why?" he asked.

"Because it was the reason," I said and turned around and walked away.

"It sucks, and all," he called after me. "I mean, you getting expelled and stuff. But that guy totally had it coming. He should be the one getting expelled."

"Maybe if I played more football," I said over my shoulder.

THE DISCIPLINARY HEARING

I opened my eyes. The principal of Hampton Park sat at the far end of the table, looking at me, waiting for me to say something.

This was not like Templeton College. This time around, the principal didn't read a report on why I was being expelled. Instead, I was interviewed by a committee consisting of him and two school trustees. Jim Worley sat with me, to help me with the process.

I believe he now thought of me as his client.

I came before them at 4:30, to a meeting room beside the teachers' lounge, on the day after the fight. I sat at one end of the conference table with Mr. Worley. They sat at the other end. Chairs ran down the wall behind me, empty save for one, in which my father sat and smouldered.

"Do you have anything to say in your defence, Mr. Wyland?" the principal asked me after he read out a report of the fight.

"I'm here against my will," I replied.

"No, you're not, Freddy," said my father.

Jim Worley touched my arm. "Try again."

"I don't want to be expelled," I said.

The principal nodded, but his expression didn't change. "Why do you want to stay here at Hampton?"

"Because I love to," I said a little loudly, then quickly closed my mouth.

"You love to?" the principal said slowly.

"Freddy," Jim Worley counselled, "relax. Take your time."

"I want to stay at Hampton Park Senior Secondary," I said slowly, in one long exhale.

"We understand that, Mr. Wyland," said one of the trustees. Her name was Martha Turkel. She was decorated in jewellery and wore a hat that covered her silver hair. "I want you to tell us *why* we should let you stay here at Hampton," she said.

183

"Because I have a chemistry class partner."

Martha Turkel frowned, uncertain. It's likely she was expecting a more abstract reason regarding regret and desire to be a better person. I am more literal.

"Is that the only reason you want to stay here at Hampton?"

"Yes," I said, because it was true.

"Do you not like attending Hampton Park?"

"No," I said. I was getting annoyed. I sensed a lack of communication, which was disastrous for me. A lack of communication almost always preceded a prolonged discussion, in which I would have to take an active role. It was a tiresome task.

"No, you don't like attending Hampton, or no, you *do* like attending Hampton?"

"Neither," I said. She stared at me.

A moment passed. They continued staring.

I took a deep breath. "I neither like nor dislike attending Hampton Park. It doesn't have any unique characteristics. I like attending this school as much as I would like attending any school."

"And do you like attending any school?"

"No," I said. But I don't think she understood.

There are few upsides to autism, but the forbearance of strangers is one of them. People around me tend to react with patience, once they come to know I'm on the spectrum. People around me tend to give me the benefit of the doubt when I say something rude. I think it worked in my favour at that moment.

"I'm sorry, Freddy," said Principal MacLeod. "We're all getting a little confused. I'm asking why you want to stay at Hampton, but all I'm getting from you is that you have a good chemistry partner."

"Yes," I said. "I want to keep her as my chemistry partner. I believe I'll get better grades, and so will she."

"Ah," said Martha Turkel slowly. "*She* . . ."

The three exchanged glances.

"Who," asked Principal MacLeod, "is this girl?"

"Saskia Stiles," I said, and behind me, my father gasped, then choked on his gum.

He coughed for more than a minute.

SASKIA IN MY MIND

Saskia has seen my bedroom. I have seen hers. Back when our parents still made us put on pyjamas before one of us had to leave, we would retreat to the bedroom and ignore each other like very good friends should do.

Within the slim definition of "play" that applies to autistic children, Saskia Stiles and I played. We bounced around rooms at Excalibur House, without bumping into each other, without talking to each other, without interacting with each other. Most people thought we were ignoring each other, but if you asked me what I did for the day, I would have told you that I played with Saskia. She would have said the same.

When we played, I was happy. She let me do the things that I wanted to do, with no other demands. I let her do the things that she wanted to do, with no other demands. We were glad for each other's company. It was enough.

Communities form from their shared experiences, good or bad. So it was that Linda and John Stiles met my mother and father at a therapy session, each family coming to terms with a brand new diagnosis. They quickly became friends.

"They like the same things we do," my mother said, the first time after they came to visit, and threw the beer cans and wine bottles in the recycling.

"Did we leave the table even *once* tonight?" my father asked.

Often, we played at my home, and often we played at Saskia's home. Our parents sat in the living room at her house or around the kitchen table at our place, laughing loudly, drinking bottles of beer, eating bowls of potato chips.

When we played in my room, I often went downstairs, but Saskia didn't mind. She hopped around my bedroom while I sat on the kitchen floor and watched our parents. Saskia found nothing interesting about downstairs, and she was right. I did little more than sit. The adults rarely acknowledged me and sometimes I didn't even listen. Yet it was enjoyable *because* they ignored me: I could be around them without having to answer questions.

I could sit and not have to pay close attention. There was no need to be ever alert for an impending conversation, nor was there the agony of labouring to understand what they were saying.

I could *blend*. I could sit in the background and not be an object of their attention. I could sit on the floor, my book on my lap, flipping pages. Two forward. One back.

I could be *me*.

My parents sat at the table with John and Linda Stiles. They drank beer, they laughed at each other, and my father smiled at me if I walked by him to get a drink of water. Sometimes, if I came within arm's reach, he grabbed me and hugged me, causing me to push him away, to squirm until he let me go.

It never bothered me that he tried to hug me. I was acting by rote. When someone grabs me, even my father, I try to get away. But I *liked* that he grabbed me. Ten years later, I wondered if that was why I poured myself so many glasses of water.

When Saskia's family came to visit, my father drank beer and tried to wrap me in his arms.

And he smiled. I went downstairs to see my father smile.

———

John Stiles and my father spent a lot of time together, until the day before I said goodbye to Saskia.

After that day, I never saw Linda and John Stiles again. My father enrolled me in Templeton College, a private school, and I never went back to Excalibur House.

After that day, my mother was gone.

Correlation is not causation. Even when you know it's not causation, you still can't stop thinking about it.

I opened my eyes and I was seventeen. Bill sat in the driver's seat of the truck, gripping the steering wheel, his lips pressed together so hard they were white.

He yelled at me all the way home.

"Saskia Stiles," he said through gritted teeth. "You're kidding me, right? You're just freakin' kidding me."

I didn't answer. I knew he wasn't wondering if I was joking.

"Saskia goddamn Stiles?" he shouted.

"That's not her middle name," I said.

"Stop," he barked, pointing a shaking finger at me. "Just stop that. Not right now. Not right fucking now do you make stupid-ass comments like that. You know what I mean. You know *exactly* what I mean."

But I didn't know. I didn't understand why he was so angry that I was chemistry class partners with Saskia Stiles.

"You could have told me," he said, his hand gripping the wheel so tight the knuckles were as white as his tightly pressed lips. "You could have bloody well told me. How long, Freddy?" He looked at me, a little too long for someone who should be concentrating on driving. "How long have you two been hanging out?"

"Eight weeks, six days," I said.

"Two goddamn months you're seeing this girl, and you don't think once of telling me?"

"Yes," I said. "I thought about telling you eleven times."

He took a breath, held it, exhaled slowly. "So why the fuck didn't you?"

I didn't answer.

That night, I stared at the clock on the wall while downstairs my father slammed cupboard doors.

When we got home, he said, "Just go to your damned room," and stomped to the kitchen. "Get out of my bloody sight before I do something I can't take back."

I would not sleep, I knew. The threads lay heavy, blanketing my mind like fresh snow. I thought back to when we walked out of the committee room. The principal had dismissed my father and me without making a decision on my status. For the time being, they said, I was suspended, and they would decide if they were going to expel me. That made me afraid.

It was a brand new type of fear that I had never felt before.

For the first time, I was afraid of losing someone. I was afraid that, upon being expelled, I would have to go to another school, and Saskia Stiles would no longer be my chemistry partner. I knew I would get a new chemistry partner, but I knew that it was unlikely it would be someone whose company I wished to keep.

I sat on my bed, flipping pages. Downstairs, my father muttered in short bursts. I knew he was drinking; I heard the *spritzzz* of each opening can of beer.

My father drinks. My mother left us. I flip pages to calm myself. Academics call my family situation dysfunctional. I call it life.

———

A text.

> are you up
> **Yes.**
> are you having a good day
> **No.**

say, do you want to go swinging in the park
Do you want to go swinging in the park?
yes
say, do you want me to come too
Do you want me to come too?
yes
Okay.
when are you coming
when are you coming
when are you coming
Now.
squeak

I sat on my bed, turning pages and wondered how I could go swinging in the park with Saskia.

I hadn't been to a park for years. I hadn't been on swings in even longer.

When Saskia and I went to Excalibur House, there was a playground in the back and we played there on our break. Saskia rode the swing the entire time. Sometimes I pushed her.

Memories arose, and I thought of a time at Excalibur House in the playground. There were six of us, in a circle. I stood beside Saskia, who was debating the merits of riding the swing with her interventionist.

"You can ride the swing after your exercises, okay?" Saskia's behaviour interventionist told her.

Saskia nodded. "Okay."

"Good, then, let's—"

"But I want to ride the swing now," Saskia said and walked toward the swings. The BI ran after her, chiding her along the way.

I observed this peripherally but was distracted by my propeller arms. My own behaviour interventionist knelt down before me and said, "Look at me, Freddy."

We were all supposed to be playing a game, but the fresh air was exhilarating. We jumped up and down. I waved my hands in a clockwise motion. Clockwise was good. My BI said something to me that I did not hear. I was too busy thinking about what would happen if I waved my hands in counter-clockwise motion rather than clockwise motion. I didn't hear her and didn't realize she was talking to me. To be more precise, I didn't hear her *because* I didn't realize she was talking to me.

———

Listen: I was four years old when I watched my first Charlie Brown special, *A Charlie Brown Christmas*, and it was the first time I heard Charlie Brown *listen* to his teacher.

The teacher said to Charlie Brown: *Mwa Mwa, Mmmwa mwa MWAH MWAH.*

When someone is talking to me and I don't realize it, I hear the same thing. This is why I liked Charlie Brown: he heard noises in a way that I sometimes did. The only difference between Charlie Brown and me was that, when he heard the teacher speak, he understood her and could Pay Attention. Charlie Brown was, evidently, someone I could learn a great deal from. He could have advised me on what to do.

That was what I heard from my BI, a bunch of sounds. I didn't know they were directed toward me, so I didn't pay attention to them. My BI said, *Mwaa Mwa mwaMwaaWaa.* And I had no idea if that even meant anything.

We had come outside to practise standing in line, by taking turns going down the slide. We were supposed to line up in an orderly fashion, go down the slide, then go to the end of the line. But I kept losing track of where we were in the chain of supposed-tos.

Saskia was tired of the game and argued about the merits of riding on the swing. Others ran around, screaming, flapping their arms. I swung my arms in circles until my interventionist put herself squarely in front of me, and told me to go stand at the slide.

Instead, I went and stood at the swing. I didn't like slides. I didn't like swings, either, but I did like being near Saskia, and I wanted to stand and watch her swing.

"Freddy," said my interventionist sternly, "look at me."

"Mwaa mwaa, mwa mwa MWAH mwaa," I replied.

Tonight, after Saskia's text, I felt a tug, a pulling I hadn't felt in a long time, a yearning to go back to a park with her and watch her swing. Just watch her swing, and not think about anything else. Without interventionists telling me to look at them. Without my father telling me to stop ruining his life. Without a principal telling me I was a threat to students everywhere.

I wanted to stand and watch Saskia swing. Maybe I would push her, too.

My phone vibrated.

> are you coming
> **Yes.**
> i know your secret
> **What?**
> shhhhh
> it's a secret
> **Okay.**
> i've known you all my life
> you were my friend
> you stopped coming to excalibur house
> **I stopped.**
> i said see you later
> you said see you later
> **It took ten years.**
> the last day i saw you it rained
> **Yes.**
> i was under a blanket
> **You were not.**
> my mom cried and i cried
> say, why did you cry
> **Why did you cry?**
> shhhhhh
> it's a secret

I opened my eyes and I was seven, and I didn't want to go have dinner. Not yet. I wanted to stay in the living room, with my book, and stare out the window. I wanted to turn the pages of the book in my lap.

My father disagreed. He called something unintelligible as he came into the living room and I was certain he wasn't speaking to me, because he made no sense.

This is what he said: "Freddy, DINNER!"

This is what I heard: "Mwaa mwa. MWA MWA."

Naturally, I ignored it. He couldn't have been speaking to *me*. I don't even know what Mwaa is.

He tried to close my book; I jerked it away and turned from him. This time, he spoke directly to me.

"Freddy," he said angrily, and I didn't know why he was angry.

"What," I said, still staring out the window.

"It's dinner."

"Okay," I said. Two pages forward. One page back.

"Close your book."

"But I'm getting to the best part."

He shook his head. "No, you're not. You're not even looking at your book."

"Yes, I am," I explained. I turned two more pages, continued to look out the window.

"Fine," he said. "You can get to the best part after dinner."

"Listen: I need to—"

"Just get in the fucking kitchen!" he shouted at me and grabbed my book. I refused to let go. He pulled hard, and it tore at the binding. Pages, already loosened from countless hours of turning, spilled to the floor.

"NO!" I shouted at him, but he tore the book from my grip and I began to scream. I stood up, swinging my hands at my father, pummelling him on his shoulders, his chest, his stomach.

"Freddy, stop it!" he shouted and pushed me back. I lunged forward at him and he slapped me across the mouth so hard I lost my balance. It startled me. It stopped every single thread in my mind. It brought my thoughts to a grinding halt.

What was that? they asked.

I tasted blood. Something rattled in my mouth. I spit out a tooth.

In the hall, my mother gasped. She stared at me, her eyes wide, one hand clutching the other.

"Freddy," she said, then backed up.

I scrambled after the tooth, which lay under the sofa chair.

"What the hell, Freddy?" my father said.

I held the tooth up like a trophy. "My loose tooth!" I shouted, hopping up and down. "It came OUT!"

Time seemed suspended. My hand holding the tooth triumphantly in the air. My mother, with hands to her mouth in the hall. My father, unsure of what to do with his hands, his mouth bobbing open and closed.

"Okay, Freddy," my mother said softly. "Let's go put it under your pillow, okay?"

"Okay," I said happily and ran upstairs as fast as I could.

"What the hell did you *do*?" I heard her shouting at him.

At the age of eight, Jack Sweat started slapping the heavy bag. He was, after all, the son of the Butcher.

Jack could have been an elite boxer; he was an intelligent person, but he lacked a killer instinct. He admitted it. He wasn't concerned enough with victory that he would sacrifice anything to obtain it. The truth was, victory wasn't the goal.

"If I get in a dust-up," he told me, "and the judges call it even, and the other guy has done everything he could to beat me, and I did everything I could to beat the other guy, then that's the perfect fight."

This was a philosophy not discussed with his father, who belonged to the Old School, where your opponent was the enemy. To the Butcher, the challenge of the fight was not the fight, but the victory. If he had known that his son was more interested in the competition than the victory, he would have been disappointed. So Jack kept it to himself.

He was the youngest of three, and his older brothers were in the army. Jack lived with his parents in a three-bedroom apartment just down from the shop. The Butcher shared one bedroom with his wife, Elle. Jack had the second bedroom. The third bedroom was where they kept the trophies Jack won in competition.

The Butcher called it the Jack Room, but it was the Jack Room in name only. In all the times I visited, Jack only went in there twice.

The only other people who went into this room were the Butcher, guests who visit the Butcher, and Elle, who went in to dust.

Jack went into this room sparingly, only to put a new trophy on a shelf or hang a new medal. For a while, when he brought a girl home, he took her into the Jack Room, and hoped it would make her sexually excited to see the trophies, medals, and plaques for Best Fight of the Night. Sometimes it did, but the sexual excitement was muted by probing, poking questions from his parents. The Butcher and Elle came from hearty prairie farm stock and a love of tradition. They did not approve of young boys and girls spending time together, alone, and especially frowned on the idea that boys and girls may become sexually excited by each other.

After a while, Jack stopped showing girls the trophy room. The gains from displaying his physical accomplishments were outweighed by the losses accrued. His mother inevitably doused the flames of any passions aroused.

By the time Jack turned seventeen, he stopped bringing girls home altogether. He stopped going into the room himself, and let his father hang up his medals or find a space on the shelves for the trophies. He only took one other person into the room, years after he stopped bringing anyone else.

He brought me.

Jack Sweat showed me his trophy room when we were both seventeen, in my last semester at Templeton College. One day, after I had finished a workout and was lacing up my street shoes, he came over and said, "I want to show you something."

I looked at the Butcher, who nodded at me, indicating I was free to leave. I stood up and followed Jack through the side door and down the street to his apartment. At the end of the hall, he opened the door and told me to go in.

The room was small. A single window had no curtains. The window ledge was empty, except for the hull of a common housefly, dead after prolonged efforts to flee the room through the windowpane. The closet doors had been removed, and a chest-high bookshelf was in the middle of the closet. There were no books on the shelves. There were only trophies. The smallest were on the lower shelves, and the tallest were on the top. Nine medals were wrapped around the three tallest of them all.

The walls were covered with plaques and photographs. There were framed clippings from newspapers, describing fight cards in which Jack competed. Three of these included photographs of bouts showing Jack trading punches with an opponent.

We stood in the centre of the room.

After a moment, I understood that Jack expected me to be

195

impressed, but I was not versed in the ability to look impressed. I swivelled my head slowly. I deliberately stopped and focused on random trophies. I read the text of newspaper clippings on the wall.

"What do you think?" he asked.

"I like this room," I said.

He nodded. "Thought you might."

Thirteen plaques hung at eye level, surrounded by photographs. My eyes never left the pictures. Seven of them, framed, showed Jack in mid-round battle. Nine showed him posing, post-fight pictures, beside his father. In two of these, Jack was in his fighter stance. In six others, his father had his arm around his shoulders.

"It's quiet in here," I added.

"Yeah. I kind of knew you were going to say that." He looked at his watch. "I've got to get going—I'm working tonight. But I thought you would like to see this room."

"Yes."

He looked at me, a small frown on his face, as if he wanted to say something. Instead, he let out a sigh. "Did you want to stay in here a little longer?"

"Yes," I said, still looking at the photographs.

He nodded. "Just let yourself out."

"Okay." My eyes fell on one photograph. The referee holding his arm in the air. Jack, exhausted, leaning backward as if he was going to faint. His father supporting him, both arms around his chest in a bear hug. The Butcher looked like he was dancing. As happy as a man can look without drawing suspicion to himself.

I sat on the floor, my back to Jack, staring at this photo. A moment later, I heard the door close behind me.

I watched the picture, and on the canvas of the ring, I saw a clock rise up.

4:32. 4:33. 4:34.

I stayed for an hour.

———

After seeing the Jack Room, my workout routine changed. After the last round of sparring, I would towel off the sweat and tell Jack, "I want to see the trophy room."

Most times, Jack or the Butcher would say, "Not today, Freddy."

Other times, Jack would glance at the Butcher, who'd nod or say, "Make it snappy." Then, I would walk down to their apartment, often by myself, go in, and say, "Hi, Elle," as she made dinner in the kitchen. Sometimes she'd say, "Hi, Freddy." Sometimes she'd wave. Other times, she ignored me. I would go into the Jack Room.

I liked it in there because it was always warm, and always quiet. The window spilled into a narrow back alley. The only sounds outside were the occasional faint honk of a horn, or the rattling of a shopping cart as a homeless man scurried from trash container to trash container.

I liked to sit in the middle of the room and look at the photographs of Jack Sweat and his father. Seeing them, I felt calm. My mind quieted. It was like the early mornings, without threads rattling around in my brain.

The last time I sat in the middle of the floor of Jack Sweat's room, he came in with a new trophy. This was a break in tradition—usually only the Butcher added memorabilia. But this time it was Jack. The trophy was medium-sized. It would go on the middle shelf. Only first-place trophies went on the top shelf, and he didn't win the competition this time.

He nodded to me. I sat cross-legged, still in my boxing shorts, still wearing my hand wraps, my shirt damp with sweat from the day's workout.

He added the trophy to his collection and stood beside me. I stood up.

"What do you think?" he asked.

I didn't think anything. I understood that he wanted to know what I thought about the contents of the room. I requested appropriate answers from my memory, and quickly a list of responses came back.

After a few moments of consideration, I chose the optimum answer.

"This room does not have a chair in it," I said.

He looked around. Then he smiled. "It could use a chair, couldn't it?" he said.

Then he stepped closer and kissed me on my lips.

Listen: These are the people who have kissed me in my life.

My mother kissed me frequently. I remember every kiss she gave me, and I remember the final one, on a train platform, the ticking of rain on hot metal, the hiss of air released from the brakes. She kissed me on the forehead and said goodbye.

My father kissed me less frequently, and he stopped when I was seven. That's not right. He kissed me on the top of my head as I lay in the hospital. His last kiss was when he thought I was asleep, but I was in the midlands between sleep and wakefulness, and his kiss seemed to be from far away. His voice, barely audible, echoed through the high country of the place from which I listened and waited.

"I'm sorry," he whispered. "I'm sorry."

Ten years ago, Saskia Stiles kissed me on several occasions, at the urging of her parents.

"Say good night to Freddy," Linda Stiles said, as they put on their coats in our front hall.

"Good night," she said, looking at the floor.

"Well, *kiss* him, for Chrissake," urged John Stiles, and my mother laughed loudly and my father frowned.

Three times, before they left our house, or before we left their house, John Stiles shook my hand, but Linda Stiles kissed me on the cheek.

"Good night, Freddy," she said. "You're a treasure."

"Yeah," I replied.

Until I was seventeen, only four people had ever kissed me. Only my mother kissed me on the mouth. But then Jack Sweat kissed me on my lips. His mouth was open, and his tongue pressed against my lips.

My mind raced. I hadn't been kissed in almost ten years. I had no reference point from which to craft an appropriate response.

Only my mother ever kissed me on the lips. Jack Sweat wasn't my mother. No one kissed me before with an open mouth. Jack Sweat slid his tongue over my lips when he kissed me.

His lips held, opening just a little, pressing against my lips, warm and soft. When he pulled away, there was a bit of a pop.

He looked at me. He wasn't smiling. He stood, a few inches from my face, watching me intently. I didn't meet his look. My eyes started to water. My nose started to itch.

"What are you thinking?" he asked, and I grabbed the first relevant reply in my hastily gathered list of possible responses.

"I think you need to step back," I said to Jack Sweat. I don't think he expected that.

He stepped away from me. We stood, not looking at each other.

A few moments passed.

"Maybe you should go," he said, his teeth gritted together.

I stepped backward slowly. I turned and walked to the door, then stopped. "I like this room," I said.

"Just go," he sighed.

"Goodbye, Jack," I said. "I'll see you later."

He didn't answer.

I walked downstairs and out the side door. I think he was sad that the room didn't have a chair just then.

———

Two days later, I went to the gym as per my schedule. I changed and sat down beside Jack, who was wrapping his hands. I began to wrap my own.

"Go away," he said, without even looking at me.

"I don't want to go away," I said and began eating my sandwich.

"Sit somewhere else."

"I want to sit here."

"Fine," he muttered and picked up his towel and headgear. "*I'll* sit somewhere else."

"Is there a problem with you two Nancies?" asked the Butcher.

I said nothing, but I stared at Jack's headgear. After a moment, Jack said, "Nothing, Dad. Nothing."

"Freddy?" asked the Butcher. "What's up?"

"I just want to sit here."

"Okay." He nodded. "Why don't you do that?"

Jack shook his head. "Bloody retard," he muttered and started walking away.

"But *listen*—"

The Butcher put his hand on my shoulder and stopped me from following Jack.

In the ring, Jack was out of control. He swung wildly, dropping his guard in sacrifice. He came at me quickly, throwing punches even as I was coming to the centre of the ring, and he pushed me back. I was momentarily confused, and he connected once, twice, three times and I fell back into the ropes.

"Stop," ordered the Butcher. He motioned Jack back to his corner. Jack paused, puffing angrily, half turned away from me in contempt. "Freddy, you gotta be aware of your opponent."

"Yes," I said.

"You gotta know that they can come at you right away. Don't expect to set up first."

"Okay."

We touched gloves and he started swinging almost immediately. I backed away from him, dodging some punches, blocking others. Others clipped me at threatening angles, but none landed with any great force.

Not yet.

I had no idea what to do because this was a style I had never seen before. He gave no thought to his own defence. He focused everything on the attack.

When his left hook misses, his chin is forward. Within reach.

But his right is coming across just after it. Before the left has finished even.

So step to the hook. Let the left go by and follow it with your head.

A left jab sent me back two times. My nose was bleeding. An overhand right tagged me above the eye and I saw stars.

The left hook. It's coming.

His knee dropped. That was the tell. I stepped back and a left hook scythed by. I stepped in and his right grazed the back of my head. My cross didn't miss. It caught Jack square on the jaw where the mandible reaches into the skull, where the power of the blow runs up the jawbone and explodes into the brain at the joint.

Jack's knees wiggled and gave way. He collapsed to the canvas.

I stood over him. "Best two out of three?" I asked.

"Just go away," he whispered. "Just go away."

THE LAST CONVERSATION
WITH THE BUTCHER

When I went back to the gym on Wednesday, Jack wasn't wrapping his hands. I began to wrap mine, and the Butcher came over. His face seemed angry but it didn't seem angry. It seemed sad but it didn't seem sad. It was an expression I hadn't directly encountered before, and I didn't know what it meant.

"Jack's not in today, Freddy," he told me as he sat and finished wrapping my hands. "We'll just do pad work today, okay?"

"Okay," I agreed.

———

On Saturday, Jack wasn't there.

"He's probably not coming back," the Butcher said. "Not for a while, anyway."

"Where is he going?"

"He's going to work upstairs."

I stood up. "I'll go ask him to come downstairs."

He took my arm. "Sit," he said. "He doesn't want to come downstairs."

"Why?"

"He doesn't want to spar for a while."

"Why?"

The Butcher leaned back and scratched his chin. "He just doesn't, okay? Maybe you should take a break yourself."

"I don't want to take a break."

"I know." He sighed. "Jack is . . . well, Jack has things he has to work out, you know?"

"No."

"He's got a lot on his mind. Going to college next year. NCAA scholarship possibility. His grades." He shrugged. "You know, a lot of thinking about where he's going."

He paused. "Who he wants to be, I guess."

That night, the threads were waiting, and I got little sleep as I tumbled the questions in the dryer of my mind. Why did Jack Sweat kiss me when it made him so upset afterwards? I'd never seen him kiss anyone else, nor had I ever seen a boy kissing another boy. This was an unusual event, and I wasn't sure what I had done to enable it. Once again, my action, or lack of it, was possibly responsible for another conversational head-on collision.

I carried the threads through the weekend and then to school. I wandered through the day, not talking to anyone, paying little attention in class. I meandered through lunch, then began to go to my next class, but was unable to because Chad Kennedy had Oscar Tolstoy pressed against my locker door.

"You're gay," he said to Oscar. "Say it. Come on, say it."

Objectively speaking, Chad Kennedy was not a good person.

He had few of the characteristics of a good person: he did not treat others with consistent respect, except for those with whom there would be negative consequences otherwise. Those who could not punish him for neglected courtesy were discarded as irrelevant.

Oscar Tolstoy was such a person.

So was I. Until the moment I told him to move away from my locker.

"You're in my way," I said to the back of Chad. There were several people standing around, and they stepped away, forming a ring.

I stepped into that ring.

Chad didn't answer me. I assumed it was because he didn't hear me.

"You're in front of my locker," I said again, a little louder. When I said it, the hall fell silent.

He turned and glared at me, frowning, the same frown he used when he was about to do something to someone.

"What are you looking at?" he demanded.

"What are *you* looking at," I said back to him.

He pushed me and I pushed him back. He pushed me again. I pushed him back again and he grabbed my shirt. I looped my arm under his and bent my elbow. With a rotation, I wrapped around his arm and pulled down. His arm dropped, but he didn't let go, and it dragged him closer, bending him down with the pull of my arm.

I punched him as hard as I could and his knees wobbled. He stepped back defensively, brought his arms up, and swung at me.

He missed. I didn't.

I didn't miss the three times I struck him in rapid succession, and his knees gave out. He leaned forward into me. With all my might, I pushed him back; he stepped on his own shoelace and fell back into the glass case across the hall. The shelves collapsed on him. Trophies tumbled down, striking him on the top of the head. He sank to the floor.

He didn't get back up. His head began to bleed. He closed his eyes.

"Crap," someone said. "He's our quarterback!"

when are you coming
Tonight.

I opened my eyes. It was time to go see Saskia. I stood at the kitchen door, staring at my father. He sat at the table, a can of beer in front of him.

"What?" he barked.

"We're out of milk."

"And you think I should just go get some so you can have your precious goddamn milk?"

"Yes."

"You want milk?" he said, taking a drink of beer. "Get it your goddamn self."

He turned to stare out the window. I didn't move. After a moment, he turned and glared at me, then took another drink.

"Okay," I said. I took my coat from the hall closet and slipped out the front door.

I remember the first time I realized someone was lying to me, which means that I remember a time when I believed everything I was told.

I remember when I told my first lie, which means I remember a time when I only told the truth.

I rarely lie, because I am not good at it. I have a good poker face, but my lies crumble under prolonged questioning.

Listen: If I had told my father I was going to the store, the conversation may have gone in an entirely different direction.

"I'm going to the store," I said to my father in the scenario envisioned in my head.

"The bloody hell you are," he growled. "Go back to your room."

Or if I tried a different approach.

"Can I go to the store?" I asked my father. "We're out of milk."

"I don't give a shit," he said in this scenario. "Get the hell back in your room."

"I need to go to the store," I told my father in the third scenario.

"What for?"

"I need baking soda."

"What the hell do you need baking soda for?"

"A science project."

"For what class?"

"Yes," I replied.

"No, Freddy," he said. "Which class has a science project?"

"I don't have a science project in any of my classes."

"So why do you need baking soda?"

"I don't," I replied.

"Bloody well get back to your room, then."

Telling a lie carries too many risks. I've found it is better to not lie. So, when I told my father we were out of milk, I wasn't lying.

I knew that he would refuse to get the milk for me. He was content to sit and drink and be angry at me. I suspected he would tell me to get it myself. So, when he did, I interpreted his instructions as literally as possible.

He didn't specify which store to use, so I was free to choose the one I wanted to patronize.

I chose the 7-Eleven down the street from Saskia Stiles's home.

An hour later, I stood at the front door of the home of John and Linda Stiles.

There were four unanswered texts on my phone. The first had come in eighteen minutes ago. It was from my father.

What the hell is taking you so long

I ignored it and, five minutes later, he texted me again.

Where are you

Again, I ignored it. My phone must have rung in the meantime, but I had turned off my ringer. I don't like phone calls.

Pick up the damn phone

I arrived at Saskia Stiles's house, just as the fourth text message came in.

Freddy

I ignored it again. My mind raced with other thoughts, other questions, other threads.

I couldn't stop thinking about Jack Sweat and his trophy room. I couldn't stop thinking about the kiss he had given me. Not the kiss itself, but the feeling of the kiss.

The touch of lips on lips.

And I couldn't stop thinking about how it would feel if those were Saskia's lips, and I didn't know why I was wondering it.

I tumbled the thought over and over again.

At which point, Linda Stiles opened the door.

"Yes?" she said.

She stood in the middle of the doorway, looking at me, but I was not there anymore. My eyes had lost their focus. I was chasing a thread, following it from conjecture to conclusion, like a rabbit across a warren.

This was an inopportune time to be lost in a thought of kissing her daughter. Somewhere deep in the recesses of my awareness, I realized it, but was having trouble communicating this to the rest of my body.

"What do you want?" she asked. It was good that she did this, for little else could have disturbed me. But she asked a direct question, requiring a direct answer, and I was good at answering questions like that.

"I'm here against my will," I said, at last.

She frowned. "Excuse me?"

I began remembering the words I had practised on the way over. The words I had assembled from years of conversation practice during therapy. "Good evening, Mrs. Stiles, I would—"

But she cut me off. "I'm sorry, I don't have time for sales pitches."

She started to close the door. I said, "I'm Freddy Wyland."

She froze. I didn't know if she was going to turn around or close the door. She stared at me, her eyes wide. Her hands let go of the door and clasped each other. She leaned forward as if to get a better look at me. I wondered if she wore contacts and, if she did, if she was wearing them now.

"Freddy?" Linda Stiles said. "Freddy *Wyland*? What are you doing here?"

I stared back at her.

"Answer me, Freddy," she said.

"Mrs. Stiles," I said slowly, making sure I enunciated. "I would like to have a discussion with you and Mr. Stiles."

Her expression hardened. "There is no Mr. Stiles," she said.

I blinked. "When will he be back?" I asked, thinking I may have misunderstood the phrase; perhaps "There is no Mr. Stiles" was a colloquialism that meant he was buying groceries.

"Freddy, he's not coming back. He's—" She hesitated. "He's been gone for a decade. Didn't your father tell you?"

Suddenly I was afraid.

"Is he buying groceries?" I asked, and the words came out high-pitched and strained.

The day after I saw my mother for the last time began a stretch of days that aren't in my memory. There is a patch in my head, a blip of the timeline, in which I remember nothing at all. A black span of ten days from the late morning of September 10 to the evening of September 20.

Now, as I stood in the doorway of John and Linda Stiles's home, I felt waves of panic wash over me. I remembered. I remembered a little.

Only a little.

Linda Stiles used to wear her hair down, but tonight she wore her hair in a tight ponytail. The last time I saw her, ten years ago, Linda Stiles also wore a tight ponytail. And a blue cardigan, like the one she wore tonight. When I remembered that, I became afraid.

Ten years ago, I walked into the kitchen after school. She sat at the table with my father, where they both smoked cigarettes. Neither talked. Neither smiled. My father's hands were trembling. Linda Stiles's eyes were red. When she saw me come in, she stood up and, without a word, walked by me. That was the last time I saw her.

My father looked at me as if he didn't recognize me, as if it took him a few moments to bring me into focus.

"Sit down, Freddy," he said. "I need to tell you something."

I didn't remember anything that happened after that. But now, standing before Linda Stiles, remembering only that my father told me to sit down, I began to shiver.

I opened my eyes. Linda Stiles's living room was small, and the rug was faded. I sat in the middle of the couch and stared at a tank of fish on the other side of the room. A single clown fish ambled around, just above fake coral. Back and forth. Back and forth, like a book turning its own pages.

Linda stood in the kitchen with the phone to her ear, yelling at my father.

"He's your son, not mine," she said. "This is *your* mess to clean up."

I trembled. Threads burst into my head like panicked tenants.

Linda Stiles came out. She lit a cigarette and took a long drag. She sat on the couch beside me. "You need to go home, Freddy."

"I would like to take Saskia to the park."

"Not a chance," she said, shaking her head. "Not a chance. I don't think Saskia wants to go to the park."

"Yes, she does," I said.

"Go home, Freddy."

"But she told me to come over."

"Who did?"

"Saskia," I said. "Saskia told me to come over."

"Saskia doesn't speak, Freddy."

I nodded my head. "Yes," I said, "she does."

She massaged her temple. "Freddy," she said, letting out a long exhale. "Saskia has been non-verbal ever since—" She paused. "Ever since the last time you saw her."

"I want to take her to the park," I said.

She jumped up. "No!" she shouted and pointed to the door. "Get out! Just get out of here, Freddy!"

I stood up, too. "But I want—"

"I don't care what you want!" she screamed. "The last thing I or she or anyone needs is you smashing up someone else's life! Now get your—"

"Hello, Freddy," said a voice from the hall. Linda Stiles stopped and, mouth agape, turned to look at her daughter, who was standing with her headphones in her hand. Her arms were rigid. She was trembling with excitement.

"Hello, Saskia," I said.

"Did you have a good day?" she asked me as she dropped her headphones on the floor.

Linda Stiles, eyes wide, sat back on the couch, like she had been dumped from the back of a truck.

"I had a good day," I said. "How was your day?"

"I had a good day TOO!" she said and began to hop up and down. I felt a longing, a wishing for my past. A wave of emotion passed over me and I felt as if I might pass out, so I sat down.

A moment of silence passed between the three of us.

Silence. And then the only sounds filling the room were small squeaks as Saskia hopped up and down, and shuddered gasps from Linda Stiles as she stared at her daughter and cried.

For a few moments, we looked at each other. Mrs. Stiles stared at her daughter, her hand to her mouth, tears streaming down her face. I was content to not say anything.

Saskia, on the other hand, was like a cold engine on a winter morning, trying to start, trying to start.

"Did you—" she began. She looked down, in intense concentration, looked back up. Every muscle in her body tensing and relaxing. "I had a good—"

She looked around.

"I said, I said, I said—"

"It looks like rain," I said to her.

"Yes!" she shouted and stepped into the room, stopping at the edge of the rug.

"I want," she said, then stopped. Her muscles relaxed. "Say, can you show me a poem, Saskia?"

"Can you show me a poem, Saskia?"

Her hands came up. They started flapping. "YES!" she shouted and walked across the rug, stiff legged, barely able to contain her excitement.

"Squeaky," Linda Stiles called to her softly.

Saskia gave me her poem. She pulled it in a crumpled ball from her pocket. She uncrumpled it and read it to herself. Then, satisfied, she thrust it at me.

"HERE!" she shouted, hopping up and down. She squeaked.

I reached for the paper; she pulled it back, holding it against her chest.

"No, no, no, no, no, no," she said. She balled the poem back up and presented it again. This time, I reached for it and she let me take it.

"Thank you," I said.

She squeaked. Then she turned to her mother. Stopped and looked her straight in the eye. Still smiling. "Hi, Mom," she said. And then Saskia was walking out into the hall, up the stairs, back to her bedroom.

I looked at the wadded-up ball. The paper was faded and dry, cracked in places. It looked like it had been crumpled in a ball for years. I opened it, flattening it on the table.

This is what the poem said.

> ONCE UPON A VERY MERRY TIME, there was a girl
>   named Saskia.
> She was alone with nobody to play with.
> So, a chrysanthemum came over to play.
> But Saskia was still lonely.
> So, her best friend Freddy, a dog and a cat came over
>   to play.
> There were so many friends and Saskia wasn't lonely
>   anymore.
> So they played and played and played and played and
>   played.
> And they all lived happily ever after.
>
> by Saskia.
> age 7

I didn't see Saskia again that night. She went to her room, and her mother wept on the couch in front of me.

Linda Stiles dabbed at her eyes with tissue. Collecting herself, she said, "How do you and Saskia—" She shook her head.

"Saskia is my chemistry partner," I said. "We eat lunch together." After a moment, I added, "I wrote her a poem."

She looked up, staring at the wall behind me. "Today is the first time she's said anything for a decade, Freddy." She put her tissue down. "The first time."

"Okay," I said.

"How long has she been talking to you?"

"We send text messages."

"Freddy," she started, then stopped. She looked down at her hands balled up in her lap.

"Can I take Saskia to the park now?" I asked.

She looked up at me. "No," she said. "You can't. In fact, you need to go home, Freddy."

"I'll go home after the park," I said.

"No," she said, firmly. "You need to go home now, Freddy. You need to talk to your father."

"I don't want to," I said, and my throat was dry.

"He needs to tell you something," she said.

"Yes," I said. We stared at each other.

"Do you know what he needs to tell you?"

"Yes."

"What does he need to tell you?"

I paused.

"I don't know," I said.

She stood up, and I stood too. We regarded each other from across the coffee table.

"Please," she whispered. "Please go home."

THE QUIET OF THE
LIVING ROOM AT NIGHT

The TV in the living room was blaring. *The Daily Show with Jon Stewart.* And my father in a reclining chair. His head back, mouth open, snoring slightly. In his left hand, he still held a can of Bud Light.

The room was otherwise dark. I sat on the sofa and stared at the wall. I watched the time tick by for an hour until the Late Movie began: it was *Titanic.*

All at once I remembered a night, with my mother dancing in the living room, Celine Dion singing that her heart will go on, my father watching her with a can of Bud Light in his left hand.

My mind split itself between the past and the present. I was there. I was here. I sat and listened to the music, as my father snored in his chair, and I watched the wall. In the corner of my eye, the memory of my mother dancing; a glass of wine in her hand, she spun about the room. At that moment, remembering my mother, the fear that had been in me all evening evaporated and I felt something I hadn't known in my entire life.

It embraced me like a heavy quilt. It poured over me like early spring rain. A weight lay on my shoulders, and I sat back against the couch, aware of my breath.

Just at the edge of my vision, my father sat with his Bud Light, my mother danced, and I remembered it.

I think I felt, for the first time,
    I felt
        I felt
            sadness.

At some point I fell asleep. I awoke with a start from a dream, my hands coming up instinctively, gasping in a gulp of air as if I had surfaced from beneath the water.

The room was empty. The television was off. I didn't know what time it was. I was sweating.

It was the same dream. I was alone in the house and looking at the door, which was now ajar. This time, there were voices down a darkened hall.

"It's time for you to be a man," the voice said.

In my dream, I heard the tick-tick-ticking of a cooling engine, the hissing of metal as the rain boiled off.

A train whistle.

"It's time for you to be a man, now, Son," my mother said. "Can you do that?"

Somewhere, a voice on a radio.

It was 4:32.

I opened my eyes and I was seven years old, screaming as loud as I could. I opened my eyes only briefly, then closed them again. With my hands pressed to my ears I lay on the rug, knees to my chest. The sound of my own scream was at the same time comforting and unnerving. Not sure which was winning the tug of war, I screamed louder to see if I could clarify things.

Outside, it was raining, and thunder trembled the sky.

Inside, by the fireplace, Mom yelled at Dad. Dad yelled back at her and they tried to be louder than each other.

I tried silence, but it didn't work. Then I tried slapping my palms on my thighs. But they kept yelling.

"He needs to *be* somewhere!" Mom shouted at Dad.

"He needs to be right *here*!" Dad shouted at Mom.

"When are you going to open your eyes!"

"When? *When?* When are you going to grow up and realize you can't do anything about him?"

Everything was making noise. Everyone was making noise. Everything was competing for the attention of everything else. But if I screamed, I could compete for my own attention.

And I started. I howled, dropped to the floor, and began to kick at the couch.

That did it. The music turned off. My parents stopped yelling. Even the trolls heard me and stopped arguing.

What the devil is that noise, they asked each other.

Then my mother was kneeling beside me, picking me up and squeezing me against her.

"That's not helping," my father said. "Let him go."

I screamed louder.

"I'm not just going to let him scream," she said. "I can't."

"Did you ever think that maybe you have to?"

"No," she said firmly. "Not once."

I began kicking, squirming, struggling, and she tried to hold me tighter. Her arms around me felt good, and as she squeezed tighter, things felt better. So I kept kicking, kept screaming, because it was working.

"Dammit, Betty," he said to her and tried to pull her arms apart. "Let him go. He needs to go to his room and calm down."

He pulled me away from her arms. Now things were no longer working. So I doubled my efforts.

"Freddy," he said sternly. "Look at me. *Look* at me."

My eyes remained clenched shut. I screamed louder as my mom and dad struggled: her, to hold me; him, to break us apart. He was stronger, and finally pulled her away. Now she began screaming, too. I opened my eyes and saw him dragging her back, as she kicked and struggled. Rage filled me. I leapt to my feet and charged him, arms swinging, a guttural howl escaping my lips. I threw myself against him, striking at every angle, slapping, thumping, kicking, trying to bite.

"Freddy!" he pushed me away, and I charged him again. This time he pushed me away and I fell to the floor.

"Go to your room!" he roared at me.

I ignored him and leapt back to my feet, attacking again. One wild swing caught him square on the jaw and he winced. I saw his eyes darken, then a sweeping hand, out of nowhere, and my world exploded in stars, knocking me off my feet to the floor.

"Freddy!" Mom shrieked and ran to me, but I rolled away, stood up, and ran, screaming, crying. I swiped at pictures on the wall, knocked over a lamp, and bolted to my room. Bursting in, I ran to Gordon's cage. He was running on his wheel, paying me no attention, oblivious to my distress, unaware of the apocalyptic day I was now having.

I pushed his cage as hard as I could and it flew from my desk and tumbled across the floor.

Downstairs, the trolls were in my house, yelling at each other.

I opened my eyes and I was seventeen, staring at Jim Worley's bookcase. I was alone in his office. When I arrived, the door was ajar, so I walked in and stood in the middle of the room.

A few minutes passed, as I stared at *The Twentieth Century in Review*, on the top shelf. Finally, I took it down and sat in the duck sauce sofa chair, turning the pages. But they offered nothing of value. Today, they were only pages. Just historical facts of no interest to me. Even the texture of the paper seemed different, of no use, of no special feeling, and my hands were tired even before they began turning the pages.

I let the book lay open on my lap and stared down at it.

4:32. 4:33. 4:34.

At 4:37, Jim Worley came into the office and, seeing me, stopped.

I continued to stare at the book, one hand still holding a page, but not turning it.

Oh the humanity! the caption cried, and the Hindenburg burst into black-and-white flame on the page before me.

Jim Worley placed his hand on my arm. "You know you can't be here, Frederick," he said calmly, but I could see that he was nervous. Just a little.

"But I'm getting to the best part," I said, and he closed the book. I didn't resist, nor did I stop him from making me stand.

"It's time to go home," he said.

"I have to get notes from my chemistry partner," I told him, and he shepherded me out of his office.

"You don't need them." He glanced around. "You should be more concerned with how it looks that you're on school grounds. You've been *suspended*. You might not be expelled, but coming around here isn't going to help you."

"I don't want to be expelled," I said.

"It may be too late for that."

I became frightened. I started to breathe rapidly.

"Look at me, Frederick," Jim Worley said, but I continued to hyperventilate.

He said again, "*Look* at me."

I looked at him. He sighed and put both hands on my shoulders.

"Go home, Freddy."

"A lot of people have told me that," I said.

He nodded. "Maybe because it's good advice."

"But I don't want to be expelled."

"I know," he said sadly. "I know. Go home, Freddy."

But I didn't go home. I went somewhere else.

I do not skulk. There's no logic in it.

Skulking is crouching in the shadows of life. Waiting on chances, but hiding only to come out when the opportunity is clear and unambiguous.

Someone who skulks is someone not entirely clear on their purpose. If they were clear, there would be no need to skulk. People who are clear on their purpose *stride*. But I don't skulk or stride. Neither serves a purpose for me.

It was strange, then, that I was skulking beside a hedge at the corner of Pipeline and Paddock.

There were so many strange things about it that I could make a list:

1. The day was cold and wet. I should have had the good sense to sneak about on a day that was at least cloudy with sunny breaks.
2. I had never skulked before, and there was no way to tell if I was doing it correctly.
3. I was waiting for Chad Kennedy.

A fourth thing that made it strange: I didn't know why I was skulking Chad Kennedy. I never do anything without a reason. Yet I was here. On a cold wet day. Skulking Chad Kennedy.

It wasn't a difficult thing to do. I went to school with Chad for nine years. I knew where he lived, just like he knew where I lived. We weren't friends, but we were aware of each other. Everyone in our class was aware of everyone else in our class. We grew up with each other. Our families attended the same concerts every year. When you go to school with the same people for nine years, you start to know where they live.

Which makes it easier to stalk.

From a distance, I saw Chad, walking up the sidewalk. I stepped out from behind the hedge and faced him.

At first he didn't recognize me. Then realization came over his face like a passing cloud. He stopped.

He wore his school colours over a blue shirt with a red tie. His left hand clutched the strap of his backpack. His right hand held the hand of his nine-year-old little sister.

I had no idea what to say, because I had no idea why I was there.

We stared at each other silently. The little girl's eyes flicked between the two of us. I didn't move.

Chad spoke first. "Hey, Freddy," he said.

"Hey, Chad," I said, because that was how you reply to people.

I looked at his sister. "What's your name?" I asked.

She looked up at Chad, and he nodded to her. "Tanya," she said.

I nodded at her. "How do you do," I said, but she didn't reply. I felt this conversation was going well.

Sticking to the script.

I regarded Chad. His hair was shorter.

"Do you still have a concussion?" I asked him, after a few seconds.

He shook his head. "I had headaches for a couple of weeks. They still won't let me do any sports."

"It was a stochastic event, hitting your head," I said. "It was unpredictable that it would happen exactly then, but statistically, there was a defined certainty of it happening over a number of samples."

Nodding slowly, he said, "I guess so."

"But that's just the way it goes. Some things will never change."

"What do you want, Freddy?"

I stared at him. His sister looked up at him, uncertain.

"Okay," he said. "We're just gonna turn around and go back. Okay?" He put his hand on Tanya's back and nudged her.

"I'm sorry," I said quickly.

He stopped. "What?"

"I'm sorry," I said. "I'm sorry I hit you."

He turned back to me. A slight wind began blowing from the hill. "Really?" he asked me.

I nodded. "It was wrong. I didn't understand the situation and reacted incorrectly. I hurt you as a result. I'm sorry."

He looked around. "It is what it is, right? I know I've been a dick to you for years." He smiled and rubbed his jaw. "Where'd you learn to hit like that?"

I shrugged. "My boxing coach said I have natural ability."

"True that," he muttered.

We stood, looking at each other.

"Goodbye, Chad," I said. "I'll see you later."

He nodded back. He walked by me. "See ya, Freddy."

I said to him, "Be nicer to Oscar Tolstoy."

He laughed.

Listen: I am the person I have become because of my mother. Because that is what she would have wanted.

She was the one person interested in my welfare solely because I was *me*. She never got angry. She never swore at me. She never yelled at me. She only wanted to see me become *better*. Better at whatever I did, whether it was crawling, walking, reading, or just setting the table. She wanted me to succeed.

She told me this as she pruned white orchids in the living room. They were expensive; she argued sometimes with my father about them, and the arguments always ended the way they began: he said they were frivolous, she said they were the only thing she indulged herself in.

"It's my one extravagance," she said. "It costs a lot less than your beer."

"Beer rehydrates me."

"So does *not* beer."

He never stopped her from buying the orchids. I liked watching her trim them.

"You're just like an orchid," she told me. "Unique and beautiful."

"I'm not like an orchid," I said.

"In some ways, you are," she disagreed. "I love you both. You're both growing and changing into beautiful new things."

"I don't have petals."

"No," she agreed, "but you have the same goodness in you that an orchid has in it. You both light up my soul."

"I'm good like an orchid?"

"You are good simply because you try to be good, Freddy."

My mother always believed that I could be something, be someone, reach any level. But she was convinced that it was more important that I be good.

Other people were not so unconditionally committed to me. Even my father, who certainly loved me, and raised me to the best of his abilities, even he was not as committed, for he was often angry. Being so, his judgment was suspect. The things my father wished me to become were suspect as a result.

But the things my mother wanted me to be were not suspect, because *she* was not suspect. My mother fit the criteria of a good person. It stood to reason, therefore, that the things she wanted me to become were good things.

———

Here is what happened the day I went to Excalibur House, after my mother left.

On that day, my father came to get me, and I said goodbye to Saskia Stiles for the last time.

We drove home in silence, and I was happy. I liked to count buses as they went by, and bin them into blue buses, which are powered by natural gas, white buses, which are powered by diesel, and grey buses, also powered by diesel, but much older.

My father liked to talk on drives, but I liked to be silent and watch the roads for buses. As we drove, I stayed as still as I could in the back seat, hoping that my father would forget I was there and wouldn't try to talk.

There was no dinner that night. I went straight to my room and stood in the centre, not moving, waiting for my father to call me down to the kitchen. The call never came. I was surprised; usually, he made me sit at the kitchen table and work on my printing for ten minutes, then draw pictures for ten minutes, then colour within the lines for ten minutes. After that, dinner would be served, after which I would have a bath. I would change into my pyjamas and brush my teeth. Then I could go to my room and be by myself, which is what I wanted most of all. But that day, I got to be by myself immediately.

I waited for fifteen more minutes, but he didn't call me down to the kitchen, so I took off my clothes and got dressed in my pyjamas. Then I sat on my bed and flipped through my book.

The minutes passed. The hours passed. I flipped the pages quickly, first forward, then backward. The words and pictures washed over me like a warm current. I didn't read. I absorbed.

When I looked up, it was 10:30. Downstairs, I heard my father shuffling in the kitchen, and the clink of glass.

I closed my book, crawled under the covers, turned off the light, and went to sleep.

———

The next morning, my routine was fully broken. I sat in bed, hungry, my bladder full to bursting, and I waited for my mother to come in, turn on the light, pull back the covers, kiss me on the forehead, and tell me to get up.

She didn't come. The light remained off.

I waited.

Soon, I became uncomfortable, with a swollen bladder, but I still didn't get out of bed.

I waited.

A few minutes later, I couldn't hold it. I relieved myself in my pyjamas. At first, the urine was warm, and I was comfortable, so I waited some more. But, after the pee cooled down, and my thighs became itchy, I climbed out of bed and dressed myself.

When I walked into the kitchen, my father was standing at the sink, staring out the window.

"I'm hungry," I said, and he didn't reply.

I went to stand beside him. "I'm hungry," I repeated. "I want Froot Loops."

"We're out of Froot Loops," he said, still staring out the window. He was fully dressed, but his clothes were unkempt. His shirt was untucked. I could smell stale cigarette smoke. "Have Sugar Crisp instead," he told me.

"But I want Froot Loops," I said. "I don't want Sugar Crisp. I want Froot Loops."

"Too bad," he said and pulled a cigarette from his front shirt pocket.

"*Listen*. I want—"

"Dammit Freddy!" my father yelled at me. "There are no bloody Froot Loops. Get that through your head!"

I turned away from him and went to the cereal cupboard. There was only Sugar Crisp.

"Where's Mom?" I asked.

"She's not here."

"Where's Mom?" I asked again.

"If she was up your ass, you'd feel it."

"Where's Mom?"

He hung his head. "I don't know, Freddy," he said. "I don't know."

———

One week after that, the wind was blowing through the trees as I walked home from the school bus. There was a car in the driveway, and my mother was waiting for me on the front steps, two suitcases at her feet. She hugged me and kissed me.

At first, I didn't recognize her. She had cut her hair short, and she wore sunglasses. I thought she looked older. But I was happy to see her.

"Where were you?" I asked.

"I had to go away, sweetheart," she told me. "I had to leave. But I've come back to get you. Okay?"

"Okay," I agreed. "Can I play on the Game Boy?"

She nodded. "Of course."

I started up the stairs to the front door, but she stopped me. "We're not going inside, Freddy."

"Hey, Freddy," said John Stiles, stepping out of the car.

Listen: I remembered.

It was John Stiles who came with my mother and picked me up outside our house. My mother was smiling, but he wasn't. He got out, took her bags, and put them in the trunk of his car. As he did it, he glanced at me several times, frowning.

"Hey, sport," he said.

I didn't answer because he hadn't asked me a question. It's not necessary to answer when you are not asked a question.

My mother snapped me in my seat belt, in the back seat, behind her.

"Where's my booster seat?" I asked my mother.

"Not now, Freddy," she said, looking around as she clipped me in.

I opened my eyes and rain fell hard against the kitchen window. The day was long and had wound itself out of me. I came in the front door, tired, empty, a single thread still in my mind.

Go home, Freddy, Linda Stiles had told me the night before. *You need to talk to your father.*

Bill sat at the table before a bottle of whisky. He looked aged. I could see the tendrils of white that had crept into his hairline. He looked tired. His sleeves were rolled up. His shirt was light blue. He had just returned from work. He had come home early.

Come home early to drink.

When I walked in, he looked up, then back down at the tumbler in his hand. It held two ounces of whisky and three ice cubes.

Leaning back, he reached to the kitchen counter for a second tumbler, put it on the table, then poured in whisky. He pushed the glass toward me.

"Join me," he said and smiled briefly. "Time to be a man."

I pulled a chair out and sat across the table from him.

"Drink, drink," he motioned to the whisky. I didn't move. After a moment, he shrugged and took the tumbler back, pouring the contents into his own glass. "Suit yourself," he said.

"John Stiles no longer lives with his wife," I said.

My father nodded slowly, his face grim. He agreed with me.

"Mrs. Stiles said I should ask you about it," I continued.

He nodded again. "She did, did she?"

"Yes."

"Did she tell you anything else?"

"Yes."

He paused and took a drink. "What else did she tell you?"

"That you're an asshole."

He smiled slightly, turning up one corner of his mouth. "I've been wondering for a while when you would figure that one for yourself."

"I figured that for myself four months and nine days ago," I confirmed. "It was ancillary to the previous thing I found out for myself four months and nine days ago."

He took a drink. "And what was the previous thing you figured out?"

"That we are *all* assholes."

Four months and nine days ago, Jack Sweat threw me out of his house. He threw me out because I offended him when I didn't kiss him back. I didn't kiss him back because I felt no such desire.

There was no precedent in my life for returning a kiss from a friend. Kisses were returned in films or television only if you were related or in love or French or Arabic. I was none of these.

Perhaps I should have slapped him. That's what they do in the movies.

When I didn't kiss Jack back, he stood motionless, his eyes still looking down, his mouth firmly closed, his cheeks reddening. But his hands remained at his side. His shoulders slumped.

He asked me to leave. He asked me to leave the room, the gym, his life.

For a long time after that, I carried a thread: *Who was responsible? Why had my one and only friendship disintegrated that night?*

Was Jack to blame for kissing me or was I to blame for not kissing him? Should I have slapped him?

The answer was constructed after careful thought. Neither of us were to blame. We acted as we were supposed to.

There is nothing intrinsically offensive about a kiss. A kiss is a sign of interest at worst, and a sign of love at best. There is no reason to strike someone for kissing you; that would indicate that you are threatened by their interest at best, or their love at worst.

It may be that this was a case where I should have kissed Jack back, or a case where I should have slapped him. But how does someone know which are the acceptable cases? They aren't advertised. There is no page on Wikipedia detailing the correct way to slap someone. We can't seem to agree on the correct circumstances.

We can't agree because we can't find an objective framework. We can't point to unassailable rules of right and wrong.

We can't do any of this because none of us knows all of the rules of right and wrong. We only carry approximations, fuzzy guidelines with wiggle room. Often, we will drift off course and be wrong. But we won't always know we were wrong until later, after much consideration.

That means that we are doomed to walk through our lives doing things we will only later realize were wrong.

Listen: I told my father that I learned every one of us is doomed to do wrong, no matter how hard we try to do otherwise. Every one of us will do things that we will long regret. Every one of us will do things that hurt others, sometimes on purpose, sometimes out of sheer ignorance. Every one of us will do some of these things and never get the chance to apologize.

Every one of us is an asshole.

I told my father why we were all assholes; I told him about Jack Sweat. He let out a long sigh and clinked the ice in his empty glass.

"I never did like that Jack kid," he said. "Never understood why he hung around you." He glanced up at me quickly, and an expression ran across his face. "I just meant that—" he said and stopped.

I nodded. "I understand what you meant," I said. "Muggles rarely associate with wizards."

He nodded and dropped his head, smiling with his mouth but not with his eyes. "Yer a wizard, Harry," he said softly.

———

When I was young, my parents spoke to me differently. When they spoke with others, it was quicker, with shorter words and greater inflection. With others, their voices carried emotional themes, ones they rarely used with me. With me, their words were measured, careful. My father, in particular, spoke like a HAL 9000 computer.

Even at an early age, I understood that he spoke condescendingly, although I did not have a word to associate with it, or a full meaning, or even a context. I only knew that it was different, intended to convey meaning at its most basic level.

I didn't mind being patronized.

On May 23, 2004, my mother told me that I was autistic.

"Do you know why you go to Excalibur House?" she asked me.

"No," I said, not because I didn't know, but because, at the time, I was still uncertain what the word "know" meant. Saying "no" was an appropriate response to most things. If I said "yes," I would have to justify myself.

If I said "no," my mother would explain things to me, and I wouldn't have to talk. After she explained things, I repeated back to her what she said. I could do this—it was relatively easy. I have a good memory.

"Remember how sometimes I yell at you and tell you you're not listening?" Dad asked me.

"Yes," I said. I was rarely asked to explain something I had remembered.

"Do you know why I yell at you and tell you that you're not listening?"

"Because I'm not listening," I said. I knew the answer to this because I had been asked the same questions many times.

"Do you know why you don't listen?" Mom asked.

"Why," I said.

"Because you are autistic. Do you know what that means?"

"What."

"It means that you have difficulty processing information, and difficulty communicating with others. Do you understand?"

"Yes."

"What did I just say?"

"You have difficulty processing information, and difficulty communicating with others."

My mother shook her head. "*I* don't have that problem, Freddy. *You* have that problem."

"Yes," I replied.

She nodded. "Some people have red hair. Some people have blond hair."

"I have blond hair," I said.

She nodded again. "Some people have blue eyes."

"I have blue eyes," I said.

"Some people wear glasses."

"I wear glasses."

"No, you don't."

"I wear sunglasses."

"Yes, Freddy, you do. Sometimes."

"I don't like to wear sunglasses."

"That's why you don't wear them."

"That's why I don't wear them."

She took my hand. "Listen closely."

I stepped toward her. Her eyes shone on me and I fell into them.

"Some people wear glasses because it helps them see. And some people can't see."

"They can't see?"

"They're blind. And some people are deaf, which means they can't hear."

"I can hear."

"You're not deaf, Freddy."

"No."

"Some people can talk to others easily. Is that you?"

"Yes."

"No, Freddy, it's not."

"No."

"Do you know why you have trouble talking to other people?"

"No."

"Because you have autism."

I looked around. I fished in my pocket. "Where is it?" I asked.

She tapped me on the top of my head. "It's in there, Freddy," she said. "It's in there."

I opened my eyes. I was seven years old. My mother, gone for a week, was now back, and I was in the car as we drove to the train station. John Stiles kept glancing back at me, as my mom tried to calm me down.

"Are you all right?" John Stiles asked her.

"Never better," she said.

"Betty," he said to her. "You never said you were bringing Freddy. They're expecting only you."

"He can sleep in my bed," she said.

"It's just—"

She put her hand on his forearm as he drove. "John," she said, "did you think I would ever go without him?"

The sky was darkening, and it was raining hard. I wasn't confident this would be a fun car ride.

"Where's my booster seat?" I called out.

———

It's necessary to ask questions about things that cause you concern. Sitting in the back seat, the thing that was of great concern was my booster seat. It came with me every time I went for a good car ride. How was it possible that I could have a good ride without the seat? It was *important*. It's absence caused me *concern*. I asked questions about it.

The first thing I asked when I got in the car was: "Where's my booster seat?"

"Sweetie," my mother said, "I'll get you a new one, I promise."

This wasn't working for me. "But I need my booster seat," I repeated.

She cupped my face in her palms. "Freddy, this is really, really,

really important," she said and kissed me on the nose. "Please, we need to go." She patted my cheek, closed my door, then got in the front seat.

"What happened to your eye?" I asked. I reached up and touched it. It was swollen, spongy to the touch, a deep shade of blue and ochre.

"I'll tell you some other time," she said.

Mom suggested, on several occasions, that arguing was one of my Favourite Things. It isn't. In fact, it's one of my unfavourite things. But there isn't a word for the opposite of favourite.

Too often, however, I have to go through one of my unfavourite things to get to the Favourite Thing. It appeared that this would be one of those times.

The car pulled away from the curb.

"I want my booster seat," I said, and Mom turned her head and looked at me sharply.

"Freddy," she warned.

"Why is he here?" John Stiles said.

I opened my eyes and I was seventeen again, and the rain pattered against the kitchen window. My father sat across from me, the ice cubes in his glass chattering. The candle on the table was the only light in the room. It cast shadows across his face. It made him look angry. It made him look dangerous.

The memory of the night in the car washed over me like the tide coming in.

I asked my father, "Did you hit my mother?"

My father lit a cigarette and took a long drag. Then exhaled slowly. He nodded. "Once. Twice, maybe."

"Why?"

"Because I was and still am an ass." He sighed. "Back then, I was an even bigger ass. Sometimes we fought, and sometimes she threw things at me, and sometimes she hit me. Sometimes I wrestled her down. Sometimes I shoved her away. I guess I smacked her once or twice. Some couples are like that."

He shifted position in his chair and looked out the window. "Some couples like to fight. Some couples like to make up. Sometimes, people like to make up so much, they don't mind the fighting."

"Is that why she left us?"

He straightened up, frowning. "She wasn't going to leave. Not for good. She'd done this before. I guess you don't remember but she did it every once in a while. Just packed a bag and went to her friend's for a few days. Freddy, if there's one thing I hope you remember about your mother, it's that she was a fireplug. She was high drama. Always. And she was always coming back."

"She wasn't coming back."

He nodded. "Of course she was. She was coming back just as sure as I'm sitting here. The only thing different is she thought that John Stiles was in love with her. But he just wanted to sleep with her. It was going to come to a crashing end fast enough."

"No," I said. "I was there. She wasn't coming back."

"Christ, Freddy." He finished his drink and poured another. "What are you going on about?"

And I was remembering more.

MOMENTS

I remember moments. They burst forth like patrons from a show. Scattered memories, scattered moments. As my father sat at the kitchen table and stared up at me, I remembered so many more things.

I opened my eyes and I was seven, lying in bed, staring at the ceiling. Gordon ran on his wheel, which squeaked and shrieked. *Oil me*, it called out. I'll do it later, I told it.

Outside, the wind lashed wet rain against the window. A streetlight shone through my window, the branches of a tree cast shadows against the wall.

Downstairs, my parents argued.

"I can't keep doing this," my mother shouted.

"Doing what? Ignoring me?" he shouted back at her. "Acting like everything's wrong? And then, just like that, thinking that nothing's wrong?"

"*Nothing's* wrong? You think that I believe *nothing's* wrong?"

Later that evening, I awoke to the sound of smashing of glass. My mother cried out. I sat up and looked at the Darth Vader clock beside my bed.

It was 4:32.

But that's not right. It makes no sense.

I opened my eyes and the streetlights rushed by me. I counted them as I argued with my mother about the missing booster seat.

"Sweetheart," she tried to reason, "it's just this one time. Do you understand what 'important' means?"

"Yes." I nodded, counting the streetlights—eighty-six, eighty-seven . . .

"And if something is important, little things that are different can be ignored for just a little while. Right?"

"Yes."

"This is important. It's very important that you come with me," she continued. She undid her seat belt, reached around, stroking my hair.

"But I want my booster seat."

"Hi, Freddy," said Saskia Stiles. "Are you having a GOOD DAY?" She was sitting in her booster seat.

"What are you looking at, sport?" she asked me. No, she didn't. I don't know.

I opened my eyes and Chad Kennedy threw a basketball at my head in gym class as I walked by.

"What are you looking at?" he said, then laughed at me, when I stopped and stared at him. I was annoyed, because rhetorical questions make me uncomfortable. I end up answering questions I shouldn't and not answering questions I should.

"I'm looking at you," I said, because it was a true fact.

Chad Kennedy wore a thick green coat. But that makes no sense, either.

I opened my eyes and my father threw a shot glass at me.

"What the hell are you *looking* at!" he roared, and I don't know when that was. But I was younger.

"Where's Mom?" I asked him, and he laid his head in his arms.

I closed my eyes. I didn't want to see any more. My head hurt. Not like a headache, but the painless hurt that falls over you when you don't want to think anymore about it.

And I didn't want to think anymore about it.

But I opened my eyes again and I still didn't have my booster seat and my mother was arguing with John Stiles.

But Saskia talked to me. She sat on the driver's side. I reached out my hands, and our fingers touched. I stopped thinking about my booster seat.

"Did you have a good DAY?" she asked loudly, grinning widely. Her feet kicked at the back of her father's seat. She wore a blue polka-dotted dress. Red shoes. White socks.

"I had a good day," I replied to her. "How was your day?"

She laughed and kicked her father's seat harder. "I had a good day TOO!" She laughed, until her father turned his head back to her, a scowl over his brow.

"Saskia, *please*! Stop kicking my seat."

He turned to me, frowned, saw that I was now staring past him, at the light approaching. "What are you looking at, sport?" he asked.

And the sound of a train whistle.

THE CHANGING LIST OF
MY FAVOURITE THINGS

My mother came off the list of my Favourite Things on April 5, 2012, when I replaced her with boxing. There were already four things that I thought about more than my mother. Boxing was now the fifth thing.

It was no longer clear why I should think so much about my mother. I hadn't seen or heard from her in seven and a half years. I couldn't say with certainty that my heart would race faster or if I would feel eager anticipation to see her again. Clearly, it was more prudent to move boxing onto my list of Favourite Things.

Moving her off the list was made easier by the knowledge that she abandoned me. That she perhaps stopped loving me. Her leaving was, therefore, egregious.

Now, here I was, seventeen, and I sat in the kitchen. My father, getting drunk again. Telling me why she left.

A thread awoke and told me.

She still loves you.

It told me. It didn't ask a question, like a thread always does. It had been there for a decade and now awoke.

Your mother didn't stop loving you, it told me. And I knew it was true.

She still loved me. She left because
    because
        because
           because

My father was drunk, staring at me from across the kitchen table.

"Why did I stop going to Excalibur House?" I asked him.

He looked down at his glass for a while before answering. "I moved you to a private school. It was best for everyone concerned."

"Who was everyone?"

"You. Me. Linda."

"Why?"

He took a deep breath. "Your mother didn't abandon you."

I stared back, my muscles frozen.

"She died, Freddy," he said, and the time was now 6:19 PM, March 27, 2015.

THE TRAIN

I opened my eyes and my mother was screaming, and John Stiles instinctively stood on the brakes, even before he began to turn himself around to face forward again.

When the windshield exploded, it was like cold snow bursting through an open window.

The car spun like a top, and I heard, so close, the pounding of train wheels on the track, the screeching of steel on steel.

And then it was quiet.

Then a ringing in my ears. Then the patter of water as it fell on the roof, the ticking of hot metal. Then voices outside. I felt the cold air streaming through where the windshield once was.

Saskia kicking at the back of her father's seat. "Daddy," she called. "Daddy, HELLO."

John Stiles didn't respond.

I heard the opening and closing of car doors. "Is everyone okay?" someone shouted.

"Daddy!" called Saskia. "Hellllloooo!"

My mother lifted her head slightly. Blood poured from her scalp. I could see a ridge of bone above her ear. "It's time to be a man now," she said. "Get on with your life."

And then there were hands on me, on her, people calling to us, saying things too quickly for me to understand.

"Don't hurt him," my mother said and closed her eyes.

And Saskia Stiles calling to her father.

"Helllooooo!" she called out. "Daddy, hellllooo!"

The clock on the dashboard.

It was 4:32.

My father lit another cigarette. He offered me one. I didn't respond. He shrugged and put the pack in his front shirt pocket.

"She was going to a battered women's shelter," I said.

He snorted. "Bullshit," he said, without conviction.

"She wasn't in love with John Stiles," I continued. "He was driving her to the place where she would get away from you."

"Freddy," he said, low and angry. I recognized the tone of his voice. It meant *stop*. But I kept talking.

"John Stiles was taking her away from you," I said. "Not me. You."

"Shut up," he said. He rubbed his forehead. Outside, the wind was increasing, and waves of rain pelted the window.

My father poured himself another shot of scotch and drank it quickly.

"You little insufferable shit," he said. "You mongoloid bastard."

"A bastard is a fatherless child," I said.

"Shut the fuck up will you," he said.

"She didn't leave because of me," I said. "She left because of you."

I said it carefully, the words coming out slowly, as the threads exploded in my mind. Suddenly, it felt like my world had rotated 180 degrees. Up was the new down.

"You," I repeated.

He slammed a hand on the table. "She couldn't take *you* anymore!" he shouted. "*I* almost couldn't take it, either. You were a twenty-four-hour job, Freddy. We never had a moment of quiet. We never had a moment when we could let our guard down. If you weren't into one thing, you were into another. If I said do one thing, you said you wanted to do another. If I said do the other thing, you said you wanted to do the first thing."

"She was leaving you, not me," I said.

243

He hit the table so hard his glass tipped over and ice spilled on the table. "She was leaving *you!*" he roared. "It was *you* that drove her out. *You* that put such a strain on our marriage that it broke. It was *you* that pushed her over the edge. Jesus, Freddy, if you weren't so fucking *you*, she'd still be here with us today. If you weren't so fucking retarded, she'd never have wanted to fuck John Stiles and run away with him."

He sat, panting, glaring at me. After a moment, his head dropped heavily. He poured himself another drink.

"No," I said.

He took another drink. "No, what?" he growled.

"No, it's not true!" I shouted, stood up, grabbed the table, and turned it over on him.

THE FIGHT

My father liked to listen to country music, but only a subset of the genre. When he drove me home from Excalibur House, he played it loud.

"I listen to *real* country music," he often told me.

"You only listen to real country music?" I asked.

"Hell, yes," he laughed and turned up the car radio.

I sat in a booster seat in the back, on the middle of the seats, where I had a grand view of the road ahead. From there, I could easily see my mother and father, and they could see me. She could turn her head to look at me and smile. He could look at me in the rear-view mirror and wink. I could try to wink back. I had no idea why we winked. But it was interesting, so I did it.

"Real country music," he continued, "is music that speaks to the unique American condition. And there's not a lot of that out there these days."

"There's not a lot out there?" I asked.

"That's right." He laughed again. "There's not a lot of real music, period. Where are the George Joneses? Where are the Willie Nelsons?"

I considered this. "Are they in the glove compartment?"

"I guess they're just in your heart, Freddy."

And then there was Johnny Cash. His favourite singer was Johnny Cash. His favourite song was "A Boy Named Sue."

"Just when you think you got it tough, kid," he said. "Just when you think it can't get worse, remember that someone once was a boy and his name was Sue."

After that, whenever things got worse, I remembered this.

Someone is named Sue, I thought.

So what? said the threads.

I opened my eyes, and my father sat across the table from me, and a thread spoke to me.

Freddy, it told me. *It's you. You are Sue.*

"No, it's not true!" I shouted, stood up, and turned the table over on top of my father. He fell off his chair and crashed against the kitchen cupboard. I walked deliberately over to him, to stand over him, to tower over him. To glare righteously.

Or to try and glare righteously. Having never been angry before, I wasn't sure how to be angry. But I had seen it enough times that I knew the range of typical angry steps involved.

"Are you kidding me!" I shouted down at him.

His foot shot out like a piston, driving into my ankle. I tumbled to the floor.

"Goddamn it, Freddy," he roared, kicking me in my hip, then standing up. "What the goddamn bloody hell are you—"

I grabbed a chair and slammed it into his thigh. As he staggered back, I leapt to my feet and stood, knees bent, in a perfect stance. We were two arm's lengths apart. I knew how to close the gap quickly, where to step if he threw a punch at me, and where to strike when he missed.

But before I could move toward him, his arms swept the two glass tumblers from the counter at my face. As I threw my hands up to protect myself, he launched himself at me. Before I could register, he was upon me and drove his fist straight into my cheekbone. My vision exploded. Bright flashing lights blinded me and I fell back against the fridge, and he pinned me there, his hands closing around my throat.

I smiled.

I heard music.

There are foolish things people can do to me. One of them is to grab me with both hands. It means that they have left themselves undefended.

As my father pressed me against the fridge, leaning into me, clamping down on my windpipe, I brought both my arms under his and wedged my hands up between the insides of his elbows. Lifting up, I forced his arms apart, forced his elbows to bend, and pulled him closer to me.

I smashed my forehead into his nose. He stumbled back, and I hit him several times in the face, left and right, left and right, until one fist found the sweet spot where the first knuckle strikes the middle of the mandible, at the precise angle, the doorbell to the brain.

Hi, my fist said. *I'm here.*

My father slumped back, his eyes fluttering, and his hands released me. I pushed back from him, dragging in my breath. He staggered and tried to regain his feet.

Still gasping for breath, I stepped forward and lay on him like a hammer on a nail.

I opened my eyes and I was seven years old.

The night before she left for the last time, I heard them arguing downstairs. His voice was slurred, dragging out the soft consonants.

"It's time for me to move on," she told him. "It's time for *us* to move on."

"Move on to where," he wondered.

"Not *to* where," she said. "*From* where is what you should be asking. Look at us. Is this who we want to be? Is this where we want to be? I'm tired of beer in the fridge. I'm tired of a recycling bin full of wine bottles."

Silence.

"I've been talking to people," she said. "I think maybe you—"

"Oh, good Christ," he muttered. "Here it comes. This is just great."

"When I say move on, I don't care *where* we move on to. I just care that we move on from *this*. But right now, I'm trying to move on, and you're still there, and I'm moving on without you."

He made a spitting noise. "We do pretty good. We got a house. We got a good life. You like it here. I like it here."

"Does Freddy?"

"What?"

"Tell me, Bill," she said, her voice rising. "Do you think Freddy likes it when we're hungover Saturday morning and he has to watch TV for hours? Do you think he really likes it?"

"Hell, yes. He loves it."

"Don't you think he'd rather be hanging around us?"

"Flapping his hands and staring at nothing? He'd rather watch TV. He'd rather watch it all day."

"And do you think that would be good for him?"

"Maybe."

"Bill?"

"You're not making sense. How did we get from drinking to you accusing me of giving him too much TV?"

"Not you. *Us*. Every time we do something to ignore him. Every time we can't crawl out of bed to spend time with him. Every time we forget we promised to take him for a walk. Every single goddamn time, Bill. We're crushing him. Any chance he's got, we're wrecking, because we won't stop."

"Fine," he said. "You want to stop? Great. Let's just stop. There. Done. We've stopped. Okay?"

Silence.

"We both know how that's going to turn out," she said. "We both know how it *always* turns out."

"Well then what the FUCK do you want?" he yelled at her. "Stop drinking! Don't stop drinking! Make up your mind, for the love of Christ!"

Silence again. Then, "I have, Bill," she said. "I have."

I opened my eyes and I was seventeen, and my father bled before me.

The house was quiet, except for the low-throated humming of the furnace blowing slightly warmer air into the room. Outside, the wind abated. The trees no longer tapped at the window.

What did you do? they asked and their branches rattled like bones.

My father lay on the floor. His face was matted with blood. His breathing was ragged. His cigarette, discarded, smouldered under the table.

I pulled him to a sitting position and leaned him against the cupboard under the sink.

I looked him in the eye. "My mother never left me," I said.

He didn't reply. He just licked his lips and looked away. I pulled his face back to me.

"Look at me," I said, and he did. "My mother never left me," I repeated.

"No," he whispered. "She never left because of you, Freddy." Blood trickled from his right ear. "Your mother left *me*," he said. "Not you."

My throat felt like it was closing. "She left because of you?"

He nodded slowly. "I was certain she was coming back. She always did. Maybe she was gathering the courage to leave me, I don't know." He looked away. "But she always stayed because of you. She always left because of me."

"Did you make her angry?" I asked.

"Sometimes." He shook his head. "Other times she made me angry. But it wasn't anything horrible. People make each other angry all the time. Then they get over it. We just stopped loving each other."

"Mom never made me angry," I said.

"She never did, Freddy," he answered. He reached to the table, pulled a cigarette from the open pack, lifted it to his lips, and lit it.

His fingers trembled. He took a drag, coughed, and flicked the ashes on the floor.

"No one ever makes you mad, Freddy," he said. He smiled slightly. "Until now, I guess. But that's it. You can handle people. And that's a blessing I wish we all had."

He sat and smoked his cigarette. I watched the smoke rise from the burning tip. I asked, "Why didn't you tell me she was dead?"

He stubbed out the cigarette. "I did, Freddy," he said. "I've told you so many times."

Then a memory.

I opened my eyes and people moved slowly, single file, eyes downcast. A song by U2 played softly in the background. A song she sometimes danced to in the living room.

I want to run, I thought. I want to hide.

I sat on the aisle chair of the first row and people shuffled by. Some of them touched my shoulder, because that's all they knew how to do.

"She's in a better place," someone said.

I brushed his hand away. "I don't know you."

My father sat to my right, wearing a black blazer, black tie, white dress shirt. His hands were clasped together in his lap, flexing. Clenching until they were white. Releasing until they were red.

I turned to him. "Where's Mom?" I asked.

He didn't answer. After a moment, I turned away and stared straight ahead.

There were flowers on the coffin. Orchids.

I opened my eyes and I was seventeen one more time, and my father leaned against the kitchen wall and coughed. He spit out blood.

"I used to tell you all the time, Freddy," he said. "It never took root. A few days later, you would come back and say, 'Where's Mom?' I'd tell you all over again. Sometimes that's all I needed to do. Other times, it drove you berserk and you'd start throwing things.

"And then one day, after a few years, I told you she left us," he said softly, looking down. "It wasn't planned. It just came out. But after that, you stopped asking where she was. You didn't have your tantrums. After that, you seemed to accept where we were."

"Where were we?"

"We were left behind," he said. "We were alone together. You and me."

I stood up.

"No," I said. "Not anymore. Just you."

I opened my eyes, and Linda Stiles stood inside her door, the chain still on.

"Why are you back here, Freddy?" she asked

"I know something about John Stiles," I said.

"That's very nice," she sighed. "Go home."

She began closing the door, but I quickly said, "He wasn't leaving you."

She stopped and stared at me for a moment. The wind pushed the rain against my back.

"What are you talking about?" she said.

"He was driving my mom to a shelter. He was taking her there because she was leaving my father."

She continued to stare at me. Her eyes wide. "Why didn't John tell me that?" she said quietly. Her fingers rubbed against the side of the door.

"I don't know," I said. "He never told me."

"Then what did he tell you?"

I shook my head. "Nothing," I said. "He told me to put on my seat belt."

"Ten years," she said slowly, distantly. "For ten years, I've lived with that. Did you know that, Freddy? Ever since the day he died, I thought he was taking Saskia and leaving me. Did you know that?"

I said nothing.

"For ten years," she said softly.

She looked me in the eye. Strangely, it didn't hurt.

"Where's Saskia?" I asked her.

THE WEB

What are you doing?
i'm waiting
Do you want to know something?
yes
I'm going somewhere.
are you going swinging
No.
are you going for ice cream
No.
where are you going
where are you going
I'll take you there.

There is a web between people. The strands are the bonds that they make with each other. The stronger the love for another, the stronger the bond and the stronger the thread.

Two people with a strong bond have an advantage over those without one. The closer they are together, the more they love each other, the more they understand each other. The more they understand each other, the more they can read each other.

The bond allows them a new level of communication, because they can read the language of each other's bodies. Where once there were only two eyes, now there are four.

The bonds of a culture are the threads of the metaphorical web that people build among themselves. It locks them into a community. Sometimes a bond will weaken and disappear. Sometimes it will grow anew with someone else. Sometimes it will stay, locked there forever, like a limb on an oak tree.

The strands of the web tell the story of the family. The strands of the web define the family.

I have no strands.

People who say they feel no love tend to be overly dramatic. The inability to feel love is a developmental delay at best and a pathological condition at worst. You're either delayed or a sociopath.

Love is a set of physical characteristics: a racing heart, a nervous tightness in the pit of the stomach. An ever-present sense of antici-pation. People in love feel the same general physical symptoms. I have felt those symptoms in the same combination. Therefore, I am "capable" of love.

There is a difference, I believe. Most people are unable to dis-tinguish love from symptom, so they call it love. I am unable to distinguish symptom from love, so I call it symptom.

I stood at the edge of the park at the end of the field, under a tree.
The air was still, and the rain gone. Clouds above were thinning,
and the promise of blue elbowed between them.

I saw Saskia at the far end of the field, sitting on a swing. She
rocked, kicking at the cedar chips that blanketed the playground.

I texted her.

> **Did you know?**
> i dont know
> **I remember.**
> you remember?
> **I remember. I remember the car accident.**

She lifted up her phone and put it back down in her lap. She
lifted it up again and put it in her pocket.

> **You were in the back seat. We were in the back seat.**

She took her phone from her pocket. I could hear her grunting,
as if she was trying to say something she had no idea how to say.

At last she texted me back.

> i said daddy wake up
> **I know.**
> he was mad at me
> i kicked his seat
> **He wasn't mad at you.**
> he wasn't mad at me?
> **He only wanted you to stop kicking his seat.**
> dad i will never kick your seat again
> **He knows.**
> he knows?

He loves you.

From across the park, she laughed out loud.

> **It's time for me to go.**
> are you going?
> **Yes.**
> Tell me you want me to come with you.
> **No. Stay with your mom.**
> Okay.
> **But we can swing, if you want.**
> Squeak.

I walked out from under the trees.

I opened my eyes. The Butcher stood behind the counter, his head tilted to the side. I stood in the middle of his store, my hands at my side.

"Well, well," he said. "If it ain't the cat, and if the cat ain't dragged itself in."

"I'm not a cat," I said to him.

He wiped his hands on his apron. "Ain't seen you since months. Where you been?"

"I got stuff."

He nodded. "Is that a fact?"

"Hey, Dad, we need to order more gloves," said Jack, walking out from the back, carrying a bucket. When he saw me, he came to a complete stop.

His father looked between the two of us. The only sound was the ticking clock above the counter.

"Well, this is awkward," the Butcher said softly and turned away from us.

Jack sniffed. He set the bucket down.

"So," he said.

"So," I repeated back to him.

"Did you graduate?" he asked.

I nodded. "I'm enrolled at Douglas Technical College. I start in September."

"Not bad, not bad." He looked around. "I'm taking some time off. Help around the shop."

"You were runner-up in the Golden Gloves."

His eyebrows went up. "You been stalking me, Freddy?"

I shook my head. "I googled you. I was your sparring partner. I have a specific interest."

He smiled, and his shoulders relaxed. "Sounds like something you would do."

"You know," said the Butcher, "I recorded Ali versus Norton last week. Maybe you might want to come and watch it with us, Freddy?"

I shook my head. "I can't."

"Sure you can," he said gently.

"No. I have to meet a friend. She's waiting for me."

Jack laughed. "A girl. You *dog*."

"I'm not a dog."

"I know." He nodded. "I know."

Silence. The Butcher turned away again and began wiping the counter.

"I could come tomorrow," I offered.

The Butcher looked at Jack, who looked at him, then at me.

"Sure. We've even got beer."

"I don't like beer."

"You like beer when you sit with us," he said.

"Okay."

Another silence.

"I need a job," I told Jack.

Jack looked at his father. "We do need someone to clean up in the evening."

His father nodded. "That we do," he said. "That we do."

My mind continues to race.

I was there. That night. I was right behind her when she died.

I was in the back seat, and my last memory is a fleeting thought, the instant before the car slammed into a truck, stopped at the train crossing. The collision ploughed the truck into the train's path, and it was carried down the track. The car I was in took the truck's place in line. Tick-tick-ticking.

At the moment of impact, there was a thought. It faded away even after everything went black. The thought was this: my mother, in the front seat, has blocked the flying glass.

If you asked me what was the last thing I remember about that night, I would answer this: I remember thinking that my mother was protecting me. I remember her scream, the stuttering of the car as John Stiles stood with all his force on the brake pedal, the spray of glass and a thundering noise as I was thrown forward against my seat belt. Then I remember my eyes closed, and I saw nothing, and heard nothing.

But I remember one last thought, still lingering, that she had, once again, protected me.

My mother wore lilac perfume. It smelled purple. When I nestled against her, watching TV, her scent enveloped me like smoke around a campfire. Sometimes, if I pass someone in the hall at school who is wearing my mother's perfume, I stop and become alarmed. I feel her presence with me, as if she were right behind me.

I have long since given up turning around to see if she is there.

After the night when I remembered, Linda Stiles visited my father only once. She came in the evening, and they sat in the kitchen and drank. They thought I was in my room. I was on the stairs.

"Did you know?" she asked him.

"About where they were going? No. I didn't."

The clink of ice cubes. The clunk of a bottle on the table.

She sighed. "The thing is, I've lived ten years, Bill. Ten years thinking he left me. Thinking that he didn't leave because of Saskia. Thinking that he left because he couldn't take life with *me*. And he took Saskia with him."

"I spent ten years thinking the other way," he said and laughed softly. "I guess we're trading each other's story."

When she left, my father didn't get up from the table to see her out. I was sitting on the stairs that led down to the front door.

"Hello, Freddy," she said. "You're looking well."

"Am I?" I asked.

Listen: There is no evidence of life after death and, therefore, no reason to believe in life after death.

There is no evidence of God's existence, but that doesn't mean the world isn't consistent with Him. Because it is. The things you expect in a God-filled world are here: unexplained events, good triumphant over evil, prayers answered, and other astonishing happenings.

In science, it's called stochastic. In religion, it's called a miracle. Regardless of the label, it's still there. These things happening in this world.

There is no evidence that my mother is anywhere but buried in the ground. There is no evidence that my mother still exists on some other spiritual plane.

But my need to justify the existence of God is clear. If there is no God, I will never see my mother again. If there is a God, I will see her again.

This is sufficient. This is enough to believe.

All of this is important. It is my justification. It is the only thing that keeps the threads about my mother to a minimum.

We're going to go now, the threads say.
I know the perfect place to leave you, I tell them.

I open my eyes and I am sitting with Saskia Stiles. We are in the forest behind my old house, high up the mountainside. We are sitting at the foot of the cliffs, under an overhang, looking across the valley as the rain falls around us.

In my left pant pocket is my father's talisman. I took it when I left. He doesn't need it anymore, but I do.

On my lap is my old friend, *The Twentieth Century in Review*, and I am flipping the pages back and forth, back and forth.

Saskia takes her phone from her purse.

The woods are lovely, dark and deep.

"I'm dry," I say. "Are you dry?"

I'm dry.

We sit together, and I feel our shoulders touching. They have been touching for a few minutes.

I've just noticed this.

She continues to type text messages. I sit and listen to her tap at her phone, and I count twelve text messages sent. At last. At last I have to ask.

"Who gets those messages?"

She pauses, hunched over her phone.

God.

I don't respond. An earlier version of me may have pointed out that she didn't have God's contact information.

Then she sends another message to God.

"What did you say to him?"

She pauses again and looks up, out across the valley. The mist is rising from the ground, and the mountains in the distance are dissolving in white.

"What did you say to him?" I ask again.

She looks at me. "Amen," she says.

And she leans in to me, until she is close enough to me that I feel her light breath tickle my upper lip. She is looking directly at me, straight into my eyes.

I tumble into their blue.

Her eyes close.

High above, thunderclaps rolled across the sky. Up the side of the mountain, I hear the clamouring crashes as trees bend and snap, the trolls slowly walking down the mountain.

And it's okay.

ACKNOWLEDGMENTS

Listen: These are the people who form the chain.

I know that this book would never have been written if it weren't for my wife, Joanna. She was the first person who made me want to be more than I was. She was the first person who made me want to finish this book, because she was the first person I wanted to read it.

My first and greatest mentor was my mother, Donna Milner, who has this strange ability to make those things I struggle with look easy. This book got out of the gate because she read the first chapter, early, early on. If her emailed response could have had volume, it would have been turned up to eleven: *keep writing this damned thing*.

The author Anthony Dalton was the first to tell me "You are going to be published." He was the first outside my family to say that this was a good book, the first to say that someone needed to read it, and the one who introduced me to Taryn Boyd, my publisher.

Taryn Boyd was the first person to see me as more than someone who wrote something they liked. She saw me as someone she could make money off of. Every writer's ultimate goal. She also saw me as something no one had called me before: *literary*. Every writer's and all that.

Taryn demonstrated some kind of prestidigitatious genius when she paired me with Colin Thomas, my editor, because he turned out to have an unnerving knack of knowing where the bullshit was. My book has been a lengthy process of cutting off the unnecessary fat, and Colin was a master at separating the tissue from the bone.

I need to thank more people than there is room here, but I'll include most of the cream: Wanda Ann La Claire was the first person outside of my family to read and edit my book, and her help was much appreciated. Tracy Wilkinson, my boss, who put up with my angst during our weekly reviews. And then there was the stranger at the Surrey International Writers' Conference, when I was pitching the book to agents, who overheard me and said, "Are you the guy writing that book about the autistic kid?" I said I was, and she said, "You keep going. Everyone's talking about it." That was the moment I glimpsed that maybe this book could eventually be read by complete strangers. Again, every writer's ultimate goal.

Be sure to visit aaroncullydrake.com for outtakes, bloopers, and deleted scenes.

AARON CULLY DRAKE has written for newspapers and magazines, and is a former reporter and editor. He lives in Vancouver, British Columbia, with his wife, son, and autistic daughter, all of whom keep advising him to shut up. *Do You Think This Is Strange?* is his first novel. To learn more about Aaron and the book, please visit aaroncullydrake.com.